Photo credit: Stephen Armishaw Photography

JEEVANI CHARIKA (pronounced 'Jeev-uh-nee') writes multicultural women's fiction and romantic comedies. She spent much of her childhood in Sri Lanka, with short forays to Nigeria and Micronesia, before returning to England to settle in Yorkshire. All of this, it turned out, was excellent preparation for becoming a novelist.

She also writes under the name Rhoda Baxter. Her books have been shortlisted for multiple awards.

A microbiologist by training, Jeevani loves all things science geeky. She also loves cake, crochet and playing with Lego. You can find out more about her (and get a free book) on her website www.jeevanicharika.com.

Also by Jeevani Charika

Playing for Love
Christmas at the Palace
This Stolen Life
A Convenient Marriage

Picture Perfect

JEEVANI CHARIKA

ONE PLACE. MANY STORIES

HQ
An imprint of HarperCollins*Publishers* Ltd
1 London Bridge Street
London SE1 9GF

www.harpercollins.co.uk

HarperCollins*Publishers*
1st Floor, Watermarque Building, Ringsend Road
Dublin 4, Ireland

This paperback edition 2022

1
First published in Great Britain by
HQ, an imprint of HarperCollins*Publishers* Ltd 2022

To my family, always

Chapter 1

Nirosha reread her email before she hit send on her latest commission. She hadn't been able to concentrate properly since she'd seen that damn invitation, and it would be far too easy to do something stupid like send the wrong email to the wrong client – something she couldn't afford to do as a freelance graphic designer.

Email sent, she sat back and rubbed her eyes. The image from Mick's exhibition invitation was there, waiting behind her eyelids. Ugh. It had been a long time. She had thought she was over it. Over him. Then something like this happened, and the hurt started stinging all over again.

Downstairs, the front door slammed. Oh good, Sam was home. Niro checked the time. It was a bit early for Sam, but it was romcom movie night, so maybe that was why.

Niro stood up and stretched the stiffness out of her shoulders. She shook out her arms. Romcom movie night would be just the thing to drag her out of her gloom.

She padded downstairs in her fluffy slippers. The flat she shared with her cousin, Sam, was small but homely. Niro had helped Sam decorate it when it was new and then, when things went wrong with Mick, Sam had let Niro move into the small room.

'Evening.' Niro closed the blinds in the living room. It was already dark outside. She leaned over the arm of the sofa to reach the plug socket and switched on the fairy lights she'd put up earlier that week, because Sam maintained that Christmas lights couldn't go up until it was December. Niro stood back up and pulled her jumper straight. There – things looked more cheerful already.

The living room was also the dining room and only a thin counter separated it from the narrow kitchen. Sam was standing at the worktop, looking through the post, frowning. Unlike Niro, who was shaped like a generous apple and had dyed purple and blue streaks into her black hair, Sam was slim with a sleek black bob. Since her business had started doing well, she looked even more corporate than before. She wore more make-up now and generally came across as a very polished brown lady. Light brown, compared to Niro's deep brown. If Niro didn't love her cousin to bits, she would have found her intimidating.

Niro eyed the pile of post. The invitation was at the bottom, the card thinner and shinier than the other envelopes. Niro had jumped on hers, torn it up and thrown it in the bin, but she couldn't do anything about Sam's. She wafted into the kitchen and put the kettle on. 'Good day?'

Sam was the first person she'd spoken to all day. She hadn't even had any online meetings or phone calls today. It felt a little strange talking to anyone, let alone someone three-dimensional.

Sam looked up from the letter she was reading. 'Are you wearing pyjamas?'

Niro glanced down at herself. 'No. I found these in the bottom of my trouser drawer. I wore them as part of my costume in a play once. They still fit.' The trousers were made of polycotton and had colourful stripes on them. They also had an elasticated waist, thankfully. When she looked back up, Sam was studying her, frowning. 'What?'

'Niro,' Sam said, her voice soft and cautious. 'Have you been out of the house today?'

She didn't need to think about that, but she pretended to. 'No.'

'Yesterday?'

'Um …'

'The day before that?'

'Yes. Yes, I did go out that day. I went to get more milk and the newspaper.'

Sam was studying her with that mixture of exasperation and sadness again.

'Stop looking at me like that.' Behind her, the kettle boiled, giving Niro a good excuse to turn around and bang about while getting out mugs. 'I'm fine.'

'Niro …'

She opened the pot of teabags. 'Ugh. We're out of teabags. I'm going to have to use the nice ones from Sri Lanka.' She opened the cupboard and found the box. They usually used them only when someone's parents were over. This box hadn't even been opened. She scrabbled at it with her nails. 'Dammit.'

Behind her, Sam made a sympathetic clicking noise with her tongue. 'Love, it's been nearly two years now. You have to get back out there.'

'Do you think I haven't tried?' She tore at the packaging and blinked back the tears that were muscling into her eyes. Why would you make a packet of teabags so bloody difficult to get into?

'Not … recently.'

'Aargh. Gotcha, you little bastard.' She tore a corner loose and used it to peel a strip off the plastic.

'Niro.'

She slammed the box down. 'What, Sam?'

'I've just seen it. Do you want to talk about it?'

Niro looked down at her hands on the worktop, which were blurred now through tears, and shook her head.

'Oh, baba.' Sam rushed over and put her arms around her.

'I should have taken us both off their mailing list,' Niro said, into Sam's shoulder. Tears loosened themselves from her eyes and ran down her cheeks. She pulled back to wipe them away. She didn't want to ruin Sam's nice work clothes.

Sam released her and picked up the exhibition invitation again. It had a photo of Mick's artwork and Niro could just about make out the words 'building on his acclaimed exhibition last year, Mick Vickery showcases'. Seeing his name in connection with that particular gallery had shot Niro right back to that dark place she'd been struggling to get out of ever since she'd found out about Mick's betrayal.

Sam put a hand on her arm. 'Niro. He's an arse. The only reason he gets exhibitions at that gallery is because he's sleeping with the curator.'

'He is actually quite good,' Niro said, quietly. He was.

'So are you.'

Was she? She had thought she was, but then ... then she'd seen the messages between Mick and Clarice, the curator at the gallery. The explicit ones about what they wanted to do to each other had been bad enough, but worse had been the way he'd talked about her to Clarice. *She's very insecure about her art – with good reason, obviously* and *I feel sorry for her. She's trying hard with her art, but she's not aware of her limits.* And Clarice had agreed!

'Oh please,' said Sam. 'You don't honestly believe that weasel's opinion is anything to go by?'

Niro shrugged with one shoulder. 'I don't know. Maybe. All I know is that I simply can't take photos like I used to. The ...' She waved her hands around, trying to find the right word. 'My inspiration is gone.' Photography was where her heart lay. She had started taking on graphic design work as a way to make ends meet. Now it seemed that was the only skill she had left.

Sam blinked but didn't say anything, waiting for an explanation.

Niro didn't have one. 'It's like ... the things I wanted to photograph. They meant something to me. Spoke to me. And now they've just ... stopped. I could take pictures of things, but they would just be pictures. No heart.'

'You took some lovely photos of my bags for my website,' Sam said.

'That's craft. I haven't suddenly lost my skills.' That came out too sharp. 'Sorry. I mean, those are just pictures. I can light them properly and take a good photo. That's different.'

Sam's expression said she had no idea what Niro was talking about.

Niro tried again. 'All the technical stuff – that's still there. I can take competent photos. But the thing that makes them mine – the uniqueness. That's gone. I don't know where it came from before and all I know now is that it's not there anymore.'

'Maybe you need to photograph something different from what you used to do. Go somewhere different. How about that competition you mentioned the other day? That could be a good opportunity.'

'What competition?' Niro frowned. She had no recollection of what this might be.

'Buildings in the landscape or something like that.' Sam waved a hand. 'There was a picture of a big house in the jungle.'

'Oh! Architecture in the environment.' She'd idly taken a screenshot of the contest requirements and showed it to Sam, mainly because the example photo from their last competition was so beautiful.

'You're eligible to apply, right?' said Sam. 'You've got some examples that you can submit? You've always done things to do with how humans affect their environment.'

'Yes, but ...' Her old photos had been of the small things that people left behind in public spaces. Each item an artefact from a life. Each photo a story. You had to see the meaning in something before you could capture it. Her cousin just didn't get that.

Sam leaned forward. 'You can't let him win. He wanted to undermine you and he's succeeded. You're brilliant. I know you are. That artist is still in there, somewhere. We just need to shake her out.'

Niro looked down at her hands. Sure, the artist might still be in there, but she couldn't find her. It wasn't like she hadn't tried. Every so often, she would kick herself out of her funk and try, really try, but all that came out were flat, boring pictures. No heart. Nothing that made you look twice. Each time, she sank back a little deeper into the melancholy.

'Niro, you have to do something. Or else you'll have to give up and let the Aunties choose you a husband so that you can get married and raise children with some nice suitable Sri Lankan man.'

'Not,' said Niro, 'that there's anything wrong with that.'

'No. But is that what you want?'

She threw up her hands. 'I don't know what I want!' She walked out into the living room area and flopped onto the sofa.

Sam came and sat on the arm of the sofa. 'What did you used to want? Before …'

'I wanted to be an artist. To sell my photos in galleries. To be invited to take part in stuff. To do a photo book.' She eased out a cushion that was wedged uncomfortably behind her back and hugged it. 'Right now, I just want to stop feeling shit.'

'Maybe you need a project? Something to focus on. Something fun and different, I mean. Not like the graphic design stuff you do for clients.'

Even that was suffering. She was giving people what they asked her for, but she used to give more. She had once designed some packaging that made an art director squeal out loud. On the other hand, she knew where Sam was going with this. 'You're trying to gently lead me to say I'll apply for that competition, aren't you?'

To her credit, Sam didn't deny it. 'So? Is that such a bad thing?' She leaned forward and put her hand on Niro's knee. 'I hate seeing you like this. I want the fun, nothing-is-impossible Niro back.'

When Niro didn't reply, Sam added, 'Besides, you were there for me when I needed help with my business. I want to do the same for you.'

Niro looked up at her cousin. Sam was right. She really did

have to shake herself out of this and get back into her art, or at least try to. Otherwise, she was letting Mick win. She groaned. 'I hate it when you're right.'

Sam grinned. 'So, you're going to enter the competition?'

'I don't have any money to travel – and I'll need to travel, if I'm going to take photos of anything extraordinary.' The competition called for photos of unusual buildings that complemented their landscape. You didn't find many of them in London.

'There was a travel grant from that charity ...' Sam pulled out her phone and started scrolling through the messages that Niro had sent her. They messaged each other most days, but dammit, Sam paid far too much attention to her throwaway daydreams.

'Yes, but that would need a bit of coordination.'

'Ah. Here it is. Hang on ...' Sam tapped on her phone. 'Closing date is the end of this week. You could still apply. Get on it while you're still inspired. You just need to come up with a decent pitch. Luke and I can help you with that.'

Niro stared at her cousin, taking in her earnest expression. She and Sam had been the family losers, the ones with the strange non-standard ambitions. Niro with her interest in art and Sam with her eye for fashion. Their parents had expected them to have traditional jobs – as doctors, lawyers, teachers, accountants.

Even Sam had spent some time doing a 'real job' until a few months ago, when her business took off. Being an entrepreneur was a scary thing to do and Sam had made a success of it. Niro had supported her in all kinds of ways at the beginning. Now Sam was trying to pay her back.

Niro sighed. 'Fine,' she said. 'I'll apply for the travel grant. If I get it, I'll enter the competition with the photos from the trip.'

'There you go. Not so hard,' said Sam.

'Chances of me getting the grant are a bit slim,' said Niro.

'They'll be slightly better if you actually apply.'

A fair point.

'Now then,' said Sam. 'What are we watching tonight?'

Chapter 2

There was a muffled cheer from one of the meeting rooms down the corridor. Vimal looked up from his computer, where he was logging the changes he'd made to the latest algorithm he was compiling.

Faheem, who sat opposite him in the open-plan office, rolled his eyes. 'Let me guess, one of the posh boys sold one of our algorithms for a lot of money. What's the betting that yet again, we don't get any acknowledgement?'

Vimal shrugged. He was used to it. Sabatini Putnam Woolf were an investment bank. He got paid well to create models and algorithms that predicted the stock market. If someone with better people skills than he had was able to go out and get others to pay a ton of money for them, then great. They could have all the glory.

He wouldn't want to do that job in a million years. The idea of all the schmoozing made him shudder. The sales department was full of ex–public school, ex-Oxbridge people of a certain type. The loud and irritating type, in Vimal's opinion, but they seemed to manage to charm fund managers, which was what the job required. Chief among them was Lucien Fothergill Yelvington, who was currently selling the algorithms made by Vimal and his team.

When Vimal had been with Kerry she had made him go to after-work drinks and parties to 'network'. At first, he'd made the effort. It might have been useful for his career and it would have been nice to have proper friends at work. But it had taken him so far out of his comfort zone that he'd hated every minute of it. What few friends he'd made had really been Kerry's friends, so those relationships had petered out when he and Kerry split up. Lucien had been friends with Kerry, and had always made it clear that Vimal was only welcomed because he was Kerry's partner. So now, Lucien was merely a work colleague to him.

'Wonder which product it was,' said Faheem.

'Lucien was taking one to the City of London pensions last week,' Vimal said, and there were murmurs of agreement and nods from a few others. He had been pleased with that particular algorithm.

'Probably that one, then,' said Faheem. 'Lucien nearly always closes the deal.'

'Yeah,' said Richard, a nondescript guy who had been there a lot longer than Vimal had. 'He's good. And he's a nice guy. I got to know him a bit when I went to that soirée of his. He's interesting and fun. Gives other departments the time of day, you know. Not like some people.'

Vimal smiled and turned back to his computer screen. They'd all heard about Richard's going to Lucien's 'soirée' before. Vimal was slightly less impressed by it than Richard seemed to think. He himself had been casually invited to Lucien's upcoming party, as Kerry's guest. Obviously, he wasn't anymore. He was quite glad he hadn't broadcast the news of that. He finished what he was doing and picked up his mug. 'I'm doing a coffee run.'

He gathered up two more mugs, put them on a tray and made his way down the corridor to the kitchen. He had to pass the meeting room on the way. There were a bunch of guys in expensive suits in there; he recognised Lucien, leaning against the table, holding court. The others sitting around him were juniors, hanging on his every word. Vimal carried on walking.

There was a time when he'd cared about what people thought of him and being in with the right crowd. When he had first started at the investment bank, he had come in as a direct hire from another job, slotted into place without first going through the company management trainee scheme. They'd hired him for his skill with numbers, but many people in the business were fast-talking, confident types who appeared to know exactly what they were doing. It had taken him years to realise that although they knew less than him, their self-confidence was blinding. Especially in sales. They treated the office floor much like they would have treated the school playground. But he didn't have to join in the games. Somewhere along the line, Vimal had stopped wanting to be friends with these people and just settled for doing his job. Which was much more fun anyway.

The filter in the coffee machine needed changing. Of course it did. As he put in a new one and waited for the coffee to brew, he thought again of Kerry. In the beginning, she had been as much of an outsider as he was, but she'd embraced the whole London City People vibe. She did her best to be invited to the right parties, go to the right events, be seen in all the right places. Since they'd split up, he hadn't a clue what was in. Come to think of it, he hadn't actually been to any events at all, since then. What was the point? People were exhausting. He wasn't great with conversation. Without Kerry there to be dazzling, he was just … out of place.

He checked the level of the coffee. He needed a bit more to make three mugs, so he waited, listening to the gurgle and drip of it. The lack of Kerry in his life was a gnawing pain in his heart. Once upon a time, he'd thought they understood each other. They had been happy for four years, hadn't they? But it turned out, quite suddenly, that he didn't know her at all. He sighed. It would have been five years this New Year's.

High heels clicked behind him. He pulled himself together and smiled. The woman who had come in was looking at her phone.

She gave him a quick smile in return and went back to reading whatever it was she was reading.

Vimal relaxed. Oh good. He didn't have to make small talk. He quickly poured three coffees and picked up the tray.

He'd almost made it past the noisy meeting room when the door opened.

'There he is!'

Oh god, it was Lucien. Vimal slowed down, clutching the tray extra hard. 'Hi, Lucien.'

'Come in, man.' Lucien put an arm around Vimal and ushered him into the room. 'This guy,' he said. 'He's the genius who came up with the algorithm.'

There was a smattering of applause from the others.

Vimal inclined his head. 'Thank you. I take it the last algorithm of mine that you sold is still performing nicely?' He knew it was.

'It is, yes. Happy customers all round,' said Lucien. 'I think this calls for drinks after work, chaps.'

There was general agreement to this. Vimal waited a beat. No one suggested that he join them. Go figure.

'I should get back to the office,' he said, lifting the tray a fraction to indicate that people were waiting for their coffee.

'Oh yes. Of course. Just wanted to give credit where credit was due.' Lucien opened the door for him.

'Thank you.'

'Oh, by the way,' Lucien said, once Vimal had passed him, 'I saw our mutual friend the other day. Kerry? Works over at Miller and Brown now.'

Kerry. His heart gave a little skip at the thought of her. Why was Lucien referring to her as 'our mutual friend'? He knew damned well that Kerry had been more than a friend to Vimal. Lucien was looking at him. He should say something.

'Kerry. How … how's she doing?' He wanted to scream, *What did she say about me? Does she miss me?* but he managed not to.

'She was all right, actually. Doing well. She was with my good friend Simon Woolberg.' He nodded to one of the other guys in the room. 'Hey, Arlo, you know Woolly, don't you?'

The mention of a man with Kerry landed like a blow to the windpipe. That was not the guy she'd been dating the last time he'd heard. She'd had at least two boyfriends since splitting up with Vimal. Was she seeing a *new* guy now? Or were they just friends?

'When you say *with* …' Vimal began. But Lucien had already moved back into the room. The conversation was clearly over.

'Uh. Okay. I'll see you later, then.' He hurried back to the office.

*

When it got to home time, people left in ones and twos. This office wasn't the sort of place that emptied promptly at five. Vimal rubbed his hands over his face and glared at the screen. He just couldn't focus. His mind kept drifting back to Kerry. He'd done a furtive google of her name on his phone earlier, but there was nothing new. He had also searched Simon Woolberg, who it turned out was the son of a baron. If Lucien knew him, he must be a big noise – either in banking or because he was plain rich. He could do more research, but then what would he do with the information? Torture himself with it?

Sighing, he saved his work and locked his computer.

Faheem looked up. 'Leaving early?'

It wasn't early. 'It's nearly six o'clock.' He stood up and gathered his stuff. 'I have a thing.'

He left before anyone could ask him what the thing was. He hadn't thought that far into his lie. Lying didn't come naturally.

Richard was leaving too. They walked down the corridor side by side, neither of them speaking.

'Hey, wait up.'

Vimal turned to see Lucien hurrying down the corridor, his suit jacket undone – slipping into after-work mode already. Beside Vimal, Richard lit up.

'Lucien. Hi.'

Lucien spared him a glance. 'Hi. Actually, I need to talk to this guy.' He indicated Vimal.

Richard seemed to deflate a little. 'Well, I'll see you tomorrow.' He resumed walking down the corridor.

Vimal tilted his head to one side. What on earth did Lucien want?

Lucien put a hand on his shoulder. 'Listen, Vimal. About my little New Year's bash in my uncle's new place in Switzerland?'

Okay. That was not what he was expecting. 'Um … yes.'

'Just checking that you've got all the info you need for flights and stuff. What time will you be arriving?'

What? He didn't have a flight booked. He hadn't even thought about it. 'I thought now that I wasn't with Kerry … I didn't think I was invited.'

A group of guys from sales appeared at the far end of the corridor. They were wearing their coats and chatting. There was much jostling and stopping to punch each other in the shoulder. Clearly they were all heading to the pub.

'Of course you're invited,' said Lucien. 'And you'd agreed that you were coming.'

Vimal stared at him. Surely that hadn't been a serious invitation. 'I don't—'

'Oh, come on, man, you can't back out now. I've had you on my confirmed list for months.'

He felt terrible. It simply hadn't occurred to him that Lucien would want him to come if he wasn't with Kerry. He didn't want to be rude. And it was rude, wasn't it? Another thought outshone the others. Kerry was going to be there. At New Year's. He might never get the chance to spend concentrated time with her again.

'I must say, I thought you were better than that. You'd put me in a really awkward position if you pulled out like that.' Lucien shook his head. 'I suppose I can rearrange a few things … but it's not ideal.'

'I …'

The sales guys were closer now. Their laughter bounced ahead of them.

'Obviously, no charge for the accommodation,' said Lucien, as though that was the only possible issue. 'It's a fair way from the airport, but that shouldn't be a problem. There are taxis.'

He was speechless for a second. How did smiling and nodding in response to 'oh, you must come to my New Year bash' translate to a genuine agreement? Even if it had been, without Kerry, he barely knew the guy. Why on earth did Lucien still want him to come?

Lucien made an impatient click with his tongue. 'Kerry said you were still friends.' His eyes gleamed. 'So I thought that was all good.'

Was it all good? His heart was barely holding it together, while she thought they were friends? 'I … suppose so.'

'Capital! There's a whole bunch of us going early in the five days around New Year's Eve. Including Kerry.' Lucien got out his phone and scrolled through. 'Here.' He showed him a picture of the interior of a villa – all blond wood and white furnishing. 'Of course, we'll be hanging out together there for a while before the party. An extended soirée.'

Lucien was known for his soirées … and had a habit of inviting people he worked with to them from time to time. So his expecting Vimal to come probably wasn't that weird. Almost a week, hanging out with Kerry. Vimal's breath hitched. Given that she'd been out with so many people since they'd split up, she hadn't found what she was looking for. Maybe this was his chance to show her what she was missing.

'Glad you didn't welch on me, old chap.' Lucien raised a hand to acknowledge the group from sales. They were almost upon them.

Vimal nodded. Welching on a deal was tantamount to treason around here. 'Yes. Sure. Why not? It'll be fun.'

'Great. I'll email you details.'

The guys flowed around them. Lucien said, 'Catch you later' and joined the flow. A few seconds later, Vimal was standing alone in the middle of the corridor as the group rounded the corner and disappeared in the direction of the lifts.

He stared after them for a second, then his heart gave a little skip. Excitement spread, tingling through his body. Details didn't matter. He was going to see Kerry again!

Chapter 3

Niro hit 'submit' on the grant application page on the Arts Council website, waited for it to go through then closed her laptop. It felt good to have done something positive. She spun her chair round and looked at her room. What now? Unlike normal, her room was tidy – the bed carefully made, clothes actually put away rather than piled in the 'clean stuff' basket. That was the plus side of procrastination. She checked her list of freelance projects. Nothing too urgent. So maybe … a walk?

She had got as far as getting her boots on before the ennui caught up with her. Did she really want to go for a walk, when she could just sit on the sofa and watch something for a few minutes instead? It had been over an hour since lunch, so she could have a cuppa and a biscuit.

Her gaze fell on Sam's empty coat hook. On the other hand, if she went for a walk round the block, she could be smug when Sam asked her if she'd gone out. Yes. Ten minutes.

Once she was outside, she was surprised at how chilly it was. She should have worn a hat. Stuffing her gloved hands into her pockets, she started walking. It was a sunny day, with only a faint hint of the fog that had cloaked everything that morning. Everything felt wintry. There was no snow or ice, but railings and pavements gleamed with a sheet of moisture from where last night's frost had melted.

Niro strode quickly, avoiding the empty wheelie bins that hadn't been taken back in after the bin lorry had been past. Once upon a time, she would have seen three things to photograph by now. When had she stopped noticing the world? She turned the corner and walked past the house with the black railings. Someone had picked up a child's glove and put it on one of the spikes. People often did that, to get it off the ground and make it easier to find if the owner came looking for it. What was unusual today was that there was a second glove next to it – a man's leather glove, bigger and heavier, with the middle finger sticking up from the spike being fed into it. The big glove was rude and childish and the child's glove was standing up with dignity. Niro pulled her gloves off and stuffed them in her pocket before getting out her phone to take a photo.

She looked at the image. It was ... okay. It needed something else. There was only so much she could do using a phone camera, but she could do better than that. She moved closer, changed angles. Now the bigger glove loomed over the smaller one, vaguely threatening. Better. If she squashed herself closer in, maybe she could get it so that the light—

Her phone rang. She almost dropped it.

She swore and stood up, moving away from the railings. It was probably best, anyway. If the owners of the house looked out, they would wonder what the mad woman with the purple-and-blue streaked hair was doing to their railings. Besides, it was her mother calling her.

'Hello, Amma,' she said, as she resumed walking.

'Hello, Nirosha darling, how are you?'

'I'm okay. Actually, I'm just going for a walk.'

There were a few seconds of silence. 'Really? That sounds lovely. Where?'

'Just round the block. It is nice, actually. I might try and do

17

this more often.' A couple of years ago, she had walked around the city all the time – camera around her neck, alert to possibilities. Another thing she'd lost after Mick's betrayal.

'You sound … happier.' Amma's voice was cautious, as though Niro would shatter if she said any more.

The strange thing was, she really was feeling happier. The conversation with Sam had shifted something. *I want the fun, nothing-is-impossible Niro back.* Niro had believed that once. In fact, she'd often said that to Sam when things had been going wrong in Sam's business. Sam was the poster child for seemingly impossible things working out. After all, she had managed to get her business off the ground and bag herself a gorgeous boyfriend within a year of leaving her 'safe' job.

She told her mother about applying for the travel grant. 'If I get it, I'm going to go to Bilbao to photograph the Guggenheim. And then I'm going to enter it into the competition. I would also use the photos for a series on art galleries by rivers – so I've put together an itinerary and an outline. Sam helped me. So did Luke.'

'Oh, that is nice that Samadhi is still helping you with things. She must be very busy now.'

'She is. But she's still there for me.'

'And how is her young man?'

'They're very happy.' It was a little sickening sometimes, but they did try to keep their hands off each other when she was hanging out with them. Niro genuinely liked Luke. He was exactly the right sort of guy for Sam.

'Speaking of young men …'

Niro stopped walking. That tone of voice didn't bode well. 'Amma … I said not to arrange any set-ups for me. I'm not ready.'

'I know, darling, I know. But it has been a long time since you split up with … Mick.' The pause before she said his name was full of implied cursing. 'And anyway, Kumudhini Aunty proposed this one, not me. He's suitable and she thinks he's a catch. She's already invited him to the party at the weekend.'

'Amma, no. I was looking forward to that party as well.'

'It will be fine. There will be a lot of people there. You only have to meet him. Who knows, he might be nice.'

Niro snorted. 'Kumudhini Aunty thinks he's a catch. That just means she thinks he's rich.'

'Nirosha! Don't be rude about your aunty.'

'Sorry.' The apology was a reflex. Kumudhini Aunty had been a fixture all her life. At some point Niro had even thought her glamorous. Now she knew she was just a judgemental pain in the arse. But Kumudhini Aunty was Amma's friend, so being respectful went with the territory. Besides, the Aunties had always been there when she'd needed them.

'Please just be nice to this boy. Just say hello. Give him five minutes and then move on.' Amma gave a little laugh. 'Unless you like him, of course.'

Niro sighed. 'Fine. What's he called? How old is he?'

'His name is Vimal and he's thirty. Just a few years older than you are.'

The walking and talking had taken her round the block and she was approaching the house again. 'Okay,' she said. 'I'll meet him. I can promise you, it's not going to work out.'

'Don't be so negative,' Amma said. 'It might.'

Not if she could help it.

*

Vimal heated up some leftover pasta and sat on the sofa with his tablet, so that he could research what there was to do in the area where Lucien's party was going to be. If there was going to be skiing, he would need the right gear. He had been skiing once before, with Kerry. He hadn't enjoyed it much – but the hot drinks afterwards had been fun. But if there was skiing, he would ski. If it was winter walking, he would walk.

He thought of Kerry's voice accusing him of being boring.

Thirty going on fifty, she'd said. *You never do anything interesting or spontaneous and I'm sick of it.*

Well, he wasn't boring. He worked hard, but that was part of his job and he was good at it. He was fit and healthy. He enjoyed going places and seeing new things. The places Kerry wanted to go had a certain pattern to them – sure, they were in different countries, but the hotels were similar and the experiences felt well-worn and fashionable. It wasn't that he didn't like it. He just wasn't keen on people, like she was. So being seen in the right places by the right people stopped being interesting after a while.

But if that was what it took for her to take him back, then he would do it. The guys she'd been out with since leaving him had been rich and posh and dynamic, so that was what she thought was exciting. He couldn't do posh, but he could do rich, if he wanted to. He'd been brought up to be careful with his money and he was. But perhaps he could ease up on that. He earned a lot and most of it went into savings. He had practically paid off the mortgage on the flat he owned and let out.

He looked around at the flat he lived in right now – it was all he could find to rent at short notice when he'd moved out of the one he'd shared with Kerry. It was nice, suited for only one person. It was not the sort of flat a rich person would live in. He'd have to do something about that in the new year. He could give notice to the tenants who lived in the waterside apartment he owned. He hadn't done so until now because a small part of him was still hoping that this split with Kerry was only temporary and that he would be moving back in with her.

Vimal chewed his dinner thoughtfully. He didn't like giving up. Kerry had clearly not found what she was looking for. So maybe she'd realise that she'd made a mistake. He could meet her halfway. Show her that he wasn't boring. Just being at Lucien's holiday would be a start for that. He nodded to himself. Yes. This would be a good thing. If it didn't work, then at least he knew he'd done his very best.

His phone rang. Putting his food down on the coffee table, he fished the device out of his back pocket. It was his mother.

'Ammi. Hi. I'm just having my dinner.'

'What are you having?'

'Pasta. With sauce, before you ask. And yes, I bought it from the shop. I don't have time to make sauce from scratch.'

'You have to eat properly, putha.'

'Ammi, I'm thirty years old. I can feed myself.'

'I'll bring some things over when I come down next time.'

He smiled into the empty living room. There was no way to stop his mother bringing food. 'That will be nice. Thank you,' he said.

'Listen. I'm calling you for a purpose today.'

Vimal leaned back against the sofa. 'O-kay …' This sounded like trouble. Ammi sounded breathless and excited. He hoped she wasn't ill.

'Do you remember my friend Kumudhini? You met her when we went to that Christmas party that time.'

'No … not really.' He had met so many Sri Lankan Aunties at various times, they all blurred into one. Besides, 'that Christmas party that time' didn't narrow it down much.

'You were about fourteen.'

Well, that might explain why he didn't remember. 'Right. I still don't recall, but go on.'

'Anyway, she called and there's this girl that she thought might be a great match for you.'

'Oh no.' Vimal groaned. 'Not this again. Ammi, I'm not ready. I've only just come out of a relationship and—'

'Putha, it's been a year. You haven't met someone else, have you?'

'No. I haven't. And it's not quite a year. It's seven months.'

'Same thing. You're not getting any younger and you have to find a woman you can marry. Let us help you.'

'I appreciate the offer, I really do, but I'm not ready.'

21

'Well, when will you be? You're thirty now. And I know you're lonely.'

He was about to say, *I'm not lonely*, but he was, wasn't he?

'Why don't you go to Kumudhini's Christmas party and meet this girl,' Ammi said. 'If you like her, then that's great. If not, at least you'll have got out and met some people. There might be other people there your age. In fact, I think this girl is related to that Ranaweera boy that you know from work.'

'Gihan?' Huh. He liked Gihan. Although he didn't remember meeting him as kids, they had met again as adults, at a training thing, and got on well enough to keep in touch. His firm sometimes worked with Vimal's – when that happened, they met for lunch.

'I think they're cousins or something. See. You already have something in common with her.'

Vimal tipped his head back with a chuckle. To hear his mother talk, you'd think he was twelve. 'Okay. Fine. Yes, I'll go to this Christmas do and meet this girl. Where is it? What's her name?'

'Her name is Nirosha. She's an artist or something like that. Very good, apparently.'

Vimal rolled his eyes. Aunties weren't above embroidering the truth a bit. That could mean anything from the woman was a professional artist right down to *she painted a flower once*. 'Okay.'

'I'll send you the details for the party.'

With that important business concluded, Ammi moved on to talking about other things. Vimal closed his eyes and let it wash over him, making appropriate listening noises at the right places. When he finally hung up, his meal was cold. He picked it up and went into the kitchen to reheat it.

The kitchen in the flat was narrow and he didn't like it. When he settled down, he would have a kitchen big enough to fit a table. He had spent most of his childhood doing homework or reading at the kitchen table, while his mother moved around cooking. He felt a kitchen should be a hub for the family to gather. In this poky little kitchen, there was only enough room for him. And his mother was right. He was lonely.

If he managed to win Kerry back, then he would solve that problem as well.

Chapter 4

Niro finished pulling her hair into the most severe plaits that she could manage and examined her handiwork in the mirror. Yep. That should annoy her Aunties no end. No make-up either. Just moisturiser. She slicked on some lip gloss though, because there were limits.

From downstairs, Sam shouted up, 'Niro. We really are leaving now.'

'I'm coming, I'm coming.' She grabbed her bag and thumped down the stairs.

Sam, in the middle of tugging her coat on, stopped and stared. 'Why are you dressed like a children's TV presenter?'

Niro sat on the bottom step and pulled her boots towards her. 'Because Kumudhini Aunty wants to introduce me to someone.'

Sam's boyfriend, Luke, shot her a puzzled look. 'Is this some other Sri Lankan thing I need to know about?' He was clutching a box of cupcakes. It was his first time going to a proper Sri Lankan house party, poor bloke.

Niro stood up and reached for her coat. 'Just the Aunties trying to marry me off. Now that Sam's bagged you, I'm the last spinster left on the shelf.'

Luke opened his mouth and then shut it again. 'I have no idea how to respond to that.'

'Probably best not to then,' said Niro. 'You need me on side this evening to put in a good word here and there. You don't want to antagonise me right from the start.'

'I wouldn't dream of antagonising you, Niro,' said Luke. 'I wouldn't dare.'

Sam, who would normally have joined in with the good-natured bickering, merely flapped her hands and shooed them out of the house.

As they stood on the drive waiting for Sam to lock up, Niro leaned towards Luke and whispered, 'How's she doing?'

'Stressed. Possibly more stressed than I am,' said Luke. 'Which is saying something.'

'You'll both be fine,' said Niro, loudly. 'My mum has been going on and on about how you're a power couple with your businesses. Everyone thinks you're a match made in heaven.'

They got into Luke's Mini, with Niro in the back. It was a good job she didn't need much leg room.

'So who are you being set up with?' Sam asked.

'Dunno. Some guy. I told her I wasn't interested, but apparently, that's not relevant.'

'You never know, you might like him.'

'Not likely though, is it?' Niro brushed lint off the blue corduroy pinafore that she was wearing. 'I'm not saying the Aunties setting you up is a terrible way to meet people, but it is weird.'

'Yeah,' said Sam. 'I'm glad my stepmum didn't try to set me up.'

'I've got off lightly so far, I suppose,' Niro conceded. 'I don't know why the sudden interest from Kumudhini Aunty. It's not like I'm going to fall off a cliff or something. I have a few years before I even hit thirty.'

'Well, I hope things work out,' said Sam. 'Speaking of things working out, have you heard about the grant yet?'

Niro pulled out her phone and checked. 'Nope. Nothing yet. They should be announcing the successful applicants today or tomorrow.'

'Let's hope you find out you've got it in the middle of the party, then you can tell everyone that you're spending a week in Bilbao, taking photographs.'

Niro looked at her phone again before she switched it off and slid it into the pocket of her pinafore. 'That would be so nice. I hate it when people say, "So, what are you doing right now?" It's not like I can say, "Doing social media templates on Fiverr to make ends meet."'

'You could say "freelancing", said Luke.

'I do,' said Niro. She flopped back in her seat. 'I haven't done any proper art in ages. Nothing I can sell anyway.'

Sam twisted round in her seat to look at her. 'But if you get this grant, you can travel and take photos of buildings and then if you win the competition, you'll be an award-winning photographer.'

If she got the grant, at the very least she'd get a holiday. She hadn't been away for a couple of years. Niro snorted. Chance would be a fine thing.

When they got to the party, Sam patted her boyfriend's arm and told him to be himself. In honour of the occasion, Niro refrained from making any snarky comments. Poor Luke looked so frightened, she didn't think he could take a joke right now.

'Right, then. Let's get this over with.' She marched up to the door and rang the doorbell. Looking down at her rainbow-striped tights and bright blue pinafore, she briefly wondered if she'd overdone it a bit. Oh well, too late now.

'Oh my god, what are you wearing?' said Kumudhini Aunty, by way of greeting. 'How am I going to introduce you to someone when you're dressed like a rag doll?'

'You don't have to introduce me to anyone, Aunty,' Niro said, breezily. 'Lovely to see you. Look. Here's Samadhi and her lovely new boyfriend.' She slipped past and went into the house in search of her mother. She found Amma at the dining table, taking cling film off a tray of fish cutlets.

'Amma.' She swooped in to give her mother a hug.

'Hello, darling.' Her mother looked at her outfit and raised her eyebrows. 'Nirosha,' she said reproachfully. 'You're only cheating yourself by trying to hamper Kumudhini. He sounded like a very nice man. You might have liked him … if you'd met him under normal circumstances.'

'Hmm. Chances are a bit slim though, aren't they?' She held up the bag of party food. 'I was going to make spicy chickpeas, but I ran out of time. So I'm afraid I've only got tortilla chips.'

'Can you find a bowl and put them out?' Amma looked past her. She dropped her voice to a conspiratorial whisper. 'Is that Sam and Luke? He looks very nervous.'

'Yes,' Niro whispered back, glad that Sam was providing such an excellent distraction. 'I like Luke,' she added, making good on her promise to help him. 'He's nice and he absolutely worships Sam.'

'Ah, that's lovely,' said Amma. 'Let me go and say hello.'

And just like that, the heat was off Niro. Thank goodness.

Niro's mother, Sam's stepmother and Kumudhini Aunty were firm friends. They had been in and out of each other's lives for decades. A paralegal secretary, an administrator at a grief counselling service and a physiotherapist, respectively, they were nothing like each other, but somehow their friendship seemed to work. Amma and Sam's stepmother, Ruvani, were sisters. Kumudhini Aunty was … an honorary aunty.

The 'Aunties' always had a Christmas party, which you had to attend if you were in London, unless you were dying or having a baby. Kumudhini Aunty was hosting this year and everyone had been given arrival times so that she could terrorise everyone in order of how much she loved them. Unfortunately for Niro, she was very loved. Which meant she was early. It also meant that Kumudhini Aunty could loudly worry about her prospects before the rest of the guests arrived. At least it was better than her doing it in front of everyone.

Niro went in search of her father and found him talking politics with some other uncles in the front room. He stood up when he saw her and when she bent her head, kissed the top of it. Even though she could see his eyes widen when he took in her outfit, he didn't comment on it. She loved him all the more for it.

She made small talk for a few minutes, answering 'What are you doing now?' with 'Freelancing', which worked surprisingly well. She made her escape before they asked for details. She headed for the kitchen, grabbing herself a glass of wine from the drinks table as she went past. She had the feeling she was going to need it.

Her aunt Ruvani was in the kitchen, plating out food. 'Hey, Lokuamma.' Another hug. Another look of surprise at her outfit. Yeah. She'd definitely overdone it this time. She wondered if she could borrow a cardigan from someone. Kumudhini Aunty would probably offer her something, but Aunty was tiny and it was unlikely that anything of hers would fit Niro.

'Is Samadhi here?' her aunt asked. 'And Luke?'

'I'm sure they'll come and find you soon. They're probably still at the front door, talking to Kumudhini Aunty.'

Ruvani Lokuamma made a face. 'Do I need to go rescue them?'

'I think Luke will cope.'

For a second, her aunt hovered, uncertainty written all over her expression. 'Is ... is Samadhi happy?' she asked, cautiously.

'Very,' said Niro, firmly.

'That's good.' Ruvani Lokuamma's shoulders seemed to drop, ever so slightly. 'That's very good.'

Niro gestured towards the Tupperware containers full of food. 'Do you want me to do that? You go talk to them.'

'Oh, thank you, darling. Yes. Let's do that.' Ruvani handed her a tub full of home-made sausage rolls and bustled out.

Niro hid in the kitchen, laying sausage rolls on trays and making a salad. Guests drifted in as they arrived and ended up staying for a chat. She loved this part of the Aunty Parties; she got to catch up with people she hadn't seen all year.

But she couldn't hide in the kitchen forever, so she eventually braved the living room, which was now full of bodies and noise. Eventually, Kumudhini Aunty found her as she stood by the food table, grabbing a plateful of snacks.

'Come, come,' she said. 'Let me introduce you to Vimal.' Kumudhini Aunty's accent, worn away after three decades, always came back when she'd had a bit to drink. 'You'll like him. Come.'

Niro let herself be dragged over to meet this guy. Aunty was so keen on him that Niro was 99.9 per cent certain he wouldn't be her type at all.

Kumudhini Aunty tapped a man on the shoulder. He turned.

Niro took him in, from the trendy haircut to the very tasteful Christmas jumper and chinos. He wasn't bad-looking. Okay, maybe even good-looking in a Dev Patel sort of way. But everything about him said *I have money and I know how to spend it.* Yup. Definitely not her type.

His gaze flicked all the way down to her rainbow-striped tights, and back again. He smiled politely. 'Hi.'

Even though he was smiling, his eyes looked tight, almost scared.

She gave him her cheesiest grin. 'Hi.'

'Nirosha, this is Vimal. He works in a bank. Vimal, this is Nirosha. She's an artist. Very talented.' Aunty raised her eyebrows, to show how impressed she was with Niro's talent.

'I work *for* a bank. Not actually in … um. Doesn't matter.' He seemed to remember where he was. 'Hi. Nice to meet you. I'm Vimal.' He held out his hand.

'Niro. Lovely to meet you too. Delighted.' She carried on smiling and shook his hand. There was no way Aunty could accuse her of being rude.

Aunty gave her a warning glance. 'I'll leave you two to talk,' she said firmly. Another pointed glare at Niro, and she drifted off to pick up some food, still within earshot.

Right. Making conversation. She studied him. He still looked

29

scared, which was fine. The outfit and the fixed smile were doing their work.

Vimal clasped his hands in front of him, then seemed to change his mind and joined them behind his back. 'So. Aunty says you're a friend of her friend.'

'Yeah. My mum and Kumudhini Aunty are best buddies. How about you?' She relaxed her fixed smile. The poor guy seemed so uncomfortable, she felt sorry for him. After all, he was probably being forced to be here, just as she was.

'Similar, I guess. My parents know her from ages ago. I used to live up north, so we didn't get down here that much.' He put his hands in his pockets. 'Oh. And I think my friend Gihan is somehow connected …?'

'Gihan? Oh yeah. My cousin.' She hadn't expected him to know someone she actually liked. 'How do you know him?'

'He and I work in the same sort of area. So we've met. You know.' He looked around the room, no doubt hoping for a way out. 'Is he here?'

Okay, this was now getting even more uncomfortable than usual. She had been hoping she could talk to him for five minutes and never see him again. But if he knew Gihan, then there was a risk she'd run into him again. 'He's supposed to be here. He's in London this week,' said Niro. 'But he's late.'

Vimal nodded. 'As usual.'

Again, the slight dissonance of his obviously knowing her cousin jarred. But this time her smile was real. 'Yeah.'

There was a moment they both stood there looking out at the rest of the party, avoiding eye contact. Across the room, a tall man in a suit walked in.

'Gihan.' Niro waved to him. Thank goodness.

Gihan, Sam's tall and lanky big brother, weaved his way through people until he reached them and gave Niro a quick, one-armed hug.

'Vimal, mate. Good to see you again.' He clapped Vimal on

the shoulder. 'I see you've met Niro already.' He looked at her. 'Who appears to be dressed as an extra from *Teletubbies* today.'

'It's a long story.' She grabbed the chance to escape. 'You guys must have a lot to catch up about, so I'll leave you to it. Nice to meet you, Vimal. I'll catch you later, Gihan Aiya.' And she hurried off to a different room where Sam and Luke were chatting to some friends of the Aunties.

*

Niro managed to avoid Vimal for the rest of the evening. Every so often, she'd catch sight of him, chatting to Gihan or standing around awkwardly making conversation with someone else. Despite his polished appearance, he looked so uncomfortable that she felt the urge to help. She had to give herself a stern talking-to. Her desire to rescue people was not useful at this point. Not with Kumudhini Aunty watching her every move.

Despite her best efforts to be the useful one who topped up glasses and did the jobs in the kitchen, she ended up having to have the 'What are you doing these days? Have you got a man yet?' conversation several times.

Finally, it got to the point in the evening when people with small children started to leave. The older adults were getting quite squiffy already. There would be singing soon.

Sam tapped her on the shoulder. 'A few of us are going to the pub. Are you coming?'

'Stupid question. Of course I'm coming. Let me just say goodbye to Amma and I'll be right with you.'

Not finding her mother downstairs, she hesitantly tried upstairs. Kumudhini Aunty had been a widow for almost a decade and lived happily alone. The spare room had been turned into the coat room for the party. From the main bedroom, voices could be heard. It sounded like the Aunties had decided to have a quiet chat upstairs.

31

Niro raised her hand to knock when her mother's voice made her hesitate.

'I don't know, Kumudhini, she's just not interested in getting married.' A sigh. 'I don't know what's got into her lately, she's getting more and more stubborn and distant.'

'Maybe she's getting lonely now that Samadhi isn't around so much anymore?' This was Ruvani Lokuamma.

'Could be. We used to talk a lot. We don't so much now. I'm getting a bit worried about her to be honest.'

'Shall I ask Samadhi to talk to her?'

There was a pause as her mum considered this. 'No,' she said, finally. 'I'll talk to her in the new year. It's been nearly two years since she split up with Mick. She's clearly not getting past it on her own.'

'But WHY doesn't she want to get married?' Kumudhini Aunty demanded. She believed that marriage was The Only Goal for anyone single. 'Don't think I didn't notice that she dressed like a clown specifically because I said there was someone I wanted her to meet.'

'She had her heart broken once,' said Ruvani Lokuamma.

'Pah, love,' said Kumudhini Aunty. 'Love is optional. Marriage is useful.'

'It's not like it was when we were young. Or more to the point, when our parents were young. You don't need to have a husband to get along in life now. Women can manage just fine on their own,' said Niro's mother tightly.

Outside the door, Niro did a silent air grab in support.

'That's true,' said Ruvani, the peacekeeper of the group. 'Girls nowadays have more options.'

Kumudhini Aunty sniffed. 'Some do,' she said. 'But Nirosha … She's an artist. That's not a real job. She doesn't have a good job or prospects. She doesn't even have good looks to fall back on. She's so dark. And she's getting fatter. What options does she have, really?'

32

There was a sharp intake of breath and tut from one of the other two.

Even Kumudhini Aunty recognised that she'd gone too far. 'I'm sorry. I didn't mean it like that. Looks aren't everything. The girl can cook and she has nice clear skin. She will make a fine wife for someone who doesn't want someone … conventionally perfect.'

Niro quietly took a few steps backwards until she was at the top of the stairs. Something was stirring in her chest and she didn't want to have witnesses when her heart cracked open. She had to say goodbye and get out of here. She pushed her feelings down, took a breath and called out, 'Amma, are you up here?'

She strode forward again as loudly as she could in stockinged feet and knocked on Kumudhini Aunty's bedroom door. When she opened it, she saw her mum and aunt sitting on the edge of the bed. Kumudhini Aunty was on the dressing table stool. All three turned towards her and smiled.

'I'm heading off.' Niro pointed over her shoulder. 'Going to the pub with Sam and Luke.'

'Ah. Of course. They'll be looking for me,' said her aunt. 'I'd better go downstairs.'

'Me too.' Kumudhini Aunty got to her feet, slowly. 'I will see you in the new year, Nirosha. Have a lovely Christmas.'

Niro looked at the ground. 'Thank you, Aunty. You too.'

When the other two women had left, her mother said, very softly, 'You heard?'

Niro nodded.

'She didn't mean it like that. You know what she's like.' She stood up and put her hand to Niro's cheek. 'I am worried about you, though. You're very … sad, these days. Do you want to talk about it?'

Niro took a second to lean into her mother's palm. She suddenly felt very tired. If she didn't leave now, she was going to start crying. 'I'm okay, Amma. Just tired. It's been a long year.' She leaned forward and gave her mother a hug. 'I'll see you after the new year, okay. Have a great trip to Colombo. I'll see you when you get back, yeah?'

Before her mother could say anything more, she turned and fled.

The others had already left for the pub, so Niro put her hands in her pockets and strode determinedly along by herself. Kumudhini Aunty's comment rankled. It wasn't the first time she'd said some-thing like that. Mostly, Niro ignored it. It had taken her years to stop dwelling on remarks about her weight or dark skin tone. People were going to say things regardless of how she felt about them. She reminded herself that she got to choose whether she cared about what they said or not. Sure, she was overweight, but she was healthy. It wasn't like she hadn't tried dieting. She just naturally gravitated towards this shape. And there was absolutely nothing she could do about being dark-skinned. So Aunty and her opinions could just go take a flying jump.

She turned the corner and saw her cousins ahead of her. She didn't bother trying to catch up with them. She needed to regain her composure before she faced them. Sam and Gihan would be sympathetic. They'd both been at the sharp end of Aunty's barbs before. At some point in their lives, each one of them had also been at the receiving end of her kindness, so they'd all learned to forgive her.

Niro sighed. Kumudhini Aunty's comment aside, it seemed everyone had noticed that she wasn't her usual positive self. She really needed to do something about that.

*

Vimal was grateful when Gihan suggested the pub. He wasn't good at parties and Sri Lankan ones made him feel inadequate. There hadn't been much of a community where he'd grown up, so he'd missed out on knowing Sri Lankan people. Now, being at a party surrounded by people who looked like him felt strange.

34

Not good or bad, but strange. On the one hand, it was comforting. It reminded him of his parents. On the other hand, he was sure he was messing up all the time. Saying the wrong things, doing the wrong things … basically being a bad Sri Lankan.

He eyed Gihan with envy. Gihan was a man comfortable in his own skin. He knew what he was and where he fitted. They walked down the road together. Gihan's sister, Samadhi, and her boyfriend were a few steps behind.

He cast about for a topic of conversation. 'So, how's Helen?' He had met Gihan's girlfriend a few times before she moved overseas for work.

'Oh, fine,' Gihan said, breezily. 'More importantly though, how are you bearing up? Sorry to hear that you and Kerry split up.'

The sympathy in his voice told Vimal everything he needed to know. Of course Gihan would have heard the gossip. The grapevine worked fast. It sounded like everyone knew that Kerry had dumped him and that he wasn't taking it well. 'I'm good, thanks.'

'I … er … saw Kerry at a work thing a few days ago.'

Vimal winced. She seemed to be going to a lot of social 'things' now that she wasn't with him. Had she been with this new guy that Lucien mentioned? 'How is she?'

'Seemed fine, actually,' said Gihan. 'She said you guys were still friends.'

Kerry had asked that they stay friends. He had not agreed. It was easy to say 'let's stay friends' when you were the one severing ties and moving on. Especially if you moved swiftly on to a new partner. 'I suppose.'

There was an awkward silence as they walked along.

'So,' said Gihan, brightly, 'what are you doing this Christmas?'

Okay. This was a better topic of conversation. 'I'm going to Lucien's New Year's do.'

Gihan gave a low whistle. 'Oh, nice.'

'What's that?' said Sam.

They'd reached the pub. Gihan held the door for the others

and then joined them at the back. 'This guy, Lucien, he works in the same place as Vimal. Well, I say works ... Anyway, he's the second son of a lord or a marquis something or other. Really posh. He has these strange exclusive parties in the most bizarre places. He always invites different people and it's a bit of a coup to get invited. How on earth did you manage it?' This last was directed at Vimal, who felt a warm wash of smugness.

'He actually invited me ages ago, when I was still with Kerry. I thought he wouldn't want me to come now that Kerry and I aren't a couple, but he does. I've been working with him on a couple of projects lately. He sold a few of my models and one of the projections made a hefty amount for the client. So ... I guess I know him in my own right, now.' Vimal waved a hand, as though being suddenly accepted into the loud and confident crowd was a natural progression. It really wasn't. He was the numbers guy. They liked him if the numbers told them what they wanted. The rest of the time, they just tolerated him. Lucien's attention had come as a surprise. Vimal still wasn't sure if it was a good thing or not. If it hadn't been for the chance to win Kerry back, he might have been firmer about refusing the invitation.

'The places he holds his parties at are always a bit out there.' Gihan found a table and shrugged off his long overcoat. 'Like that time he had a dinner party on the edge of a cliff. Or the one in the huge Scottish castle.' There was a hint of wistfulness in his voice.

Vimal wasn't used to being envied. Maybe he could make this project of reinventing himself work. If Gihan was impressed with his social progress, then maybe there was a chance he could impress Kerry too. 'This time it's in Switzerland. It's a short holiday with a New Year's party tagged on at the end.' He pulled out his phone. 'It's a house built into the hillside. It's quite impressive.' He found the website for the place and showed it to Gihan, who gave another low whistle.

Sam wanted to see, so Vimal's phone got passed across to her.

'Oh, that's beautiful,' she said. 'I love how they've made it invisible from some angles.' She pushed the phone back across the table. 'You know who you should show that to? Niro. She's doing a photography thing, to do with architecture in natural landscape. She'd be really interested in that place.'

Vimal thought of the girl he'd met. In her rainbow tights and loud blue pinafore, she didn't look like the sort of person who photographed beautiful buildings. She looked more like someone who made things out of loo roll inners and sticky back plastic. But he didn't want to be rude, so he said, 'Okay.'

As it turned out, she came in a few minutes later, looking harassed. Gihan insisted that Vimal show her the website of the place in Switzerland.

Her expression was sceptical at first, but then the frown lines vanished. 'Oh, wow. That is beautiful.' She looked up at him. 'May I?'

Some of the brittle anger that he'd sensed in her before was gone now. He let her have his phone. She scrolled through the website, looking at the photos. 'That's a really impressive building. They've worked hard to make it blend in with the surrounding landscape.' She handed the phone back, with a small smile. Unlike the fake grin she'd given him earlier, this smile was warm. He smiled back.

Niro gave her cousin a suspicious look. 'Why did you guys just show that fancy house to me?'

'For your project about landscape and architecture,' said Gihan.

Niro glanced across to where Sam and Luke were at the bar. 'Sam told you, then?'

'Yeah. It sounds really good. You've got a real eye for that sort of thing.'

Vimal didn't know what Gihan was like with family, but even to him, he sounded over-effusive. There was something going on here, between the cousins, that he couldn't quite understand. Was it something obvious that most people could pick up? Was he dim for not seeing it? Kerry often told him he couldn't read the room. A long time ago, she'd found it cute.

He forced his attention back. He had to stop doing that. Second-guessing everything while he was at work was an occupational hazard. He didn't need to impress the people here. They were … well, not his friends exactly, but people whose approval he didn't need. They didn't need his, either. He only really knew Gihan. He'd met Sam and Niro when they were all children, he was sure of it, but none of them remembered each other, beyond that vague 'child of my parents' friends' way. They were, as far as he could tell, nice people.

He tuned back in to Niro and Gihan bickering.

'You don't have to show me pictures of random houses,' Niro was saying.

'It's not a random house,' Gihan shot back. 'Vimal's going there after Christmas.'

She turned and looked at him. Her eyes were huge in the low light of the pub. 'Nice,' she said, making the word stretch. 'What a lovely place to go for a holiday. It must cost a fortune to stay there.'

'I'm not renting it myself,' he said. 'I'm going to a friend's party, which is being held there.'

Her eyes flicked to his hair and back again. 'Lucky you.' She turned her attention back to Gihan and Vimal felt dismissed. Was he that uninteresting? *You're so boring.* He suddenly wished he could leave. There was nothing waiting for him at home, apart from his bed. Although, an early night would be nice …

Niro said, 'Anyway, I'm not doing the landscape and architecture challenge. I didn't get the travel grant.'

'Oh what?' Sam returned. 'When did you hear?' She passed Niro a drink and sat down next to Vimal. Her boyfriend brought three pints over and handed one each to Vimal and Gihan.

'About twenty minutes before we left Aunty's house.' Niro waved her phone. 'High quality of applicants … blah, blah, blah.' She put her phone facedown. 'So, no trip to photograph nice buildings for me.'

There was a chorus of commiserations from around the table.

Feeling that he ought to contribute, Vimal said, 'That sucks, I'm sorry.'

She inclined her head in acknowledgement and took a long draw from her drink.

Sam giggled. 'You look so weird with your hair like that. You look far too young to be drinking.'

'Actually, I hate these plaits.' She flipped the plaits in front of her shoulders and started unravelling one. 'I did them so tight that my scalp has been hurting all evening.'

'So, why ARE you dressed like that?' said Gihan.

'Aunty said she had some guy lined up for me to meet, so I thought I'd be as off-putting as possible. Sorry, Vimal.' She shot him a grin and started working on her other plait. Released, the hair fell on her shoulders in regular waves. She seemed to be morphing into someone different in front of his eyes. What a strange girl.

'I wasn't wanting to be introduced to anyone either,' he said. 'So you really didn't need to go to so much effort on my behalf.'

Niro gave him an amused look. 'Kinda wasted my time, huh?'

The mischievous gleam in her eye made him smile back. 'Just a bit.'

'Especially as you're both in the pub together right now. Talking,' Gihan pointed out.

And now it was all awkward again. How was he supposed to respond to that? He couldn't insult Niro by saying he wasn't interested at all, even now. But he genuinely wasn't interested. He hadn't been interested in anyone since Kerry, because he had given his heart to her.

Niro solved the problem for him by looking him up and down and saying, 'No. I think we can agree we're safe.'

Vimal realised his shoulders were up around his ears and relaxed them. 'Yes. Let's agree on that.'

He and Niro clinked glasses. Everyone laughed and the

atmosphere settled into something comfortable again.

Vimal listened as he was told about Sam's business and Gihan's travels and possible changes happening with his work. He was several pints in and feeling more relaxed than he had been in a long time when his phone rang. He didn't think before he answered.

'Vimal? Lucien.'

Bloody hell. He sat up straighter. 'Er. Hi.'

'Just running through some logistics for the New Year's bash. You're still coming, right?'

'Yes, yes. I'm still coming.'

'Will you be bringing a plus one?'

'What?' The words didn't make sense. Vimal's mind went completely blank.

'The girlfriend. I've got you down for a double room.'

When Vimal didn't reply fast enough, Lucien said, 'I mentioned your friend Kerry was coming, didn't I?'

'Kerry?' The mention of her name made him feel light-headed.

'Yes, she's bringing Woolly. Apparently, they're together now. Is that going to be a problem? I know you and she used to be a thing. I felt it was only right that I should tell you that she's bringing her other half and ... you might want to bring your other half too, see. Unless you're still single, of course. In which case, I'll have to shuffle some people around. Bit inconvenient, really, but needs must. So. Both coming?'

Several scenarios ran through his mind. He could go by himself and try to impress Kerry, but that would look pathetic. If he had a girlfriend, he would look less pathetic and, importantly, not boring.

'Going to have to rush you, old man.'

'Oh. Yes. Of course. I'll bring my girlfriend. Sure.' His mouth seemed to have attained sentience all by itself. 'She'll love it.' What was he saying? He couldn't find a girlfriend in the next three weeks. That was madness. 'I'll ... er ... check with her and confirm tomorrow, yeah?'

'Top banana. Tomorrow, then.' There was a click and Lucien was gone.

Vimal slowly lowered the phone. 'Shit.' He stared at the now silent phone. What had possessed him? He raised his head and saw the others all looking at him.

'You have a girlfriend?' said Gihan. 'You should tell Aunty. That would stop her trying to match you up.'

Vimal shook his head. 'I don't have a girlfriend.'

'But you just said—'

'I know. I know I just said. I panicked. Lucien said that Kerry was coming to this party and she's bringing her partner, so did I want to bring mine. I had visions of sitting there, being the single one, while Kerry cosies up to her partner and I just … panicked.' He groaned and put his head in his hands. 'I'm such an idiot.'

There was a sympathetic silence around the table, until Gihan said, 'Unless …'

Vimal looked up, hope flaring in his chest. 'Unless?'

'Unless you take a fake girlfriend.'

Sam laughed and leaned against Luke. 'Like in a romcom,' she said.

'But we know, from romcom movie night,' said Niro, 'fake dating never works.'

The spark of hope died. 'I'll just have to call him back and say … the girlfriend is busy and can't come.' Vimal sighed. 'It'll be awkward, but at least I won't be the saddo who got dumped by Kerry months ago and then couldn't find anyone else.'

'Why don't *you* do it, Niro?' said Gihan.

'What?' Niro looked up from her phone. 'Do what? Be the fake girlfriend? Piss off.'

'You'd get to go to a posh person's party in that beautiful villa that would be perfect for, say, a photography competition about architecture and landscape.'

Vimal looked at Niro. She was … well, different. She was artistic

41

and unconventional. He couldn't think of anyone who looked less likely to fit in to the polished circles that Lucien hung out in. Although … Kerry had called him boring and Niro was anything but boring. Wait. What was he thinking? It was a stupid idea from start to finish. He couldn't ask a random girl to pretend to be his girlfriend. 'Gihan, mate,' he said, gently. 'You're being weird.'

'It is a very nice building,' said Sam.

'You can shut up, too,' said Niro.

'But it is. Looks lovely against the landscape.'

'You said you needed a holiday and a place to photograph,' said Gihan. 'And Vimal needs a fake girlfriend. I can vouch for him being a good bloke.'

Niro pointed a finger at first Sam, then Gihan. 'Stop it.' She turned to Vimal. 'Tell them they're being stupid, will you?'

He should do just that. But then he'd have to phone Lucien back and tell him he was coming alone. And Kerry might hear what he'd said, and she would work out he'd lied about having a girlfriend in the first place and then he'd look like a liar as well as a complete loser. Besides, no one could call him boring if he was with someone vibrant like Niro.

Niro scowled at Gihan. 'I can't believe you're trying to pimp me out. What kind of cousin are you?'

Gihan looked wounded. 'I'm only thinking that—'

'Actually,' Vimal interrupted, 'I know it's a lot to ask. It would be a big help.'

Niro's glare turned on him. If looks could kill, he would have been reduced to ash in a second. He put his hands together in a pleading manner. The glare softened, just a fraction. That was good. She was considering it.

'I would pay for everything. Even for hiring ski stuff, if you need it. And I promise, I'll be a total gentleman the whole time.' He held up his hands. 'All you'd have to do is some acting and pretend you like me.'

'I … am a pretty good actress …' She sounded less uncertain now.

'Lucien's parties are meant to be quite luxurious,' said Gihan. 'It'll be a good chance to see how the other half live.'

Niro gave Vimal a long, thoughtful stare. 'Why is this so important to you, anyway?'

Vimal raised his eyes to the pub ceiling, where strings of fairy lights sagged. 'My ex, Kerry, is going to be there. She's going to be with her new boyfriend. She's been dating the same sort of guys since she split up with me and they never seem to last long. I thought maybe ... it would be a good time to show her that she made a mistake. At the very least, to spend a bit of time with her.'

He lowered his gaze and found Niro watching him intently.

'You still love your ex?' she said softly.

He nodded. 'I know it sounds pathetic. But I'd like another chance to show her that I'm not ... that I can do interesting things and be okay in the sort of company she likes.'

'What do you mean? What sort of company does she like?'

How best to explain Lucien and his gang? 'I have worked in this team for nearly two years. I hang out with the other quants, but the sales guys and the traders ... they're our colleagues, but they're the stars. They treat us like colleagues sometimes, but never friends. So me being invited to one of these shindigs is a big deal. And Kerry was always keen to move in those circles.'

Niro wrinkled her nose. 'They sound horrible.'

He shrugged. 'They're glamorous and confident and they do interesting things. It would be nice to be part of that.' He'd never tried to be a part of that before. Maybe it was time to try something new. It would make him less boring.

'Ugh. It sounds like the popular crowd at school.'

'They are a bit like that,' said Gihan. 'I was lucky. When I was a trainee, my group had mostly normal people. If you get a group of the posh ones together it can be pretty bad. They went to school together or played croquet together or whatever and they're pretty cliquey. Lucien's not so bad though. He's friendly.'

'Still sounds like a playground.'

43

Vimal shrugged. 'Sometimes, it feels like it too.'

Niro looked at him steadily. For a second, his gaze met her eyes and he saw sympathy flash through them. She nodded. 'Okay. Fine, I'll do it.'

'Really?' He could do this. He could go to Lucien's party and hold his head up high. If he played this right, he might even be able to make Kerry see that he wasn't the staid guy she thought he was. His heart rose. 'That would be fantastic. Thank you so much!'

She gave him a small smile and a nod. He revised his opinion of her again. She was weird, sure. But she was kind. If he was going to pretend to be someone's partner, kind was a very good thing.

'There should be some ground rules, though,' Niro said. 'I'm pretending to be your girlfriend, right? So, I guess hand-holding is okay. No kissing.'

'Obviously, no kissing,' said Vimal, horrified that she'd even thought that. 'And I'll ask Lucien if we can have two rooms. Or at least, twin beds.'

'You could say it's for cultural reasons,' said Niro.

'Wait, what about kisses on the cheek?' said Sam. 'I mean, if you're together, even quite new and very chaste, it would be weird to not even kiss each other on the cheek.'

'Fair point,' said Gihan.

Vimal frowned. 'Niro? Your call.'

She shrugged. 'I'm okay with that.'

'This is going to be more complicated than I first thought,' said Vimal. He hadn't planned this properly.

'It always looks super easy in the movies,' said Sam, slurring slightly.

Niro shook her head. 'The way I see it, it's just a piece of acting. I've done stage stuff. I can act like I'm in love ... or at least in extreme like.'

'And you need to get your backstory straight,' said Luke, who had been silent so far. 'Like, how did you meet?'

When Gihan gave him a quizzical look, Luke shrugged. 'What?

44

I go to romcom movie nights, too.'

Vimal and Niro looked at each other. 'How about … the truth?' he suggested.

'What? An aunty introduced us?'

'Yeah. And we didn't object to each other and decided to make a go of it. That way, if we don't look super in love, we have an excuse. We're in a sort of arranged-match scenario.'

'Oh, I like that,' said Niro. 'So my motivation is that I'm tired of being single and I'm making a go of this because you're as good a bloke as any. That's good, because if your ex gets jealous, then she'll also know that she's in with a chance if she wants you back. Clever.'

Kerry getting jealous and wanting him back would be a great outcome. So he nodded.

'So, what sort of a woman am I?' said Niro. 'Sophisticated? Wild? Sweet and demure?'

Gihan laughed. 'You couldn't carry off sweet and demure for a whole week. You're not that good an actress.'

'I bet I could,' said Niro. 'But fair point about having to stay in character for twenty-four-seven.'

'How about, you just be a version of your real self?' said Vimal. 'That way there's less chance of one of us slipping up.'

'So … artist. Creative type,' said Niro, nodding.

'But less argumentative than your usual self,' said Sam.

'I'm not argumentative!'

Gihan snorted into his beer.

'I'm sure you'll be fine,' said Vimal, although he wasn't sure of anything of the sort. 'Just be the most charming version of yourself that you can.'

'Charming. Gotcha,' Niro said, then looked at her cousins who were both laughing now. 'Shut up, you two.'

'I owe you a drink,' said Vimal. 'In fact, I owe all of you a drink.' He escaped to the bar. The whole business of a fake girlfriend had escalated somewhat. He couldn't really believe it was happening.

Chapter 5

Niro woke up with a terrible feeling of foreboding. She frowned at the ceiling. She tried to lift her head. Oh, and she had a hangover as well, it seemed. That was a bad combination. What had she done last night?

Carefully, so as not to upset her headache too much, she looked around and did a little stock-check. She was in her own room. Good. Alone. Even better. She cautiously checked what she was wearing. Pyjamas. Result! So far, so good.

Easing herself out of bed, she found a jumper and pulled it over her head, then tiptoed downstairs in search of painkillers.

Niro and Sam's little flat had two bedrooms and a bathroom upstairs and an open-plan kitchen/living room downstairs. It was part of an old house that had been sectioned off into flats, so the ceilings were high and the rooms were big enough for them not to feel too tiny.

When she got downstairs, she heard snoring. Another frown as she prodded her memory. Oh yes, Gihan and his friend Vimal had probably stayed over. She crept in, heading for the kitchen.

Gihan was asleep on the sofa, head tucked in, snoring. There was a blanket-covered bundle on the floor that must be Vimal. The sense of foreboding was back. Something to do with Vimal.

What was it?

Nope. Nothing was going to get past her headache until she'd had some painkillers and at least one cup of coffee. She put the kettle on and searched for the pills.

A sound from the living room made her turn. Vimal was sitting up, looking very confused. His fancy hair was sticking out at all angles. It made him appear a bit less annoying.

'Morning,' she said, in a loud whisper. It came out all hoarse and husky.

He jumped. 'Oh,' he said, quietly. 'Good morning.'

'I'm making coffee. Do you want one?'

'Yes, please.' He looked down at his T-shirt and tugged it straight. Niro realised that his chinos, shirt and jumper had been neatly folded and placed on the coffee table, which had been pushed to the side. He must have slept in his undershirt and boxers.

There was a moment of weirdness as they looked at each other. What were the rules for coming downstairs and finding random men asleep in your living room? No, not random. Just men. One of whom, she didn't know very well.

'I ... er ... am going to get up now,' Vimal said.

Niro shrugged. Why was he telling her that?

'Right. Yes.' He pushed the blankets off himself and stood up. In his underwear, he looked tall and lanky and really not very polished at all.

Niro turned away and busied herself with making coffee. Slowly, memory trickled back in. A holiday. She had agreed to go on holiday ... with Vimal? No, that didn't seem right. There was more to it. The vision of that beautiful house set into the snowy mountainside popped into her mind. Oh. The villa. The incredible underground villa that was sunk into the mountain so that you could see it only from the front. That was it. She had agreed to go there with him, to some posh toff's party ... provided she was allowed to photograph the house.

She leaned against the worktop and let out a long breath. She had agreed to go on a fancy holiday with Vimal and pose as his fake girlfriend. To make his ex jealous … or something. Ugh. What a terrible idea. Hopefully, it had just been a joke. The kettle boiled. She got the cafetière out of the cupboard and loaded it up with coffee. Since Luke had started coming round, Sam had been buying a better standard of coffee.

While she waited for the coffee to brew, Niro turned her attention to the sink. It was filled with bottles and glasses. Urgh. Not yet. Coffee first. She took a bin bag out in readiness.

She had just poured two mugs of coffee when Vimal re-emerged, dressed as he had been the night before, only slightly scruffier. The shadow beard still looked immaculate, but his hair had lost all perkiness.

'Coffee.' She slid the mug across the breakfast bar that served as a barrier between the living room and the kitchen. Most of the time, it also served as a breakfast bar.

'Thanks.'

There was a strained silence as they both blew on their drinks. Niro wished she'd thought to put a bra on. Hopefully the jumper was enough to disguise the baggy mass of boob.

Vimal cleared his throat. 'Listen, last night you said you'd go to a New Year's thing with me. Do you remember?'

'That was a joke, though, right?' It seemed like it should be a joke, but … she had a feeling it wasn't.

He looked taken aback. Okay. Clearly not a joke.

'It wasn't a joke,' he said. 'But you don't have to do it if you don't want to, obviously.'

She stared at him. 'It's a ridiculous idea,' she said. 'No one does that "pretending to date someone to make your ex jealous" thing in real life. It's stupid.'

He looked so crestfallen, she said, 'Seriously, it's very unlikely you'll get her back that way.'

'I know that,' he said. 'But I have to try. I've already committed to going.' He sighed and peered down into his coffee. 'Kerry's going there with her new bloke and I'm going to be poor little Vimal, who got dumped seven months ago and still hasn't got over it. Everyone will be giving me pitying looks and it'll be embarrassing. At least, with someone else there, it would take the heat off me and I can enjoy everyone's company. I don't want to look like a total loser.'

She made a sceptical face. 'What if it doesn't work and you look like a total loser anyway? You and I?' She gestured between them. 'There's no way anyone is going to believe we're a couple. I'd never go out with someone like you.'

He stiffened. 'Well, you're not exactly my type either.'

Now she didn't know whether to be angry or disgusted. 'Glad we've cleared that up. I'm going to go have a shower.' She grabbed her coffee and stalked out.

'Wait. I didn't mean it like that.'

Niro rolled her eyes. No. People never admitted they did. She marched upstairs to the shower, not caring how much noise she was making. She knew she was fat. She was fine with that, but other people seemed to have massive problems. 'Not exactly my type. Hah.'

She lathered up the shampoo and rubbed viciously at her scalp. The cheek of the man. Besides, he was the one in need of a fake girlfriend, not her. Twit.

*

Vimal pressed his eyes shut. Okay. That hadn't gone well. He took a sip of the too-hot coffee and winced. What exactly had he said to Lucien last night? He remembered sending a message. Where was his phone? After a few minutes of searching, he found it, turned off, on the floor. He turned it back on and let it buzz and ping.

The noise woke Gihan up. He clutched his head. 'What time is it?' Before Vimal could answer, he said, 'Toast.'

49

Vimal frowned. 'There's coffee. No toast yet, but I'm sure we could see if Niro has some bread.'

'I know where it is.' Gihan hauled himself off the sofa and staggered into the kitchen in his shirt and boxer shorts.

Vimal shook his head and checked his messages. There was one from Lucien saying: *Fabulous. I have told the villa to expect two of you.*

'Oh no.' He stared at the message. Scrolling back, he could see his messages sounded entirely sensible, if you overlooked the fact that he'd just made up a girlfriend.

'What's up?' Gihan put the bread in to toast and came back.

'What did I do? Lucien's confirmed that he's expecting me and a girlfriend. I don't have a girlfriend.'

'I thought you'd arranged to take Niro.' Gihan shook out his trousers and pulled them on.

'She changed her mind.'

'Oh, what? I thought she wanted to photograph the house.'

'Hmm.' Vimal turned off the screen. Reading the message over and over wasn't going to change what it said. 'She's not wrong, though. It's a stupid idea.'

'That's one way to look at it,' said Gihan. 'The other is that it's a good opportunity for Niro to get out and do something fun ... and you get to save face. A win-win.'

'I'm sure Niro could find other ways to get out and do stuff. She seems quite ... able.'

Gihan made a so-so motion with his hands. 'She comes across as quite confident. And in many situations, she is ... but lately, she's been a little bit down what with one thing or another. Sam and I have been trying to get her to go out a bit, see if she can regain her old spark. I invited her to come and visit me and Helen, but she said no. If we can get her back into her photography, it would do her the power of good.'

'Still, pushing her to go away with a complete stranger is a bit extreme.' This had only just occurred to him. Sure, they sort of knew each other, but they didn't really know each other.

'You're not a complete stranger, though,' said Gihan. 'I know where you work. I know where you live. My parents know your parents.' He leaned forward and fixed Vimal with a stern stare. 'And I know you wouldn't dare hurt my baby cousin.'

'Obviously not.' The idea of him hurting anyone, let alone a woman as self-possessed as Niro, was laughable. 'But Niro's right. It's a mad idea. No one would believe we're together. She's creative and confident and ... let's face it, I'm quite boring.'

He noticed Gihan didn't rush to contradict him.

*

The coffee and shower did their work and Niro felt much better by the time she'd got dressed. She wrapped her hair in a towel turban rather than faff around drying it properly. It was always a little less frizzy if she let it dry naturally anyway. She checked her messages. The email from the foundation to say her grant application was unsuccessful sat right at the top of her inbox, glaring at her. She slowly sat down on the bed.

Sam was right. She was in a rut. For months now, she had been feeling numb when it came to her work. It was just work, not art. There was no challenge in photographing merchandise. No joy at all in designing Facebook ads for people. She used to feel the zing of creativity when she worked out the right frame, or managed to strike the perfect juxtaposition of light and shade to make something ordinary reveal something more. All that had somehow been smothered by real-life problems, like making ends meet. The ad hoc gigs paid the bills and she had a lot of regular clients now, but they also took up all her time. She felt like a hack. A nobody.

The mere act of putting her name down to enter the landscape and architecture competition had made her feel better. But without a travel grant, she wasn't going to be able to photograph a truly interesting building. Given her tiny budget, the best 'integrated into landscape' building she could travel to was the Gloucester motorway services with a grass-covered roof.

She pulled up the search history on her phone and found the keywords from last night. The name Villa Cachée brought up a few pictures, mostly from its website. It was the most extraordinary building. She scrolled through a few more pictures, including more informal ones taken by people who'd visited. This was the reason she'd even considered going along with Vimal's plan.

Niro lowered her phone. It was a stupid idea though. No one would believe that someone like Vimal – who had an impressive job, who looked like *that* – would go out with someone like her. She knew she was a good photographer, but that wasn't enough, was it? She had to be a great one to be properly successful. She wasn't broke, but she wasn't exactly awash with money either. All in all, she was a bit of a loser compared to her cousins.

Now that she was fully awake, she remembered most of the conversation from the night before. She had committed to this silly escapade. They'd made ground rules and everything. Niro sighed. She didn't like people who went back on their word and she'd promised him she'd go along with this scheme. She would just have to suck it up, apologise to Vimal for being rude earlier … and then see the plan through.

When she got downstairs, the living room looked normal. Everything had been put back into place. The flat smelled pleasantly of coffee and toast. The two men were sitting on the sofa, with plates of toast on their knees. Sam was buttering a toasted bagel.

'Where's Luke?' Niro got herself another coffee.

'Work,' said Sam.

'It's Saturday.' She looked around at the rest of them, who all seemed to think that working on a Saturday was a normal thing to do. Maybe it was and she was the odd one. She took her coffee round to where the guys were sitting and perched on the arm of the chair opposite them.

'Vimal,' she said. 'I'm sorry. I shouldn't have snapped at you. That was the hangover talking.'

He had just taken a mouthful of toast. He chewed frantically so that he could reply. She took the opportunity to keep talking.

'I know it's a silly thing to do, but I said I would do it,' she said. 'So I will. Tell me the details again, though, because I'm not sure I remember everything as clearly as I'd like.'

He swallowed his toast. 'I'm sorry I snapped at you, too.'

She waved the apology aside and took a sip of coffee.

'And,' he added, 'if you don't want to do it, you don't have to. Obviously, I'd like you to.'

She looked at his earnest expression and felt sad for him. He was terribly, terribly sincere. A guy like that could be easy prey for people who liked being mean. She couldn't let him down. 'I gave you my word,' she said, firmly. 'A deal's a deal. Besides, it's been ages since I did any acting. It'll be fun to try that again.' The thought cheered her up. She loved acting. Before meeting Mick, she'd done some stage acting. Having to do the same show for several nights was a bind and the emotional roller-coaster was exhausting, but she did enjoy it.

Vimal smiled at her. 'Thank you.'

'You are welcome.' She held up her coffee mug. 'Cheers.'

He picked up his mug and clinked it against hers. 'Cheers.'

*

Vimal rang Lucien as he walked from the Tube station to his little flat. He and Niro had ironed out their plan between them. He was feeling slightly more confident that this would work.

He had expected Lucien's phone to go to voicemail, but to his amazement, Lucien picked up.

'Oh. Hi, Lucien, it's Vimal.'

'Ah. Vimal. How's it going?' Lucien has laughter in his voice.

He must be with people.

'Um … good. Good. I'm just calling to confirm that my girl-friend is coming to your party.'

'What?' The laughter was gone now.

'I said last night, I'd check with her and confirm so …'

'Oh. Right. Yes. Capital.'

'One thing though. We … uh. Is it possible for us to have a room with twin beds?'

A snort. 'Twin beds?'

'Yes. Even bunk beds are fine. It's a little awkward to explain. Cultural thing.' This had sounded much less weird when he'd thought about it earlier.

'Cultural thing.' The hint of laughter was back in Lucien's voice. 'Of course. I'll see what I can do. You'll have to explain that to me when you get here.'

'Oh. It's just that we're quite new to this relationship.'

'Yeah? Sounds interesting. Tell me at the party. Listen, old boy, I have to go. Might see you at work.' There was a click and Lucien hung up.

A bit abrupt. Perhaps he was busy. Vimal put his phone back in his pocket and fished out his keys. Now that he was committed to this course of action, he had to throw himself into it. He had no doubt that Niro would do her part. Persuading Kerry that he'd changed was all up to him.

Chapter 6

The next three weeks went by quickly. On Boxing Day, Niro packed her chunky winter wear into a big suitcase and got Luke to drive her to the airport. She had only seen Vimal a couple of times since they'd made their arrangement, but he had sent her a list of things she needed to take and even arranged for her to hire ski wear. On the few times she'd spoken to him, he had been serious and polite, like she was a business colleague. It was reassuring in a strange sort of way.

Vimal was waiting for her in the main concourse, frowning at his phone. As always he looked like he'd stepped out of a Ted Baker photoshoot, all clean lines and well-groomed aesthetic. Niro immediately felt scruffy. She was taking a mixture of her own clothes and hired stuff. They had decided that quirky was good, so she didn't need to do anything about the blue and purple streaks in her hair.

Besides, Sam had told her that her perceived frumpiness was all in her head. She took a deep breath. This was a project. A role to play. She could do this. When she started walking, she pulled herself up so that her back was straighter and her stride was longer. 'Vimal. Hi.'

He looked up from his screen. Niro's step faltered. He looked like he hadn't slept. There were bags under his eyes and even his skin looked dull and grey.

'Bloody hell. Are you okay?' It came out before she had a chance to censor it.

His eyes widened. 'Yes. Why? Do I look like something's wrong?' His voice was tight and he seemed to be breathing too fast.

Oh dear. He was panicking, wasn't he? In the few times she'd met him, she'd come to realise that he was straying a long way out of his comfort zone with this trip. He must really love this Kerry woman. 'No. No,' she said. 'You look tired, that's all. Have you had breakfast?'

He blinked at her. 'No,' he said, slowly, as though he was thinking. 'I have not.'

'Well, shall we check in and then go find breakfast?' She put as much cheer as she could into her voice. She couldn't do this if he wasn't putting in the work from his side. She'd mentally prepared herself to go and take those photos. They couldn't back out of this plan now.

'Right. Yes. I was just waiting for you.' He grabbed his suitcase, hitched up a trendy satchel onto his shoulder and pointed to the desk. 'It's only just opened.'

There was a queue to the single desk that was checking people in for the short-haul flight. They joined it. Vimal in front, Niro right behind him.

He suddenly turned around. 'Nirosha,' he said. 'Is this a terrible idea? Should I cancel? You can still go. I'm sure I can book you somewhere to stay in the village so that you can photograph the—'

She put a hand on his shoulder. 'Vimal,' she said, firmly. 'Breathe.' She drew a deep breath herself and prompted him to do the same. They both breathed out. Under her fingers, she felt his shoulder relax a fraction.

'But it feels ... dishonest.'

'It is dishonest, I guess,' Niro said. 'But it's a thing you feel you have to do and it's not hurting anyone. We've agreed to make

56

sure our families don't know about it, so they're not going to be upset. It's just a project. We do it and move on. No harm done.'

The queue moved forward one. Niro let go of his shoulder. They both moved along the line.

'I'm not cut out for dishonesty,' Vimal said.

'You work at an investment bank.'

He gave her a look of acute disappointment. 'I run numbers and build models. I don't do the gambling bit. Other people do that.'

'Like Lucien?'

'He used to, yes. Now he's doing more client-facing work. He's really good at getting people to trust him. You'll see what I mean when you meet him.'

She murmured, 'I look forward to it.'

He looked down at his shoes and then back up at her. 'Look. Thank you, for agreeing to do this. If it gets too much, or you want to leave at any point, you can, okay?'

She shrugged. She'd taken that as read. Before she left she had made sure to pack her credit card, so that if she needed to come home in a hurry, she could.

'I mean it.' He reached into his jacket and pulled out a folded piece of A4. 'Here. This is your ticket. It's a flexible one, so you can change it with just a small admin fee. You can bail any time you want to. You don't even have to talk to me, if you don't want to. Although, obviously, I'd hope you would.'

She took it from him and put it carefully in her handbag. 'I won't bail,' she said. 'A deal is a deal. We shook on it.'

He gave her a look that lasted a fraction longer than necessary, then nodded. 'A deal is a deal. Yes.'

*

Vimal poked at his full English breakfast. He hadn't eaten this much heart-attack fodder in one sitting for ages. He normally tried to eat healthily, although that had slipped a bit since he'd split up with Kerry. He had a sudden memory of going for a jog to Borough Market and buying her still-warm croissants. They'd sat on the tiny balcony of her flat and had them with bananas and melted chocolate. Sadness washed over him, not as all-consuming and bleak as it used to be, but still depressing. He missed her so much that it had worn a hollow inside him.

He looked up as Niro was walking back to the table carrying her breakfast. It was almost the same as his, but with no toast and no egg. 'Don't like eggs,' she'd said.

Niro was completely unlike Kerry. She was short and chubby and had the most bizarre taste in clothes. But she was noticeable. Her personality preceded her like a storm front and her smile was dazzling. Gihan had assured him that she always kept her word. Given the way she'd calmed him down when he'd freaked out about his own hare-brained scheme, it would seem that his friend was right. Once Niro committed to something, she committed fully. At least he could rely on her to see the plan through.

'Feeling better now?' She plopped her tray down diagonally across from him and sat down.

'Yes, thanks. Much calmer now that I'm having breakfast.'

She nodded. 'Good stuff.'

He turned his attention to his plate. Niro hummed quietly to herself while she squeezed ketchup out of the sachet. He sneaked another glance at her. Right now, she had her hair tied up in a chunky bun. The blue and purple stood out in streaks. She was definitely nothing like either of his previous girlfriends. And no one would call her boring.

After they'd eaten in silence for a few minutes, Niro pushed her plate away and delicately dabbed the corners of her mouth with a napkin.

'So, if we're going to be convincing, we should go over our backstory and stuff.' She put her handbag on her lap and pulled out a small notebook. 'Let's see ...'

'Wait, you wrote it down? What if someone found the notebook?'

She rolled her eyes and turned it round. 'Good luck making it out.'

It was a jumble of letters and numbers and what could have been handwriting or ... just a bunch of lines.

He peered at it. It wasn't any language that he recognised. 'What is that?'

She shrugged. 'It's a combination of shorthand and my own terrible handwriting. I use it all the time to make notes.' She turned the book around.

The mathematician in him wanted to look at it again, to see if he could spot patterns in it.

'When did you learn shorthand?'

Niro shrugged. 'Taught myself one summer.' She tapped a finger on the page. 'So, we were set up by the Aunties. Neither of us is getting any younger, so we've agreed to see how it goes.' She put her book down. 'So, how do you think it's going?'

Vimal pushed a hash brown round his plate. 'I suppose it should look like it's going well. At least at the start.'

'Fine. What does that look like to you?' She made a sort of waving motion with her hand. 'What's my motivation here?'

He raised his eyebrows at her.

'Humour me,' she said. Her eyes creased at the edges.

He smiled back, not entirely sure how to deal with this. 'Um ... I guess we're fond of each other ...'

'Holding hands all the time fond? Constantly snuggling fond?' She frowned. 'We've established not kissing fond.'

'What? Oh god no.' He recoiled. That was not what he had in mind at all.

She rolled her eyes. 'Gee, thanks.'

Now he'd offended her. He didn't want to kiss her because he had no feelings for her whatsoever. Not for any other reason 'No. I meant—'

She shook her head. 'I know what you meant. But seriously. This is a role we're playing. We need to establish the basics.'

Define your parameters. She had a good point. He pulled himself together. 'Okay. So … we've been together a few weeks? Say … six weeks?'

'Okay. That's a good length of time, but not too long. We could play it either way. Comfortable with each other, or just in the first flush of attraction.'

'Shall we go for comfortable? That sounds easier.'

She tapped a finger on the notebook and said, thoughtfully, 'Yes. So holding hands. The occasional arm around each other. We could deem kissing in public a cultural no-no.'

'Yes. That would tie in with my asking for separate beds.'

She nodded. 'Okay. So details. Do you have any brothers or sisters?'

'A sister. Much older than me. We're not close. How about you?'

'Just me. But when I was a teen, I spent so much time with Sam, Gihan and their big brother that they're practically my siblings now.' She looked at her incomprehensible scribblings. 'So tell me about you. You studied … economics?'

'Maths. Then I did a master's. Worked for a start-up for a while. Got headhunted by a bank. And I'm still there.'

'Did you get a first?' She said it as though she was teasing him.

He felt a flush of awkwardness. He knew he was a geek. She didn't have to rub it in. 'Yes, as it happens.'

She nodded. 'Well, I did an art degree, specialised in photography. Got a two-one. I've been failing to make a living as an artist ever since.'

'But you make a living somehow, from what I saw.' The flat that she lived in with Sam was nice.

Niro sighed, and suddenly the light that powered her seemed to dim. 'I've been doing bits and pieces. I haven't sold any work in a long time, so I've been designing packaging and making social media templates for small businesses for small amounts of money here and there. Sometimes there are enough gigs to make it work, sometimes not.'

He sensed the frustration behind her words. 'Tell me about this competition you're entering.'

She waved a dismissive hand. 'Sam made me enter. I'm not really good enough.'

That didn't make sense. Gihan had told him she was quite good. In fact, the photos on her website were amazing. 'I like the stuff you have on your website. Quite reasonably priced too.'

She curled her lip. 'Not good enough to sell, though.' She stood up. 'Are you finished with your plate? I'll tidy up.'

'I'll help.'

They walked together to the clearing-up trolley and slid their trays in. In those few minutes, Niro seemed to recover her composure.

Vimal had bought a bar of chocolate-covered marzipan for pudding. He offered her some.

'Oh, no thanks. I don't like marzipan.'

'What? How can you not like marzipan? You like cinnamon, right? Otherwise you're going to hate Christmas treats. And that seems very wrong.'

'Cinnamon, I'm fine with. For the record. I also don't like peppers.'

Why was she telling him that? Oh. Right. Verisimilitude. If they were a real couple, they'd know this stuff. He had known lots of things that Kerry liked. But what did she dislike? He pondered this as they left the café.

Kerry tended to have strong but short-lived enthusiasms. Last month's cool thing would be out of favour the next. It was a moving target, so he knew to stick to the few things he was sure of when it came to presents. He had got into the habit of checking with her before buying her birthday or Christmas presents.

'What about you?' Niro interrupted his train of thought.

'Oh, I eat just about anything. But not pickled stuff.'

She looked horrified. 'Not even lime pickle?'

'Nope. Nor acharu.' He thought for a second. 'Or cornichon. Anything that smells strongly of vinegar. And I don't have vinegar on my chips.'

'Okay. Fair enough, I guess.'

He thought of something else. 'And I don't like Nutella.'

'Are you allergic to nuts?'

'No. I just don't like hazelnut spread. Something about the texture.' He gave a small shudder. 'I like chocolate. It's only that stuff that I don't like.'

She shook her head. 'That's so weird.'

'You don't like marzipan. You're one to talk.'

She smiled. 'Fair point. No hazelnut spread. Noted.' As they walked out to the waiting area, she said, 'So, tell me about Kerry.'

'What do you need to know?' They reached the seats and he politely waited for her to sit down first before he took the seat next to her.

'Well, you want her to be jealous. So I need to be ... someone who has something she wants. Obviously, one of those things is you.' She gestured towards him. 'But what else? What does she like? What does she wish she had that she doesn't?'

That was a tough question. Vimal frowned. He could tell her what Kerry liked, but what did she wish she had? He looked up at the ceiling and thought for a minute. She must have told him at some point. Maybe if he talked about her, he would remember. 'Shall I start with what she likes?'

Niro nodded.

He leaned forward, resting his elbows on his knees and clasping his hands. 'She likes exercise and runs every day. She loves white roses. And walking by the river. And art galleries, even though neither of us really understands contemporary art. She likes sweet things. Cakes, chocolate ...' He smiled. 'She's going to love Switzerland, I think.'

When he glanced sideways, he saw Niro's expression. She was

smiling in a slightly patronising way.

'What?'

'You guys have been split up for seven months and you still feel this way? That's sweet,' she said. 'Why did you split up? If you don't mind my asking.'

He shifted position. This was always embarrassing. 'She said I was boring and she was stuck in a rut. She needed ... space and something more ...'

'More what?'

'She didn't specify. Just *more*.' He shrugged. 'I said I'd do whatever she wanted, but she said that was part of the problem. And then she moved out and found a new guy within weeks.'

From the expression on her face, he could tell Niro thought Kerry had left him for the new guy. He had wondered that himself, but there had been a gap of a few weeks. Besides, he liked to think he knew Kerry. She wouldn't do that.

'Are you sure you want her back? That doesn't sound very nice.'

Vimal didn't even have to think about the answer. 'Yes. I want her back. I miss her every single day. I hate coming home to an empty flat with no one to talk to. No one to sit next to on the sofa. Home isn't home without her.' He swallowed the lump that always formed in his throat when he let himself think about Kerry for too long. 'I've been working silly hours just to avoid going home.'

'Is it all the working that made this Lucien fellow notice you?'

Probably. 'Yeah. Unexpected bonus.' He had thought that the mere fact that he'd been invited to Lucien's party would mean he wasn't boring. All he would have had to do was survive the short holiday. Kerry could never call him boring after that. Except somehow he'd ended up with this ridiculous charade of having a made-up girlfriend, just to save face.

Niro looked thoughtful, her features scrunched in concentration. 'So, you need her to see you doing interesting and spontaneous things. Perhaps something to do with art ... because that's something she aspires to?'

He considered this. Kerry did aspire to understanding art. She read blogs about it and listened to podcasts about it. In private, she would admit that she didn't feel like she 'got' it. But people she liked, liked art. It was important to be seen to care. Vimal couldn't be bothered. Maths *was* art anyway. He loved art that was mathematical and fractal. He had taken about a thousand photos when they'd visited the Alhambra in Spain.

'Yes,' he said. 'That sounds about right.' He looked sideways at her. 'You're very good at this.'

'Romcom movie night is good training.'

'You guys keep mentioning that, what is it?'

Niro grinned. 'Exactly what it says on the tin. Once a week, Sam and I sit down and watch a romcom together. Nowadays, Luke joins in too, if he's not busy. Sam loves a fake-relationship trope, in case you hadn't guessed.'

He tried to parse this. 'Movies about people pretending to be a couple?'

'Exactly.'

He glanced sideways at her. She rolled her eyes. 'Don't worry. We're not going to end up falling for each other instead. You're not my type.'

That was a relief, because she wasn't his type either. His type was Kerry.

'So what's your story then?' he asked. 'How come you're free to come on some hare-brained journey to make my ex jealous.' The laughter in her eyes dimmed. He hadn't realised the sparkle was even there until it was gone. Had he touched on something painful? 'You don't have to answer that if you don't want to. I was just—'

She shook her head. 'No. No, it's fine. It's a very dull story, really. I was dating a guy – another artist. We met in college. He was older than me and he'd come back to do some teaching sessions. We dated for a couple of years. I was going to move in

64

with him, but he kept stalling. Turned out that was because he was cheating on me.'

'Oh, that's horrible.' At least Kerry hadn't cheated on him. Moved on pretty fast, sure, but not actually cheated.

Niro was staring at the floor, her hands twisting together, as though she were grappling with something. 'There's more, though. When … when we first met, he was complimentary about my style and really boosted my confidence as a photographer. We started working on an exhibition proposal together, a two-hander with his stuff and mine. He was talking to a curator at a public gallery about it. The same curator he ended up sleeping with. I found out because I saw some texts … Some of them were about their affair, but there were others about me and my art. He said a lot of disparaging things about my work. He said …' She stopped and chewed her lip.

This was clearly distressing for her. 'You don't have to—'

She raised a hand. 'He said that he'd been complimentary because he felt that it was a shame to crush someone's dreams so young and that I was mediocre at best. That my work was … vanilla.' She sighed and placed her palms together. 'And then I lost my ability to take photos. Not good ones. I'm trying to get back into it. Get my vision back, if you like. I thought a change of scenery might help.'

Well that explained a lot. She needed to be here as much as he did. He nodded.

'So, you see, I'm not doing this trip on a whim. I need it too. I promise you, I will do my best to help you. When I make a deal, I stick by it.'

'Same here,' he said. 'I'll help you as much as I can with the photo thing. I appreciate you helping me.' Her gaze met his and something shifted between them. Suddenly, it felt like they were a team.

She took a deep breath and seemed to step back into whoever she had been before. 'But fear not. I might be a terrible judge of character and only a mediocre artist, but I'm an excellent method actress. I can totally be your manic pixie dream girl who shows your ex that you are really not boring.' She gave his arm a quick pat. 'Now then,' she said, 'if you don't have anything else to quiz me about, I'm going to read my book.' She pulled an e-reader out of her bag.

'No,' said Vimal. 'Nothing to quiz you about.'

'If you think of anything, just ask.'

'Will do.'

He pulled up his news sites on his phone and they both sat back to read in companionable silence. Now, the trip didn't seem quite so frightening after all.

Chapter 7

Niro kept her face towards the window, searching for the first glimpse of Villa Cachée. After leaving the motorway, the taxi drove through increasingly narrow roads. One side of the road was snowbanks or stone walls and the other the open valley, with a river winding through it. When she looked up, there were mostly snowy mountains, topped off by a white and electric-blue sky.

Conifers stood out from the snow, spiky patches of dark against the white. In the winter sunshine, she could just about see the tops of the mountains that rose on the other side of the dip. The scale of them messed with her sense of perspective. Her fingers itched to take a photo, but she didn't want to ask the driver to stop the car.

Vimal was sitting next to her, a restless bundle of energy. She didn't know him that well, but it didn't take a genius to work out that he was nervous. Not surprising, really. He was clearly anxious about his plan. What *was* surprising was that she wasn't nervous. If anything, she was buzzing with anticipation. She hadn't felt this alive in months. Perhaps it was the challenge. Or maybe it was just that she'd needed a holiday. Okay, it was a weird way of getting a holiday, but hey, why not?

She shot a glance at Vimal, who was peering at his phone.

He was going to give the game away within minutes if he didn't calm down. Niro reached across and poked him in the shoulder.

He jumped. 'What?'

'You look like a time bomb about to go off,' she said, quietly. 'Relax. You're meant to be in love. Not sentenced to death.'

'Sorry. Sorry.' He rubbed his forehead. 'Sorry.'

She shifted position, so that she was facing him. 'Vimal. I'm looking at this as an acting job. A role to play. Now, have you ever done any acting?'

'Um … not really.'

'Role-playing games, then?'

A flicker in his eyes before he shook his head. Liar. He totally did role-playing games when he was younger. He was just too cool to admit it now. Fair enough.

'I'm not nervous about pretending we're together,' he said.

'Then what's bothering you?'

He looked down and turned the phone over in his hands. 'I haven't seen Kerry in months. I've never seen her with another bloke.'

Oh! Of course. That was what he was worried about. She watched his fidgeting with more sympathy now. No wonder he was nervous. 'After all that's happened, you still really care for her, huh?'

He nodded. 'She left me. It was over for her. For me … it never ended. If that makes sense.'

It did make sense. She remembered the devastation of seeing Mick's texts. When Mick left, he broke not only her heart, but her career as well. She had cried. A lot. Mourning what might have been, Sam called it. Clearly Vimal hadn't done that. He was still holding on to the hope that things could go back to how they had been before.

She turned away from his sorrow. 'I understand,' she said. She really did. 'Well, let's show her she was wrong about you. But you have to pull yourself together and help me, okay?'

He gazed at her solemnly for a moment and nodded. 'You're right. I've dragged you into this. I will play my part. I promise.'

Whatever he was going to say next was derailed by the sight of something outside. His eyes widened and he pointed through the windscreen. 'Look.'

Niro turned. The car had rounded a bend. They were coming into a village. The sun was low now and the sky was already tinged with pink and purple. Christmas lights glowed from snow-covered houses with shallow angled roofs. The vastness of the mountainscape made everything look tiny by comparison. The village sprawled lazily along the valley, tracing the path of a river that ran down the middle. The sky seemed higher above them than usual. She was going to have to take so many photographs.

The taxi turned off the main road and drove along a smaller road that went higher into the mountainside. Niro craned her neck trying to see up the darkening hillside to catch a glimpse of Villa Cachée. She saw a few normal houses, but nothing out of the ordinary. On the other side of the valley there appeared to be some sort of a grand house or hotel, but on this side, just scattered dwellings.

Finally, they pulled up in front of what looked like a plain concrete garage. Niro frowned. This didn't look right. At all.

'This is the place,' the taxi driver said, when Vimal queried it.

Niro got out of the car and looked at the strange concrete bunker. It was low and appeared to be set into the mountainside. The small area that protruded had a sloping roof, with a good six inches of snow on it. The forecourt that they were standing on had been cleared of snow.

She went round to collect her case from where the taxi driver was unloading the boot. A door in the garage front opened and a sprightly man in a bright blue winter jacket emerged.

'Hello, hello. You must be the first arrivals. Lucien is still en route, driving from France, don't you know,' he said in a plummy English accent. He strode up to them, beaming. 'I'm Lucien's uncle, Sebastian. You can call me Basty.'

Before Niro or Vimal could speak, he said, 'You must be Nero and Vimal. How interesting to name a man after the mad emperor, I say.'

Niro shot a glance at Vimal. Oh dear. This was not a great start. To her surprise, Vimal smiled, completely calm. 'Hello,' he said smoothly. 'It's a pleasure to meet you. I'm Vimal. And this is my girlfriend Nirosha ... known mostly as Niro.'

The older man's gaze flicked to Niro and back to Vimal. His expression barely changed. 'Capital,' he said. 'Welcome to Villa Cachée. Come. Let me show you to your billet, as it were.' He turned and strode back towards the concrete building. Without turning to look at them, he raised a hand and beckoned. 'Come with me.'

Vimal caught her eye and shrugged. They followed the man through the door.

Niro stepped inside and blinked. She had been expecting ... Well, she wasn't exactly sure what she was expecting, but she was now standing inside a well-lit area. It wasn't a room exactly, more the front of a long corridor. There was a small booth containing a desk at one side, with a set of computer screens showing the forecourt and a few other locations that she didn't recognise. A young man sitting behind the desk sat up straighter.

'This is Martin,' Basty said. 'If you need anything from the village, just ask him. He's a good chap. Local.'

Martin bobbed his head and beamed at them. 'Good evening,' he said, in strongly accented English. 'You can just dial number one on the phones in the house and it will call me.' He gestured to a phone on his desk.

They both nodded politely to him, but Basty was off. Niro hurried after him, dragging her suitcase. Vimal followed.

The corridor sloped upwards. The floor was polished concrete, and the walls were painted plain white. Framed photos of the villa in various stages of construction were hung on the wall.

Niro felt the cold nipping at her nose and hoped that Martin's little reception booth had a heater in it.

'Bally nuisance this tunnel,' Basty said. 'But I suppose they needed to keep the approach underground to make sure the place was hidden. Wouldn't be very hidden if you had a great big entrance, eh?'

'Did you build it?' Niro asked, catching up with him.

'Good grief, no. Businessman fellow built it. Or rather, had it built. He was selling up last year. I thought, "what the hell" and snapped it up. I own the hotel on the other side of the valley, see. I thought it might be a good wheeze to add this place to the portfolio.'

A photo caught Niro's eye. It was taken at dusk. The round front of the villa was glowing from the lights in the windows, a contrast to the dark-toned mountain around it. 'Oh, I like that,' she said. 'Very dramatic.'

Basty stopped and retraced his steps to come and stand next to her. 'Yes. The old place does make a dramatic photo.'

'Niro's a photographer,' said Vimal. 'She's particularly interested in how buildings fit into their surroundings.' He nudged her.

What? Oh. 'Would you mind if I photographed the house and entered the photo into a competition?'

Basty looked taken aback. 'Well, I say …'

'Imagine if it made the shortlist,' Vimal said, his tone casual. 'It would go into an exhibition. Which is going to be touring internationally, right, Niro?'

How did he know that? 'Yes.'

She turned towards Basty, who said, 'I don't see any harm in it, I suppose. Take as many photos as you want to. I'd like to see some too. Could do with a few more pictures of the old place.'

'Thank you.' She didn't really need permission, but it was nice to have it anyway. As Vimal had none too subtly pointed out, it would be good publicity for the villa.

'Come along, we should get on. It's warmer in the house, you'll

71

be glad to know.' Basty set off along the interminable corridor again. 'Tell you what you should do,' he said. 'You should pop across the valley to my hotel. There's a great view of the house from the viewing point. Quite magical, really. Especially at night.'

'I'd love to do that. Thank you.' She hurried after him.

They carried on up the sloping corridor – the floor was covered with a thin industrial-style carpet now, but it still maintained the 'underground car park' vibe – until they came to a door set into a plain wall. Niro's legs were aching by the time she reached it.

Basty typed in an entry code. 'Welcome to Villa Cachée.'

Niro glanced at Vimal, who gestured for her to go first. She stepped across the threshold ... into a different world.

After the harsh light and plain walls of the entryway, the villa felt impossibly plush. The floor was pale polished wood. The walls were ice-white with exposed wooden beams. The furniture was mostly wooden and matched perfectly. High above on one side was a dark square of a window. Alcoves built into the wall held ornaments and red-and-green accent pieces. Wow. Everything was so ... tasteful.

Basty pulled open a cupboard. 'There are slippers and over-shoes in here,' he said. 'Help yourselves.' He took out a pair of coverings and slipped them over his shoes. 'You may as well get those boots off and make yourself at home.'

Niro shrugged and knelt down to undo the laces. Beside her, Vimal did the same. When she put her hand on the floor, she found that it was warm. 'Oh.' She pressed down and felt the warmth seep into her palm.

'Heated floors,' said Basty. 'Wonderful idea. Uses some sort of geothermal pump, too. Between that and the bally great snowy mountain acting as insulation, it's remarkably efficient to heat.'

'That's amazing.' She wondered if she could just lie down and be warmed up for a minute. She looked at Vimal, who was putting his boots neatly on the rack by the door. No. Vimal would probably object. She put her boots next to his and stood in her stockinged feet. Oh god, heated floors were lovely.

'Right. You two are, I believe … in room …' Basty pulled out a sheet of paper, frowned at it, then brought out a pair of glasses and put them on. 'In room two. Yes. Vimal and guest, brackets Niro. That's you.' He peered over his glasses, as though seeking confirmation.

'That's us,' Vimal said.

He led them down the corridor and around a corner and pointed to a door marked A. 'Here we go, just shove your bags in there and I'll give you a tour of the place. I daresay you'll have it to yourselves for an hour or so before the rest of them get here.'

They did as he suggested, pushing the bags just inside the door, and followed him into the main house. 'These are some of the other bedrooms. There are more bedrooms upstairs.' Basty gestured to a few other doors. 'Place sleeps eight comfortably, twelve at a push. Over here we have the main house.' He turned through a door at the end of the curve.

'Wow.' They were in an oval-shaped room. One wall was made of windows. The room was in darkness, so they could see through the glass the last light of the setting sun as it disappeared behind the mountains. Spots of gold flickered where there were street-lights. In the distance, a big house was an oasis of light in the dark mountain. That must be the hotel he'd mentioned.

'Oh wow,' said Niro again. 'This is gorgeous.'

'Let me get the lights.' Basty found the switch and the lights rose slowly, revealing cream sofas and armchairs, with fleeces thrown over the backs of them. In one corner was a fireplace.

To one side was an enormous Christmas tree, decorated in red and silver. 'There's a remote control somewhere for the Christmas tree lights. Aha. Here we are.' He turned them on and tiny golden lights sprang up on the tree. It all looked impossibly cosy.

'As you probably gathered, this is the living room. Through here we have the kitchen, should you feel the urge to cook. But there's a catering team who will make sure your meals are provided. Just help yourself to anything in the fridge.' He pointed out the dining area, which had two tables in it. 'You can put the two together and have a really big table if you wanted to make it feel like a dining hall,' he said with a laugh. He led them through a spotless and gleaming kitchen. A corridor led off it. 'Here we have the games room, the lavatory, the library. The stairs at the front take you up to the other bedrooms. If you go up the stairs through here, there's a balcony observation area. It'll be a bit snowy right now, though.'

'What's that room?' Niro asked, pointing to a door at the end.

'Oh, you must never go in there,' said Basty.

What? Like in a horror fairy tale? She frowned and looked at Vimal, whose shoulders twitched into a tiny shrug.

Basty laughed. 'I'm only joking. Nothing sinister at all. Just a store room.' He opened the door and turned on the light. It was, as he said, just a store room. 'There's spare ski stuff and things in here. Feel free to use whatever you need, so long as you put it back.' He flicked the lights back off and shut the door firmly. 'So, that's the tour done.' He looked at his watch. 'I shall have to love you and leave you. I'm sure you'll find plenty to amuse yourselves with until the others arrive.' He headed back towards the main entrance. 'And do come by the hotel when you want to photograph the house.'

Niro was back in the living room, too busy gawping at the view to fully register what he said. Vimal clicked his tongue and went after Basty. She heard the low buzz of their voices, but ignored it. This view was incredible. She dimmed the lights so that she could see out again. Searching by the huge windows, she found another light switch. She flicked it and two rows of downlights came on outside. They curved like comforting arms around an oval courtyard, currently covered in a light dusting of snow. There was a waist-high table, a raised fire-pit or a barbecue of some sort, and seating, which was also curved to echo the shape of the courtyard. This was clearly an outdoor entertainment space. She imagined it would be very cosy sitting around the fire, with the vast sky above them. It was beautifully well-thought-out. How had nobody taken a million pictures of this place before? All she'd seen on the internet were personal photos from people who had visited and the few pictures on the official website. Well, she could photograph the hell out of it. Excitement tingled. It felt like parts of her brain were coming alive again. She gave a little squeak of anticipation. This was going to be brilliant.

Chapter 8

Vimal watched the door close and heard the beep as the lock activated. Lucky he'd remembered to ask Basty for the door code. He let out a long breath. So this was it. He was committed to this mad idea now. No backing out. He walked in slippered feet to the living room. Niro was standing in the dark, staring out at the lit courtyard. She was moving her head slowly, one hand pressed to her chest. She was obviously lost in some sort of artistic reverie. He left her to it.

He pushed open the door to their room and dragged in his and Niro's suitcases. From the entrance, there was a short hallway, with hanging space for coats on one side and another door leading into a small en suite bathroom on the other. He stepped into the main bedroom and stopped. The bed was enormous. It was wide and looked very comfortable – but there was only one of it. No twin beds. Just one bloody enormous bed. To share. Oh balls.

He stared at the bed for a moment. He had definitely asked Lucien. He pulled out his phone and messaged Lucien.

Hi. There's been a mix-up. Your uncle showed us to a room with one bed in it. Which room is the one with the twin beds? Vimal

Not wanting to rumple the bed by sitting on it, he leaned against the desk. His chest felt tight. What if there hadn't been a mistake? What if they had to share a bed? Niro would be furious. That could not happen. The scheme had failed at the first hurdle.

He pushed himself away from the desk and walked around the room. The bed took up most of the space. There was no window, but there were two light wells, now dark because it was night. Below one of them was a mirrored dressing table and a stool, all in the same blond wood and cream upholstery as everything else. He looked speculatively at the space between the wall and the bed. He could probably make a bed on the floor there. With the floor being heated, it would be comfortable enough. Even so, a few nights on the hard floor would wreak havoc on his back. The other option was the bath. He crossed over to the bathroom. There was no bath, just a shower. So, the floor it was.

His phone buzzed. He pulled it out and looked at it.

Ah yes. Meant to tell you. There are no twin rooms in Villa Cachée. Sorry. Giant bed or nothing. I'm sure you'll manage. Who knows, might even work to your advantage.

He'd added a wink emoji. Ew.

Vimal felt light-headed. Oh no. Niro was going to go ballistic. He put the phone down and gave his cheeks a sharp pat. He had to pull himself together. It wasn't the end of the world. He could deal with a few days on the floor. It would be fine. Absolutely fine.

Okay. A nice place like this was bound to have spare bedding. He opened the wardrobe built into the wall. Aha. Bedding.

He was pulling out the spare pillows when Niro arrived.

'What are you doing?' Her eyes moved across the stuff he'd dumped on the floor.

'I … er …' He gestured towards the bed. 'There's only one bed. So I'm trying to make another on the floor.'

She looked at the bed, frowned and turned back to him.

'I definitely told him separate beds. I just messaged him,' Vimal said quickly. 'He said there were only double bedrooms here. I'm so sorry. I genuinely didn't know.' He pulled the last spare blanket out and pushed the wardrobe shut. 'Don't worry. I'll sleep on the floor. There's space. It's fine.'

Niro walked to the other end of the bed and considered the floor. Her features scrunched down. Her scowl was quite frightening.

'I honestly didn't know,' he said, again. 'Look, if you want to bail now, before everyone else comes, I understand.'

She drew a sharp breath. Her gaze flicked to his, eyes narrowed. 'No,' she said. 'It's fine. Not very nice of your friend, mind. But like I said, a deal is a deal.'

'Great.' He gathered the pillows and started moving around the bed towards the space where he was going to make his bed. He was glad she wasn't bailing on him. The whole discussion with Lucien about beds was going to be awkward enough. If she left he'd have to explain that and it would be so much worse.

Niro flattened herself against the wall to let him pass. 'What are you doing?'

'Making a bed on the floor.' Wasn't it obvious?

She shook her head. 'No. That's silly. It's a huge bed, just look at it. There's plenty of room for both of us. It's stupid for you to sleep on the floor when I'm swimming about on an enormous mattress.' She pointed to the pillows in his arms. 'We'll use those and make a pillow barrier of some sort between us. I'm sure it'll be fine.'

He paused where he was. That did make sense and it would be far more comfortable for him. It was her choice to make and she was the one who'd suggested it. 'You're sure?'

She nodded. Her expression cleared and she looked tired. 'Yeah. It makes sense.' A sudden flash of her generous smile. 'Besides, Gihan assures me you're a gentleman. And if you touch me, he will kick the crap out of you. Once *I've* finished kicking the crap out of you.'

The smile was infectious. Vimal grinned and dropped the pillows on the bed. Niro folded back the duvet, so that it only covered one side, knelt on the bed and started to lay a line of pillows down the middle. Vimal laid the other duvet across his side and folded it up at the middle to form his side of the 'wall'.

The pillow wall was two pillows high at the top and the bottom half was made of the neatly folded duvets, which Vimal tucked in at the foot of the bed so that they didn't move too much.

'Good job,' said Niro approvingly. 'That should keep us out of mischief.'

Vimal agreed. He sat on his side of the bed and said, 'This is a deeply weird situation.'

Niro bounced a bit on her side. 'It is. Kinda fun though. Breaks the monotony of life up a bit.' She lay back. 'This is such a comfortable mattress. In fact, this whole place is amazing. The attention to detail is just …' She put her fingers to her lips and blew a chef's kiss.

He looked at her short form, lying stretched out on the bed. He hoped she calmed down before the others got here. She was meant to be making Kerry think that he'd gone up in the world. It wouldn't work if she went around exclaiming over things because they were more beautiful than merely functional.

'What are you worrying about now?' Niro said.

'I'm not worrying.' How did she know?

'Of course you are. You're always worrying. You're so uptight.'

'I'm not. It's just a bit of an odd situation.'

Niro sat up and swung her legs off the bed. 'I'm going to go wash up before your posh friends get here.' She turned and grinned at him. 'And don't worry. I promise I will be a perfect gentleman too.'

Vimal watched her disappear into the bathroom. She had a weird sense of humour. He was going to spend almost a week with this strange woman. What had he let himself in for?

Chapter 9

From what Vimal and Gihan had said, Niro had imagined Lucien to look like some bronzed god. But instead the guy that Vimal introduced her to was tall, thin and very normal-looking. Neatly cut light-brown hair, blue eyes, designer sunglasses on top of his head. There was a certain polish about him, though. He was dressed in a chunky jumper and chinos, but everything about him was pressed and tidy. His skin gleamed. He looked … expensive.

Lucien looked her up and down. She saw the judgement in the tiny quirk at the corners of his mouth. She was used to this, so she braced herself. His eyes met hers and he smiled.

'Niro,' he said. 'It's such a delight to meet you. I've heard … Well, I haven't actually heard a lot about you, but I'm looking forward to finding out more. Welcome to Villa Cachée.' He shook her hand and dropped air kisses by her cheeks. 'Listen. I'm sorry about the snafu with the sleeping arrangements. I hope it doesn't cause too much bother for you.'

His face bore a look of concern, but his eyes were hungry. If he was hoping to see her upset, he was in for a disappointment.

'No. No, it's fine. We'll manage,' she said.

'Wonderful.' He released her hand and turned to a blonde woman who came to stand beside him. 'This is Felicia.'

Felicia, who had just removed a pair of impractical calf-length boots, flicked her hair back and shook Niro's hand. 'Hi.' She looked young. Very early twenties at most. 'Nice to meet you.'

There was another couple, who also had that same air of 'expensive' about them. Both were looking around as though they were judging the place and finding it wanting. Lucien introduced them as Peter and Magda. Niro instantly disliked them both.

Niro did a mental headcount. The place slept twelve. There were six of them there now. 'When's everyone else arriving?'

'Tomorrow,' said Lucien.

'Wow, look at this place. It's beautiful.' Felicia was padding along the corridor, shiny blonde hair swinging. 'The pictures on the internet don't look anything as gorgeous as this.'

Niro had to agree with her. She had spent the last half hour photographing the empty house from various angles. Of course, she'd only seen it under artificial light. She would have to get up early, before the others cluttered up the place, to see if she could take some pictures of it when daylight was coming through the light wells.

In the meantime, this was awkward. She didn't know these people. Peter, Magda and Lucien were looking at the house with a dispassionate eye, as though they were used to luxury and unusual surroundings. They probably were, come to think of it. The understated designer luggage and the expensive watches were not lost on Niro. These were people with money. She glanced across at Vimal, who was looking all uptight again. Oh boy, this was going to be a long few days.

Felicia found the living room and gave a little squeal of delight. 'Oh my god, this is so adorable.'

Niro saw Magda roll her eyes. Lucien raised his eyebrows and smiled at Magda. Niro immediately decided that she was going to watch out for Felicia. These people were really not her friends.

'I don't know about you,' said Lucien. 'But I am dying for a coffee.'

81

'There's a coffee machine in the kitchen,' said Vimal. 'And a basket of pastries.'

'Fantastic.'

There was a pause, as though they were waiting for something. Then Lucien clapped his hands together and said, 'Let's have a look then.'

'Actually, I'm going to go freshen up,' said Magda. 'Come along, Peter. My hair is in a terrible state after the drive.'

Her hair looked perfect, as far as Niro could tell. She glanced at Vimal, who was looking hunted. She stepped over to him and slipped her hand in his. 'Come on, Vimal,' she said. 'Come help me with the thing.'

To his credit, he didn't say, *What thing?* but merely gave Lucien an apologetic smile and let Niro drag him into the living room.

Niro sat down on one of the sofas. Vimal sat next to her, close, but not touching. Felicia was taking photos of herself on the sofa opposite. From the kitchen, there came the sound of the Nespresso machine.

Pulling out her phone, Niro scrolled through the photos she had already taken. Vimal looked at them and nodded approvingly.

'Filly!' Lucien called. 'I'm going to go check out the room. You coming?'

'Yes. On my way.' Felicia put away her phone, shot Niro and Vimal a dazzling smile and disappeared.

On the sofa, they sat tense for a few seconds, until the sound of footsteps and giggles faded, then they both exhaled.

'You okay?' Vimal said, very quietly.

'Yep. They're interesting,' Niro said, just as quietly. 'How about you? You okay?'

He nodded. 'Why wouldn't I be?'

'I dunno. I get the impression they make you nervous.'

He raised his eyebrows and tilted his head, which she took to mean 'maybe'. He had expressive eyebrows and lovely thick eyelashes. Niro turned away. Why had she noticed that? Now she wouldn't be able to not notice every time she looked at him. Oh well. Maybe it would help with the illusion that she was in love with him.

'So what now?' she asked.

'I don't know. I guess we get on with being on holiday unless Lucien has other plans.' He leaned forward and put his hands on his knees. 'On which note, I'm going to go get my e-reader and read my book.'

'Okay. Well, I'm going to fiddle with these pictures, see if I can get anything usable from them.'

Once he had left, she pulled her legs up onto the couch and settled in. Rather than use her photo-editing app, she messaged Sam.

Niro: *Some of the others have arrived. Lucien says everyone else will be in tomorrow. That includes Kerry and her fella, one assumes.*

Sam: *What are they like?*

Niro: *Lucien is ... less superhuman than Vimal and Gihan made out. He's just a bloke. Quite charming. I think he's probably a man's man, if you know what I mean. He's got a girlfriend who looks like she's barely out of school uniform. Could be wrong, obvs. The two others seem very snooty. They looked around this gorgeous place like it was slightly smelly.*

Sam: *So, no new besties then?*

Niro: *Nope. Poor Vimal is so uptight he looks like he's going to snap any minute.*

Sam: *Oh dear.*

She wondered whether to tell Sam about the king-sized bed. No, she decided. Best not. It would just make for awkward discussions. She made a mental note to tell Vimal to do the same. Thank goodness they were already keeping this whole escapade a secret from her parents and the Aunties. The Aunties would have blown everything out of proportion.

Niro: *The house is utterly beautiful, though. I didn't spot it at all on the way through the village. You enter through this long underground tunnel. It's built into the mountainside, like a warren. There are no windows in the bedroom, but there are light wells. Everything is thoughtfully done and so tasteful. I haven't seen it in the daylight yet, but I bet it looks amazing in the snow.*

Sam: *Oh wonderful. Do you think it's impressive enough to win a photography competition?*

Niro: *Possibly. Even if it isn't, the mountains alone are amazing. I'm glad this place has Wi-Fi so that I can save stuff to the cloud. I'd be stuffed if I had to rely on the storage on my phone and camera. I've already taken a crap ton of pictures.*

And this guy, Lucien's uncle. Super posh. He owns the hotel at the other side of the village and said I could come and take photos from there if I wanted. To be honest, the houses around here are lovely — all wooden shutters and snow-covered roofs. I'm going to enjoy looking around the village, too.

Sam: *You sound excited.*

Niro: *I am. Thank you for making me enter the competition. You're right. I needed to get out of my rut.*

Sam: *I'm glad it's working out. Sounds like the photography side of things is good. We just need to make sure Vimal's problem gets sorted out as well.*

Niro: *Speaking of Vimal. He's back. I'll message you again later.*

Sam: *Keep me updated.*

*

By the time they sat down to dinner, Vimal was feeling sick with nerves. He didn't know what to do with himself. He was fine speaking to Lucien in a work context. You knew where you were with projections. But here, he couldn't think of a single thing to say that didn't sound terminally dull. Lucien was very clear that he invited only interesting people to these outings. Somehow, he'd thought that Vimal was interesting enough to be a guest and now he was going to find out how wrong he was. Kerry had been right to call him boring.

Dinner was a set of tray-baked tarts, brought in by caterers, who laid one end of the enormous table, lit candles, put out the food and wine and went away again. By unspoken consent, they left the seat at the head of the table for Lucien. Vimal took the seat furthest away from him. Niro had plonked herself next to Vimal. Peter held Magda's chair back for her as she sat down. Vimal glanced at Niro – he hadn't pulled her chair out for her. Should he have? He wasn't entirely sure how she would have reacted if he had.

Niro had put her hair up in a neat bun and was wearing a green jumper with slacks. Anyone who didn't know her would never have guessed that her preferred dress was grungier. All that really remained of the girl he'd met at Kumudhini Aunty's Christmas party were the streaks of colour in her hair and her eyebrow piercing. Here, set against the extremely tasteful clothes of everyone else, both looked impossibly daring. She turned her head, caught him looking at her, and shot him a small, tight smile. Oh. She was nervous too.

Lucien arrived a minute later, with Felicia trailing behind him. Vimal couldn't help noticing that Lucien held Felicia's chair out for her, too. He must remember to do that.

'Oh, I say, this looks good.' Lucien sat down and flicked out his napkin.

'What is it?' Felicia asked, staring at the row of tarts.

'Let me see.' Lucien picked up a folded card that had been left next to his napkin. 'That one's bacon, chard and gruyere. The middle one is cheese only. The last one is mushroom and spicy sausage.' He waved a hand. 'Do tuck in.'

Niro reached to take a slice.

'Wait,' Lucien said. 'We haven't said grace yet.'

Niro froze.

Peter snickered.

Lucien grinned. 'I'm joking. We don't usually say grace.'

Niro slowly lowered her hand. Her eyes darted across to Vimal. He didn't know what to do either.

'Perhaps we should say grace,' Peter said to Lucien. 'Just this once. Since it's our first meal together.'

Lucien raised a hand, palm up and gestured to Peter to go ahead. Peter folded his hands. Magda rolled her eyes and did the same.

Vimal ignored Niro's burning WTF glare and followed suit. Niro moved her hands to her lap and said nothing.

Peter started saying grace, in what Vimal could only assume was Latin. Magda muttered, 'Get on with it.'

Peter rattled through the words faster. When he got to 'amen', everyone raised their heads.

Felicia giggled. 'My grandpa insists on Latin grace at Christmas,' she said.

Peter raised his eyebrows at her. 'Does he indeed? Mine too.'

The others helped themselves to pieces of tart. So Vimal did too. Next to him Niro served herself some salad and passed the bowl to Felicia. He could feel the tension in her movements. If they were making Niro uncomfortable, then he wasn't imagining it. There really was a weird atmosphere here.

'So,' said Magda, in her plummy accent. 'How do you know Lucien?' She was looking at Vimal. There was the slightest emphasis on the word 'you', as though she considered it impertinent of him to know her friend.

Vimal paused, fork midway to his mouth. 'I ... er ... I work with him.'

'That's right,' said Lucien. 'Vimal is one of our super-smart quants.'

'What's that?' This was from Felicia.

'Quantitative analysts,' Lucien explained, in a voice of extreme patience. 'They run the numbers and do clever things with trends and projections, which the fund managers can use to work out which funds to move money into.'

'And you're a fund manager?' Niro said.

Vimal tried not to frown. He had told her all this. She knew what Lucien did.

'No. I work at the front end. Persuading big clients to use our algorithms for their funds in the first place.'

'Tried being a fund manager once, didn't you, Lucien?' Peter said.

There was a fraction of a pause before Lucien replied. 'Yes. Didn't suit me. I much prefer the customer-facing element.' He smiled. 'But anyway. Vimal here is one of the rising stars. He's been the quant on the team I work with for ... oh, how long now?'

Vimal's throat felt dry. 'A bit over a year.'

'So, we work together. And Kerry, who isn't here yet. She used to work with me, too. She's moved on to bigger and better things, I believe.' He looked at Vimal, as though seeking confirmation.

Vimal nodded. Kerry was doing extremely well in her new job. In the two years she'd been working there, she'd been promoted twice.

Peter's mouth twitched. 'Is that so?'

'She's going out with Woolly now.' Lucien flashed a bright smile at Peter. 'Remember him?'

Vimal tried not to react to this. Niro gave him a quick sideways glance and focused back on her food.

'Bloody hell,' said Peter. 'How is old Woolly these days?'

Vimal frowned. 'You guys both know him, then?'

'Oh yah,' said Peter. 'We were at school together. Top chap.' He shook his head. 'Small bloody world, eh?'

No wonder Lucien had invited Kerry and her new man to this retreat. He knew them both from two different places. Vimal looked from Peter to Lucien; they were swapping anecdotes about school. Felicia was watching them idly as she ate. Magda was just smiling and nodding. A small nudge against his leg, under the table, made him turn to look at Niro, who gave him a sharp glance. Oh yes. He was meant to be with her now. He smiled at her. She averted her gaze, coyly. If he didn't know the truth, he would have totally believed that she was flirting with him. He reached for the bottle of wine and topped up her glass and his own. 'Anyone else want a top-up?'

Everyone did.

Chapter 10

Niro stood at the side of the bed and stared at the pillow wall they had constructed. She had seen enough romcoms to know that there were several ways this could go. Luckily, Vimal wasn't the romcom-watching type, so he was most likely to go with the scenario where the pillow wall stayed firmly intact all night. At least she hoped so.

This really was a weird situation. She hadn't shared a room with someone in ages. What if she'd started snoring in the intervening time? Or talked in her sleep? Or had some sort of erotic dream and made dodgy noises? Telling herself firmly not to be silly, she climbed into bed. She had discovered the electric blanket and used it to make her side of the bed lovely and toasty. Niro stretched out and wiggled her toes in the warmth. She had brought her warmest pyjamas, which had penguins on them. If the bed stayed this warm all night, she might even be too hot.

The bathroom door opened and she instinctively turned away. She heard Vimal putter around plugging his phone into the charger and putting his clothes away. He seemed to be a meticulous person.

Vimal sat on the bed. 'Shall I turn the lights off?'

Niro looked over her shoulder at him. He too was in pyjamas.

Plain black ones with white edging. They looked like they'd been ironed. Or maybe they were brand new.

'Sure,' she said.

He lifted the bedding to get his legs under it and Niro felt a waft of cold.

She shivered. 'You're letting the warmth out.'

'Sorry.' He turned the lights off. The room went pitch black. 'That's … quite dark,' he said.

Niro had to agree. Her bedroom at home was never fully dark. Was anywhere, these days? She let her eyes adjust. The only light in the room was a faint glow from one of the phones as it charged. It wasn't enough to make out even the broad shapes of the furniture.

'There isn't a night light or anything, is there? I'm going to walk into things when I get up to go to the loo at night.'

'I don't think so.'

Her phone was plugged in next to her. 'It's fine. I'll use my phone as a torch.'

'Good idea.'

They lay there in silence for a moment.

'What are you going to do tomorrow?' Vimal said, suddenly.

'If there aren't any other plans, I was going to go across the village to the hotel and take some pictures of the villa from over there. Weather permitting, of course.' That way, she could get at least some of her photos, which would free her up to concentrate on acting her part.

'I'll come with you,' he said, immediately.

Niro looked into the dark. On the one hand, it would be nice to have some company. On the other hand, he would just get in the way. 'You don't have to.'

'As you say, a deal's a deal. I said I'd help you take your photos.'

'I don't really need help …'

'Yeah, you do,' he said. 'If I hadn't been there, you'd have offered to give Basty one of your photos for free. You have no sense of

90

how much your work is worth.'

She rolled over and glared at his patch of darkness. 'And you do?'

'Well … I have some idea. Kerry was into art, remember. I've seen enough photography exhibitions to know what you can charge.'

He was probably one of those people who walked around exhibition openings, nursing a glass of wine and making serious faces at the artwork, without really understanding it. Some people liked owning art. A sudden thought occurred. 'You haven't seen one of my pictures in one of these exhibitions, have you?' There had only been two, both in small places.

'I don't think so.'

'How about Mick Vickery? He takes pictures of derelict buildings and graffiti. Black-and-white with bits of colour.'

Vimal was silent for a bit. 'I think I have, actually,' he said. 'Is that your ex?'

'Yeah.' The familiar sting of humiliation was back.

'I've seen your website,' Vimal said. 'Your pictures are much better than his.'

It was a nice thing to say, even if it was completely untrue. Mick had a name in the art world. She was just a nobody. Niro smiled. 'Thank you. That's very kind.'

Vimal made a little 'hmm' noise. 'It's also true. I like your photos better. Less pretentious.' There was a rustling as he turned over. 'Anyway. Goodnight, Niro.'

'Goodnight.'

She closed her eyes and lay very still, waiting for sleep. All the while, she was aware of Vimal on the other side of the pillow wall. He was breathing steadily, but not so deeply that she could believe he was asleep. She wasn't bothered by his presence; she was pretty sure she was safe with him. It was just the awareness. It was so weird. She shifted position and tried to think when she'd last slept in someone else's room. Last year, she'd been to a few parties which had involved sleeping on sofas or on the floor. That was different. Being drunk helped, maybe. She tried to stifle a sigh and didn't quite succeed.

'Can't sleep?' Vimal whispered from the other side of the pillow wall.

'Struggling a bit, yeah,' she whispered back. 'This is weird.'

There was a pause before he said, 'It really is.' There was a sound as though he'd turned over. 'So. What did you think of dinner?'

'Food was delicious.' It really had been. She thought about the white upholstery and the caterers who quietly came in, set the table with warm food and disappeared again. 'I could get used to having caterers. If all the meals are going to be like that, this is going to be an amazing holiday. I mean, this whole place is pretty epic. It's all understated, but so fancy.'

'Yes. I know what you mean. Sort of effortlessly expensive.'

That was a good way of putting it. It was all super tasteful. Nothing was over the top. It made her feel out of place. Like she was lowering the tone simply by being there. 'Do you ... feel awkward about that?' she asked.

'Not really ... How do you mean, awkward?'

She rolled over onto her side, so that she was facing the pillow wall. 'You know. Awkward. Like you shouldn't be touching any of it, because it's too special.'

'Oh.' For a moment there was nothing but his breathing, and then a soft chuckle. 'Like the good dinner set that's "for visitors"?'

'Exactly.' Her mother had one of those. She supposed his mother must do too. 'Exactly like that. "Be careful you don't break that – it's the good set,"' she said, with a hint of a Sri Lankan accent.

'And then you're so nervous about it, you drop it anyway.' Vimal's voice had laughter laced through it.

The idea struck her as funny. 'You didn't, did you?'

'I did. Mum's eight-piece dinner set has only got seven plates.'

'Oh, you terrible son.'

He laughed, soft and unguarded. It was the first time she'd heard him laugh like that. It was the most relaxed he'd sounded in her time knowing him. How weird that it was in the pitch dark.

'I bought her a new set, when I started earning,' he said. 'She loves the new one, but the family will keep telling the story of how I broke the plate just before my sister's in-laws came to visit for the first time.'

'And they will never, ever stop.'

When he spoke again, the laughter had gone and his voice was serious again. 'I guess, if you were my girlfriend, that's the sort of thing you'd know.'

And bam! It was back to being weird again. 'True. But I'm only a new girlfriend and I wouldn't know all the stuff you'd have told your long-term girlfriend. So I don't think we need to worry too much about my not knowing your family in-jokes.'

'Actually, I don't think I ever told Kerry that story.'

'Why not? Surely your parents told her the first time they met her for a meal.'

'No. They … were on their best behaviour.'

Niro wasn't sure what that was supposed to mean. Kerry had been around for a long time, from what Vimal had said. 'Did they not like her?'

'Oh, it's not that. I think they just treated her like she was temporary. They were polite and nice and all that, but also a bit reserved … if that makes sense.'

That did make sense.

'Did your parents get on with Mick?'

Just hearing his name brought a heaviness to her chest. 'They did, actually. He was very charming. When we split up, I think they were really upset that they hadn't seen that he wasn't a good man. Like they'd let me down or something. I guess none of us saw it coming.' Her parents had been very supportive when she had showed up at home, in tears. 'I moved back home for a while. It was okay for the first few weeks. Good food, you know. But after a bit, they started driving me mad again. Luckily, Sam was looking for a flatmate and so I moved in with her.'

'You're fond of Sam and Gihan, aren't you?'

'Of course. We grew up together. I'm an only child, so they're the next best things to siblings.'

'That's nice,' he said. 'My sister is ten years older than me, so I don't really have anyone I'm close to like that.'

Sam and her brothers weren't technically her cousins. Her aunt was their stepmother. But they had all been part of the same social circle even when Sam's mother had been alive. They, Sam especially, had always been there for her. Even when things were at their worst and getting out of bed was a struggle. She had other friends, but family was different, right? 'Ah, that's sad.'

'Hmm.' He sounded sleepier now. 'I guess I don't have that many close friends now. I tended to work a lot or spend my evenings with Kerry ... so I sort of lost touch.'

Niro had lost touch with friends too ... mainly because she had shared a lot of those friends with Mick and she couldn't bear the humiliation of seeing them again. It wasn't just that he'd cheated on her. He'd cheated on her with someone they all knew. They must have known about the affair. Perhaps they'd even understood his reasons. They might even know what he really thought of her work and been in on the joke.

A flashback to that horrible feeling of smallness made her queasy. No. She wasn't going to fall in this trap again. She took a deep breath in and forced her chest to inflate as much as she could, then slowly breathed out again. She was done with feeling sorry for herself. This 'holiday' was a chance for her to be someone else. This character was the girlfriend of a hot guy and was an up-and-coming photographer. She might not actually be either of these things, but she was a good enough actress that she could bloody well play them.

Wait a minute. Had she thought of Vimal as 'hot'? She had to stop doing that, because he was just a friend. A colleague on the stage. She rapped herself on the forehead with her knuckles. It occurred to her that Vimal hadn't said anything in a while.

'Are you asleep?' she asked in the softest whisper.

There was no answer apart from steady breathing.

'Night then,' she said. 'Good talk.'

Chapter 11

When Niro woke up, Vimal had gone. It was nice to have the room to herself. She'd forgotten the sheer inconvenience of sharing a room. You could never fully relax when someone else was always around. She took her time, allowing herself to relish the softness of the bed and have a long stretch. It must have been dawn outside because there was a faint pinkish glow coming from the light wells. It wasn't bright, but it was enough for her to see her way around the room without turning on a light.

The shower turned out to be powerful and gloriously hot. This was proper luxury. She found a bathrobe and would have happily sat in it for a while if it weren't for the fact that Vimal could return any minute. So she got dressed and was sitting at the dressing table, combing the tangles out of her hair, when someone knocked.

'Who is it?'

'It's Vimal. Is it okay to come in?'

'Sure.' It was his room, too.

He popped his head around the door. 'I thought I'd check before I barged in.'

'I'm grateful,' she said. She was. It was a minimum level of politeness that she knew she should expect, but somehow the fact that he bothered with knocking was nice. What did it say about the sort of men she usually hung out with that such basic good manners surprised her?

He came in and shut the door. He had clearly been out for a run. He was in a Lycra top and long running legging-type things. He wore a headband and looked flushed and sweaty. 'It's very cold, but very pretty out there,' he said. 'It must have snowed last night. There's lots of pure white on this hill.'

'Oh cool. I'd best get a move on and take photos.'

'I ran up to the hotel. Walking distance, if you're up to it.'

She narrowed her eyes. 'Define walking distance.'

'About a mile. Maybe a bit more. Up a fairly steep hill at the end, though.' He pulled up one leg behind him to stretch.

Niro tried not to stare at his legs. 'I … guess.' She turned her attention firmly back to the mirror and her hair.

'You'll be fine,' he said. 'There's a really nice view of the village on the way.'

Niro pulled her hair up into a ponytail. Vimal finished his stretching and said, 'I'm going to take a shower.'

She looked up in time to see him wander off, stretching an arm over his head. He had quite nice shoulders. Aargh. WHY was she looking? 'I'm going to go find some breakfast.'

Once the door to the room was shut, she waved a hand in front of her face to cool it down. She was being stupid. She could not afford to fancy Vimal. The only reason she was here was because she'd made a deal. The man was clearly still in love with his ex, so finding any source of feelings for him would be very, very stupid.

Niro squared her shoulders and marched off to the kitchen. Hearing voices, she peered into the living room as she went past. Felicia, dressed in exercise clothes, was doing yoga. The voice was coming from the yoga instructor on her phone. She was lying on her back, with her legs and hips lifted straight up in the air. She looked slim and toned, like an advert for Lycra. Niro knew that she herself would never be able to do that. Her boobs would suffocate her, for a start. She left the young woman to it and crept away.

A selection of breakfast things was set out in the kitchen already. What time did the caterers come in? There were pastries, covered to keep warm, and a variety of breads, cheeses and hams and some cereal. Niro got herself a bowl of muesli and yoghurt and took it to the table, where an English language newspaper had been left at the head of the table. She pulled out her phone and sent Sam a picture of the breakfast array.

Niro: *I'm having muesli. Aren't I virtuous?*
Sam: *What's the point of being on holiday if you aren't eating pastries for breakfast? How did last night go? Sleep okay?*
Niro: *Yep. All fine. Vimal's ex arrives this afternoon. I'm going to go take some photos this morning, in case things go so well that he wants me to leave earlier than planned.*
Sam: *Chances of that are slim, though. She's coming with her new bloke. The best you can hope for is that she gets a bit jealous.*
Niro: *I dunno. Turns out the new guy she's seeing is friends with Lucien and co. These people are … interesting.*
Sam: *??*
Niro: *They're very mannered and polite, but there's a weird undercurrent. I kept getting the feeling they were watching and judging everything I do. Vimal is nervous as all hell when they're around. I don't even understand why he wanted to come on this holiday in the first place.*
Sam: *That's not your insecurity talking, is it?*

Niro stared at the text, feeling attacked. Sam knew her too well for her to pretend.

Niro: *Maybe. But the character I'm playing doesn't give a crap about what they think, so I'm brazening it out. If*

*they look down their noses at me much more, I'm going
to start being deliberately annoying.*

Sam: *Which won't help Vimal, now will it?*

Niro: *Bollocks.*

Felicia wafted into the kitchen, rolled-up yoga mat slung over her shoulder. 'Morning,' she said, brightly.

Niro put her phone down. 'Morning. Finished your yoga?' She winced. Of course she'd finished. That was why she was in here.

Felicia got a bottle of green stuff out of the fridge. 'Hmm. Yes. I always feel rubbish if I miss it.' She poured herself a glass of the green goop.

Niro stared at the drink. 'What is that?'

'My kale and spirulina smoothie. Lucien arranged for them to deliver one each day.' She grabbed a bottle of water in her other hand and swigged it.

'That's sweet,' said Niro. 'How long have you guys been together?'

Felicia laughed. 'Oh. We're not together.' She took another swig of water. 'This is just a casual thing.'

Oh. Well that would explain her complete lack of interest at dinner. 'I ... see.'

Felicia's smile dropped. 'I suppose you find that strange,' she said, her gaze assessing.

Did she? Well, yes, a bit. Though Felicia's arrangement with Lucien wasn't so different from her own arrangement with Vimal, really. Apart from the sleeping together bit ... so who was she to judge? They were both consenting adults, so why not?

'A bit, I guess,' she said. 'But only because of the age gap.'

The smile returned, cautiously. 'Pfft,' said Felicia. 'He's not that old and he's attractive. I've seen worse.'

Not sure how to respond to that, Niro said, 'So, what do you do ... when you're not on holiday?'

'I'm a student. Media and advertising.'

Niro looked at the absolutely stunning girl standing in the kitchen in her leggings and crop top and tried to work out her thoughts. Felicia seemed to be intelligent and using Lucien while letting him think *he* was using her. Niro got the feeling that Lucien was punching above his weight at every turn, even if he didn't realise it.

Felicia was taking selfies of herself looking artfully ruffled.

'You know,' said Niro. 'If you stand by that window and turn the lights on, you'd be able to get a really nice background.'

'Oh, good idea.' Felicia moved across. 'Hmm. I like that,' she said. 'You have a good eye.'

'I'm a photographer,' said Niro. 'I mostly do landscapes and buildings though. Rarely figurative shots.' Although, maybe it was time to start. She reached for her phone. 'Can I take a few photos of you?'

'Oh, sure. Can you take a couple with my phone too, so that I can post them?' She struck a pose.

Niro looked at the screen of her phone. 'No. No. Don't pose. Be natural.'

'That's so awkward to do.'

'Oh, I know,' said Niro, not taking her eyes off the screen. She zoomed in a little so that Felicia's face was better framed. 'Do you have an Instagram account? Or some other social media channel?'

'Insta. I'm on TikTok too, but I'm not that well established yet.'

'You're very photogenic,' Niro said. She really was. Felicia should be a model. There wasn't an outfit in the world that wouldn't look good on her.

'Thank you!'

Niro took several photos, including one that captured the brief moment of pure delight in response to the compliment. Felicia dropped a shoulder, tilted her head and smiled, so Niro took a couple more, then swapped to Felicia's camera and snapped a few more before handing the phone back.

'Oh, I like these,' said Felicia. 'How come they look so good?'

Niro was busy scrolling through her photos and deleting the ones she didn't like. 'Framing,' she said, absently. 'I positioned you so that your eyes are the first things the viewer sees. The light is pretty good here.' She found a picture where Felicia wasn't fully smiling, but her whole face was lit up with pleasure. She turned the photo round to show it.

'Oh.' Felicia frowned. 'That's … not that much like me.'

Niro waited. She was used to this reaction, especially to photos taken on a phone. Felicia titled her head thoughtfully. 'I really like it though.' She smiled. 'Can you send me a copy?'

'Sure. I'll take a few more over the course of the holiday. If you like.'

'That would be awesome. Yes please.'

'Would I be able to use them for my portfolio?'

Felicia's perfect brow creased. She handed Niro's phone back. 'Yes, but please don't post them anywhere without telling me.'

'Would I be able to include them in an exhibition, say, if I checked with you first?'

'Of course. So long as you check with me first.'

'Deal,' said Niro. Felicia nodded slowly. 'And if I see something I really like, can I use it for my sites?'

'I'm sure we can do that.'

They shook on it.

'I'd better go have a shower and change into something more appropriate, before Lucien wakes up,' said Felicia. 'I'll see you later.' She waved with her fingers, slung her yoga mat over her shoulder and wandered off.

Niro watched her leave. She wasn't sure why she'd asked that, apart from the fact that Felicia photographed well and sometimes, it was easier to get someone to see the art in a photograph if the subject was pretty too.

She hadn't thought of taking figurative shots before, because they didn't excite her. They were just faces. But there was something niggling at the back of her mind. Something about people

101

in relation to their surroundings. The idea was still elusive, hiding. She would have to take a lot of pictures and work out what the theme was later, when she had them all in front of her.

*

Niro opened the door to the courtyard and cautiously stepped outside. The door shut behind her and the cold wrapped itself around her. She felt it mainly in her face and on her hands, which were bare so that she could hold her camera safely. The part of the courtyard she was standing in was in shadow. The snow lay undisturbed between her and the lopsided oval of sunlight in the middle.

When she walked across, her feet made muffled squeaking noises in the snow. Reaching the sunlight was a relief. She raised the camera and felt her hands warm up, just a little. Okay. She should take some photos and get back inside, or at least get some gloves on quick.

The villa was much further up the mountain than she'd realised. Standing at the gate, where the curved arms either side were so low that it only came to her waist, she could see the stretch of unbroken white between herself and the houses far below. A little way off to the side, she could see the drive leading to the entrance of the villa.

She photographed the toy-like village. Across the valley was the hotel, also decorated in white. There was more movement there. A red car pulled up to the front. She grabbed a picture of that too. Then, zooming back out, she tried to capture the height and grace of the mountain behind it.

The light was so bright that she had to step back into the shadows a bit. Bloody hell, it was cold. She hung her camera round her neck and pulled on her gloves. They were supposed to have grippy fingertips, but they didn't fit properly, so she couldn't use them like that. They would have been perfect, if her fingers had been longer. Still, they were warm and right now that was what she needed.

A movement inside the house caught her eye. She looked up to see that Magda had walked into the living room. Wearing a green jumper and dark green trousers, she was standing in the pool of light that came from outside and glaring at her phone. There was a hint of melancholy about the sight of this immaculately dressed woman, all alone in the beautifully appointed room. Niro took a photo. She would ask for permission later. Looking at the photo in the viewer, she was pleased with it. It needed reframing a bit, but there was something interesting there in the contrast of Magda against the softness of the background and the faint dazzle of the glass windows. Yes. She would have to play around with the image later and see if she could clarify it.

Niro moved around a bit to find a different view. If she leaned out over the gate, she could get a photo of the valley, half of which was still in shadow because of the angle of the sun. It would be better to go out of the enclosed space. The area just outside sloped downwards, but only gently. It got steeper a few yards beyond, but there was a low fence to mark where it was safe. She opened the gate and stepped out of the courtyard. Oh. The view!

She took a few photos and then stopped to just … look. And breathe. The air felt different. Thinner, somehow. As though there was less stuff in it. She felt it flow into her lungs and then pushed it out in a cloud that rose above her. She'd forgotten how much fun that was. She laughed and watched her laughter puff out in front of her. She should get someone else to do that, so that she could photograph that, too.

'Hey, Niro.'

She looked up to see Vimal, leaning out of the door. 'Did you want to go up to the hotel?'

Ah. Perfect. 'Come here,' she said. 'I need to try something.'

He crumped his way across the snow warily. 'What?'

103

'Stand ... here.' She placed him in the sun. 'Face that way. Now laugh.'

Through the camera viewfinder she saw him turn and give her a sceptical frown. 'Laugh? On cue?'

She didn't lower the camera. The light was falling on him, picking out the stray strands of wool from his beanie and the tips of his long eyelashes. Behind him the darkness of the wall gave enough contrast for the cloud of condensation to show up when he breathed. This would be a beautiful shot.

'Okay, then. Just blow your breath out. You know, like you're smoking.'

He gave her another incredulous look, then shrugged, looked in the direction she'd told him to and blew. She got her beautiful shot. Then, he lowered his head and laughed, his laughter billowing out of his mouth like smoke. She caught that too.

Excitement, like she hadn't felt in a long time, rose in her chest. There were things here she wanted to photograph. Okay, she didn't normally do people photos, but why not? You had to be open to change, right? Even if the photos she took were shit, the fact that she wanted to take them was something she hadn't felt in a long time. Thank goodness for Vimal and his strange plan.

Chapter 12

Vimal would have liked to walk faster, but Niro kept stopping to take photos. He waited, arms folded, as she photographed a small sledge that had been left propped against the side of a house. He had probably run past that earlier that morning but not noticed it.

Perhaps that was what made photographers special. They noticed more. Ever since they'd emerged from the garage into the sharp winter sunshine, Niro had been exclaiming and pointing little details out to him. The view was obvious, but she'd found light glinting off the icicles hanging from a roof, frost-encrusted cobwebs, the wave pattern caused by snow drifting past the posts on a fence. She took photos of them all. He would never have spotted any of those things, but then, he wasn't an artist.

He watched her as she crouched down in the snow to take a photo through the gap between the sledge body and the blades underneath. She was frowning with concentration. Her whole body seemed to be focused on the camera in her hands. When she stood up again, she checked the picture in the display at the back and her smile lit up her face.

She was clearly getting joy from this. Vimal looked around. Maybe, if he really tried, he could spot something of interest for her to photograph.

By the time they got to the road that led up to the hotel, he was getting the hang of what to look for. Specificity; that was what she liked. 'Look,' he said. 'If you stand just here, those two houses frame that mountain.'

She came to stand next to him, her shoulder pressed up against his arm. 'Oh, yes. I see what you mean.' She raised her arms to take the photo with her digital SLR camera and he felt the movement of her arm against his. Surprised by the unexpected contact, he moved away.

Niro crouched down on the ground and took another photo. Standing back up, she looked at the picture on the display screen. 'Oh, I like that,' she said. 'Good spot.'

'Shall we head to the actual hotel?' he said. 'We do have to be back by lunchtime.'

'Relax,' she said. 'Your ex isn't arriving until mid-afternoon.' She was still looking through her photos.

He didn't want to stand here arguing about what time precisely Kerry was going to turn up with her handsome, rich and exciting bloke. He started walking. 'Come on.'

The road leading up to the hotel was steep. Vimal had to keep stopping and waiting for Niro to catch up.

'I ran up this road this morning,' he informed her, bouncing on his feet and rubbing his arms to keep warm.

'That's because you're insane.' She puffed up the hill. Apparently, she was warm enough to have unzipped her coat a few inches.

'Or I have a modicum of fitness. You *genuinely* don't do exercise?' They had talked about this before and she claimed she did absolutely none. Vimal was finding that hard to fathom.

She reached where he was and stopped. Her camera-free hand on her hip, she blew out her cheeks. 'My aim in life is to get so fat that they have to dismantle the front door to get me out.'

They started walking again. He knew she was joking, but he simply couldn't help himself. 'But the health implications …'

'Ah, but those don't outweigh the sheer drudgery of having

to exercise. Besides, if I exercised I'd have to sneer at myself for being smug and my head might implode.'

He glanced at her. She was smiling, but there was an edge to her voice. He had better not push his luck. 'I must admit, that is an angle I had not considered.'

'See. It's more complicated than you healthy exercise nutters think.'

Vimal laughed. They had fallen into this easy banter only recently. He wasn't used to people gently teasing him, but it wasn't bothering him. Her sense of humour felt familiar. He felt comfortable around her, as though he'd known her for a long time.

'Oh.' Niro stopped and looked up the hill. 'Is that Basty?' She reached for her camera. Pulling a lens out of the satchel she had strapped tightly to her side, she screwed it on. When she raised the camera to her eye, it was considerably chunkier. She needed to use her other hand to steady it.

Vimal looked up. It was, indeed, Basty. In vivid blue again. He was talking to someone at the front of the hotel. From their vantage point, they were looking up at him as he stood on the top of the hill. The hotel loomed behind him, sunlight glinting off the windows.

'Oh, I like that,' Niro muttered, snapping away. 'Come on. Closer.'

She seemed to have found a burst of energy that propelled her up the slope faster than before. Vimal followed. The camera clicked rapidly.

Basty finished his conversation, turned to them and waved. Click. Click.

'That's the one,' Niro said, and lowered her camera. She sounded pleased.

'My friends!' Basty was in an exuberant mood by the looks of it. 'Welcome to chez moi. How are you getting on at the villa?'

'It's lovely, thanks,' said Niro. 'Very comfy.'

'And everyone has arrived now?'

107

'Almost everyone,' Vimal said. Some others had pulled up as they were leaving. The only ones yet to come were Kerry and her man. Vimal looked towards the hotel, gleaming in the sunlight. 'We came to take some photos.'

'Ah yes. For the competition. I remember now.' Basty rubbed his hands together. 'Let me show you the spot I meant. Come with me.'

He led them to a place in the hotel's small garden where a bench allowed people to sit and admire the view over the valley. Everything was covered in white, punctuated here and there by snow-laden roofs and the white speckled darkness of conifers. Almost directly across from them, slightly above the eyeline, you could see an oval shape set into the mountainside. The sunlight, coming low into the valley, cast the patio of the villa into shadow, so it looked like someone had punched a hole out of the landscape.

'I should have come earlier,' said Niro. 'The light has almost moved away from it.' She was already taking photos. 'I should come here at dawn one day.'

'I'll come with you for that,' Vimal said. 'We'll have to leave before dawn, so it'll be dark.'

'Hmm.' Niro raised her camera again and took more photos. While she did that, Vimal admired the frankly astonishing view. The sky, with its strands of cloud, had a crystalline quality to it. The woodlands steamed gently in the sunshine. He breathed in the air and was amazed at how different it felt. Lighter. Crisper. His run had felt harder than his usual one in London, but he had enjoyed the change in scenery.

'I'm going to see if I can get a better shot from up here.' Niro handed him her bag and climbed onto the bench. 'Ooh. Icy.' She took a moment to steady herself before raising the camera. 'Hmm. It's different.' She took more photos. 'Sheesh, I wish I was taller. It's a completely different perspective.'

'Of course, height affects everything,' Vimal said. The thought seemed momentous. 'We all see the world from slightly different angles because we're different heights. I can see the top of some stuff that you can't.'

Niro lowered the camera. 'Well, obviously.'

'I just never thought about it before,' Vimal said. He bent his knees a bit and looked around. Yes. It did look different. Not the stuff in the distance, but the things nearby.

'What're you doing?'

'I'm trying to see the world from your perspective.'

'Piss off.' She turned away. 'Bloody cheek.'

Oh no. She thought he was taking the piss out of her. Hastily, he straightened up. 'I didn't mean it like that,' he said. 'I just, honestly, never even considered—'

She waved a hand, the other still holding the camera up. 'Yeah. Yeah.' She took a couple of steps back on the bench.

He wasn't sure what happened. Niro shrieked. Her feet flew up. The camera dropped. Vimal didn't even think. He stepped forward, arms outstretched to catch the camera and suddenly they were full of her too.

'Oof.' He staggered backwards, but remained upright.

'The camera.' Niro's voice was stricken.

He had caught it. They both looked at it.

'Oh, thank god.' Niro's body sagged into him as she untensed. She grew heavier in his arms.

'Are you okay?' He turned to look at her and almost gasped to find her face so close to his. Her eyes widened. Her gaze slid downwards and he realised the reason she felt so warm and soft was that his hand was clamped onto her boob.

It took a second for them to disentangle themselves.

Niro straightened herself out, not meeting his eye. 'Thank you.'

'Not a problem.' His own face heated up. Given that he'd spent an uncomfortable night sleeping in the same room as her, the intimacy, even through seven or eight layers of clothing, seemed wrong. 'I'm sorry, I didn't mean to grab—'

'It's fine. I'm just glad you caught the camera … and me. The last thing I need is to break a bone falling off a stupid bench. And I really can't afford a new camera. So, thank you. For catching us.' She glared at the bench, where there was a clear mark where her foot had slipped on the frosted surface.

He shoved his hands into his pockets, where they wouldn't get into further trouble. 'Did you get the shot you wanted?'

'I think so.'

There was a moment of strained silence between them as sounds from the village floated up: a car swishing past, a door slamming, voices.

He still didn't dare make eye contact. 'Was there anything else you wanted to photograph before we head back?' he asked.

'I wouldn't mind taking a few shots of the hotel itself.' Niro nodded towards the pretty building. It was several stories high, with little balconies in front of each of the rooms. Everything was tipped with snow. Even though Christmas had passed, it still looked like an advert for the season.

'Basty has been so nice,' Niro said. 'I thought it would be nice to give him a photo of the place.'

They started walking back.

The sense of awkwardness persisted. He kept thinking about the feeling of her in his arms. The warmth, the weight. He really shouldn't be thinking about that. Not when he had to sleep next to her. Especially as he wasn't interested in her romantically. He needed to get his head together.

Niro stopped to take photos of the hotel.

'I think you have a real talent for photography,' Vimal said, trying to make conversation.

She paused and looked at him sideways. 'I've only put the best ones on the website.' Turning away, she took another photo.

Be that as it may, her photos were good. Vimal had been to enough photography exhibitions to know that. Niro's pictures had a certain mood to them. They made you feel something, but it wasn't easy to work out what exactly. It was the sort of thing you could look at again and again and still be affected by it. She could charge more for them. Perversely, if she charged more, she might even sell more because the art world was odd like that. 'You undercharge, you know.'

Niro froze. 'Do I?'

'Oh, yes. You could easily charge three times what you charge at the moment.'

'Ha. Then I wouldn't sell anything.'

'I think you would. People who want to buy art, want to buy a thing of value. Your photos are good, but you don't ascribe enough value to them. Sometimes people think art is good because it's expensive.'

'And you know this how, exactly?'

'I told you. Kerry dragged me to so many art events. At first, I tried to work out what made a photo good ... and there wasn't a pattern to it. Different artists do things so differently. So then I stopped bothering to look at the art and started listening to what people were saying instead. Turns out it's about feelings. Sometimes the pictures make them feel something and that's good enough.' He shrugged. 'Other times, they just want to buy something expensive.'

'You are so weird.'

It wasn't the first time someone had said that to him. He tried hard to fit in and not come off as weird, but sometimes he couldn't help it. He liked observing and looking for patterns. It was what made him good at his job. Kerry had been fine with it in private, but would have liked him to turn it off in public.

He had a momentary flashback of Kerry saying, *You're so ... analytical. So boring! I can't stand it anymore.*

The hurt crunched into his chest. He had promised he'd try to change, but he wasn't sure how. Kerry had asked him to move out and he had done so immediately, because if she didn't want him there, it was the right thing to do. He still didn't understand where it had gone wrong. Without thinking, he rubbed his chest, even though logically, his heart wasn't actually causing this pain.

He glanced at Niro, who had lowered her camera and was looking up at the sky, smiling. At least her side of the deal was working out well. This plan they'd come up with to make Kerry jealous had better work. He didn't know what he'd do if it didn't.

Chapter 13

Basty invited them in for a hot chocolate. Niro took more photos inside the hotel. They were sitting in the bar, which was still decorated for Christmas. An enormous pine tree stood in the corner, twinkling, even though it was the middle of the day. You could smell the pine the minute you walked in. Swathes of green, decorated with lights and gleaming berries, covered the walls. There was no tinsel; Niro approved. Tinsel had its place, but sometimes it was just too blingy and cold. A place like this went for warm and cosy.

There were a few photographs on the wall. The hotel in the summer. One of Basty on the day he took over. She walked along the sides of the room. These were nice photos. Technically fine. Pretty much like the ones she took when she was doing commercial work. A tiny voice in her mind said that some of the ones she'd taken this morning were better. She ignored it and walked on.

'Oh.' She stopped at a photo of four people standing outside the hotel. One was Basty, with another older man and two younger ones. 'Is that Lucien?'

Basty looked across. 'Oh yes. That's my brother and his sons. Lord Yelvington, the heir, and the spare.'

She looked at young Lucien, who seemed less confident in this photo than in real life. Their father was beaming. He had his arm around the taller son, who was straight-backed and handsome. Lucien stood slightly to the side, wearing a smile that didn't reach his eyes. Looking at the two brothers, there was an obvious resemblance, except the brother appeared more earnest. 'Which one's the older son?' she asked.

'Oh, Jasper is. His first name's Sebastian, you know. Named after me. But he prefers Jasper. Less confusion, I suppose. Can't have two Honourable Sebastian Fothergill Yelvingtons running around.'

That would make Lucien the 'spare'. She filed that piece of information away to think about later.

A waiter brought three mugs of hot chocolate and a decanter of something.

'Would either of you like a spot of brandy in your drink?' Basty uncorked the alcohol.

Niro said yes, but Vimal said no. She eyed him, sitting bolt upright. He was getting more and more tense the closer they got to Kerry's arrival time. He could have done with a drink to loosen up, really.

'Here we go.' Basty added a hefty slug of alcohol into her hot chocolate and passed it over.

She breathed it in and got mostly the smell of brandy. A few seconds later, the warm tones of cinnamon and chocolate arrived. 'Mmm.'

'So, did you get a lot of pictures?' Basty asked.

Niro took her camera out of her satchel and pulled up the one of Basty waving a greeting, with the hotel behind him. She turned the display to show him.

'Oh.' Basty held out his hand. 'May I?'

She passed it over and watched his face while he looked at it, zooming in and out again. 'You can have that one, if you like,' she said. 'By way of saying thank you.'

'That ... would be great,' said Basty. 'I should like to have

114

that in my office. Can I see the rest?' He scrolled through them, before she could reply. 'Ah, now this is nice too. You've captured something of the spirit of the place, somehow.'

Niro opened her mouth to speak and Vimal's knee nudged hers. Surprised, she looked across. He glanced meaningfully down at his hand, where he was holding up three fingers. Oh, yeah. He reckoned she was undercharging.

'How much would you want for more of these?' said Basty.

'Erm … prints, mounted and framed?' she said, buying time. Could she really ask for more? 'Or just prints?'

'Just prints. I can use a local framer.'

Niro didn't dare look at Vimal again. She cleared her throat and named a price that was twice what she'd normally charge.

Basty seemed pleasantly surprised. 'That's very reasonable,' he said. 'In that case, I'd like this one, this one and—'

'Hang on, hang on,' said Niro. 'Let me write them down.'

They went through the pictures. Basty wanted five prints, not including the one she was giving him for free. She wrote it all down. 'I'll send you an email by way of confirming the order,' she said. 'I'll need to take a deposit, obviously.'

Basty waved a hand. 'Send me an invoice.'

She turned, wide-eyed, to Vimal. Was it as easy as that?

His eye twitched, just a fraction of a wink. Yep. Apparently, it was.

*

Vimal was getting more and more anxious the closer they got to the villa. They were still a good distance away when a blue car drove past them on the way. He sped up.

'Hey! Vimal, slow down.'

He stopped and turned back to look at Niro, who was puffing going up the hill. 'Sorry.' He swung his head back towards the villa. There was a tree in the way. All he could see was a hint of

115

blue through the branches. 'I think Kerry's here.'

His voice sounded tight even to his own ears.

Niro came to a halt next to him. 'It's okay. We're ready for this,' she said.

He wanted to agree, but … 'I'm not sure I am.'

'Sure you are. You're here having a nice relaxing holiday with your cool, rich, posh friends. And you're here with me, your quirky, arty girlfriend.'

She made it sound like a game. To her it probably was. But it wasn't a game to him. His throat felt tight. How was he going to get away with this? He couldn't bear the thought of seeing Kerry with another man. The idea that he could make her feel jealous, just by rocking up with another woman in tow, had seemed like a plausible idea in a pub in London, but right now, it seemed the most ridiculous thing ever. After all, Kerry was probably happy with her boyfriend. She'd probably just congratulate him and move on. He rubbed his knuckles on his chest.

Niro frowned. 'Vimal. Snap out of it.' She held out a hand.

He stared at it. She wanted to shake hands?

Niro rolled her eyes. 'Don't you think we should hold hands? Since we're supposed to be going out?'

Oh god, this was a terrible idea.

She punched him lightly in the arm. 'Don't look so worried. You're not alone.' She smiled. 'You've got me.'

That was a good point. He did have her to help. Somehow, the thought was comforting. He nodded.

'Great. Now come on.' She waggled her fingers at him.

They had got this far, it would be stupid to throw it all away now. He took her gloved hand in his. 'Let's do this.'

They walked slowly up the hill. It was strange holding someone's hand. He hadn't done that since Kerry. He glanced across at Niro, who had unzipped her coat halfway, because the hill was too much for her and she was getting hot. She was marching along next to him with a look of concentration on her face. Perhaps

116

this was an acting thing.

As they reached the flatter ground in front of the entrance, the car passed them again, going in the opposite direction. Two people stood by the door. Lucien and Kerry. Lucien had a hand on Kerry's shoulder. Where was the boyfriend? Perhaps he'd already gone in. Damn. He had been hoping to get an idea of what this Simon Woolberg guy was like before he actually met him.

Lucien spotted them and waved. Niro waved back. Her squeezing his hand reminded Vimal to raise a small wave too.

Kerry looked up. Her eyes widened when she saw him. Was it his imagination or did she look shocked? He glanced at Niro, still holding his hand. Surely, it wasn't all that shocking that he might have found someone else. He was suddenly very glad that Niro was there.

'Where have you two lovebirds been?' said Lucien.

'We … er … went across to Basty's hotel …' He couldn't focus on what he was saying, because he was too busy looking at Kerry. He saw her gaze move from him, to his hand holding Niro's, to Niro and then back to him. She looked away. When she looked back, her face was carefully expressionless. He knew that look so well. She was thinking, working out how to approach this scenario. He'd seen her do it a hundred times before when they'd gone to social events.

Niro was telling Lucien about taking photographs of Basty's hotel.

'Oh, you must show them to me,' said Lucien, with every appearance of sincerity. 'Have you met Kerry? Kerry, this is Vimal's new girlfriend. Niro. And of course, you already know Vimal.'

Vimal managed a weak smile. Kerry's smile was so fleeting it almost wasn't there.

'Hi.' Niro shook Kerry's hand. 'Nice to meet you.' She was smiling, as though she had no idea who Kerry was. She was quite a good actress.

He shook himself. This gawping at Kerry wasn't going to help his cause. 'How have you been, Kerry?' he said. He was pleased with how steady his voice sounded. 'It's pretty cold out here. Shall we go inside?' This was aimed in the general direction of Lucien and Niro.

'Of course. Where are my manners? Kerry, you poor darling, you must be exhausted,' said Lucien. 'Come inside. Let's get you settled with a hot drink. And you can tell me all about what happened.'

Vimal looked around. 'Where's ... your boyfriend?'

Kerry sighed and fussed around with her bag. 'He's not coming. We broke up. Long story.'

He didn't miss the slight tremor in her voice. They'd broken up? That meant Kerry was single!

Lucien put an arm around Kerry's shoulders and ushered her in, taking her case with him. Vimal glanced at Niro, who gave him a warning glance and followed. She still had a firm grip on his hand.

As they walked along the corridor that led up to the main house, Lucien kept up a stream of small talk, explaining about the villa and how his uncle had let him have it for free this week because it was all still very new and he'd had no takers over this New Year's.

Kerry was single. Vimal tried to work out what this new information meant for him. Kerry was single. The thought buzzed around in his brain. If he hadn't hastily agreed to make this stupid plan with Niro, he would have been obviously single too. He might have had a chance to get back together with Kerry. Now he'd blown it. If he'd kept calm when it first came up, he would have been fine. He glanced at Niro, who seemed to be oblivious to what was going on. He tried to extract his hand from hers, but she gripped it more firmly. Not oblivious, then. Just a damned good actress.

When they got into the villa, Niro bundled him into their room and closed the door. The first thing she said was, 'Don't panic.'

'But it's all gone wrong.' He sat on the bed. He flexed his hand. 'You've got a hell of a grip, you know that?'

'Sorry.' She sat on the end of the bed, several feet away from him. 'I just had to make sure you didn't say something stupid and ruin everything.'

'What could I possibly say that could make things worse? She's single! And I'm here with a fake girlfriend. It's a disaster.'

'Oh, come on. Don't be such a drama queen.'

He got up and started pacing. 'You're right. I need to think this through. She's broken up with What's-his-name. Recently, too, because until last night, Lucien was still talking about them both coming. She clearly hadn't mentioned it to him then.'

Niro nodded slowly. 'Nor had he. He's friends with Lucien, so he would have said something, right?'

'Right. Right.' He paced back. The room wasn't very big and not built for pacing.

Niro sat on the bed frowning. 'Is it just me, or did she seem surprised to see you?'

He stopped and turned. 'I thought she was just surprised to see I had a girlfriend. She must really have thought I was a loser if she's that amazed.'

Niro made a face. 'No ... I think she was surprised to see you. I think she noticed that before she noticed me. Or the fact that we were holding hands.'

He was confused now. 'Why would she be surprised to see me? She knew I was coming.'

'Yeah. That is weird. Unless Lucien didn't tell her and she, quite naturally, assumed that you were only her plus one on the original invitation and so would not be coming.'

'Yes, but—' He snapped his mouth shut. He didn't know what he was going to say. It seemed ridiculous that Lucien hadn't mentioned to Kerry that he was coming ... and with a partner. Lucien had gone to great lengths to make sure Vimal knew Kerry was coming with Woolberg.

'There's something not right here,' said Niro.

That was as may be, but his more immediate problem was that Kerry was single and he had a pretend partner. He could never get close to Kerry with Niro around. 'Focusing on our more important problem,' he said. 'How about this? We have a pretend row and you go home. You've got the pictures you wanted no—'

'I haven't actually. I want to go back to the hotel at dawn and take a picture when the light is just coming into the valley.'

'Okay, so you do that tomorrow and we can have an argument the day after. Anyway, you go home, Kerry and I console each other and get all nostalgic because it was New Year's when we got together and … things are good.'

Niro wrinkled her nose. 'I think you're missing something.'

He slowly sat back down on the bed. 'Okay. What did I miss?'

Niro let out a long breath. 'Okay. Well, she dumped you before she met this guy Woolly or Fluffy or whatever, right? Because she felt you were a little set in your ways.'

He hadn't forgotten that. As if he could! 'Boring. She said I was boring.'

'I was trying to be diplomatic.'

Where was this going? 'Are you saying I *am* boring? Too boring for her?' He flopped backwards so that he was lying on the bed. 'I was interesting enough for four whole years.'

'What I'm trying to say is,' said Niro, sternly, 'you haven't changed much since you split up with her. If she looks at you and sees that you're the same, she will fight against getting back with you. She split up with you for a reason, not because she met someone else. Even if you manage to persuade her to come back on the rebound this time, you're going to end up having the same conversation all over again in a few months' time.'

He stared at the ceiling and tried to slow his thoughts down enough to analyse when she'd just said. That was a good point. Nothing had changed. New haircut and new clothes, but nothing substantial. If he did get back together with Kerry, there was a good probability that the pattern would repeat again, and the blow to his self-esteem would only be worse when it did. 'Okay …' He turned his head to look at her. 'So what do I do?'

'We stick to the plan,' she said. 'Except now, the remit isn't to persuade her that you've moved on and you're happy. It's to persuade her that you've changed and you've moved on but with the wrong person. We have to get her to see that she's a much better person for the new you than I am.'

That sort of made sense too. 'But I haven't changed.'

'Pretend you have. Lighten up a bit. Throw yourself into the role. Who knows, it might actually change you.'

'Does that happen?'

Niro shrugged. 'Everything changes us in subtle ways, so yes, it's possible. If nothing else, you will be able to persuade her that you're not boring. You're going out with a mad hippy arty chick who is completely wrong for your organised, analytical self and you're making it work.'

He turned it over in his mind. 'Several problems with that,' he said. 'One. That would be an obvious over-the-top response to her dumping me.'

'That's fine. It's because you're not over her. She would be totally oblivious not to make that link. Especially, if you have the chance to talk to her and you drop some hints that you aren't over her. That you and I, we're a family-sanctioned thing … which you went for because she didn't want you and you're heartbroken or whatever.'

'I dunno. Heartbroken sounds a bit pathetic.'

She gave him an amused glance. 'More pathetic than being boring?'

'Fair point.' He closed his eyes and thought about it. 'Okay. So … I need to pretend to enjoy whatever out-there things you come up with?'

'Yes. I promise I won't do anything too wild. Just a little less staid than you seem to be comfortable with right now.'

121

'Doesn't it seem out of character?'

'Not really. You're kind and you keep to your word. If you told me you were going to try to make this relationship work, you would try to do that. Even if you're not a hundred per cent comfortable with it.' She stood up. 'You have a think about it. I'm just going to go to the loo.'

When she had disappeared into the bathroom, he tucked his arm under his head and lay there, thinking. The point she made was a good one. He liked order and routine. What Kerry needed from him was change. Or flexibility and a willingness to change, at the very least. He hated change. Argh.

'Maybe we should consult the back-office gang,' he called out.

'Good idea,' she shouted back from the bathroom. 'In a minute, though.'

'Obviously.'

A few minutes later, she came out and said, 'I've had a thought. The New Year's party – or just before that. That would be a good time for us to have a bust-up. Parties are always pretty intense and there will be alcohol. By then we'll have done all the groundwork of showing her you've changed a bit but still have feelings for her. I'll flounce out early in the evening and you get to snog her at midnight.'

Vimal looked up from his phone, where he was going through his emails.

'How do I show her that I still have feelings for her, if I'm supposed to be with you?'

She tilted her head to one side and smiled. 'Oh, you sweet baba. Just look at her the way you did a few minutes ago. It's obvious.'

He hadn't realised his feelings were so transparent. 'Oh.'

Chapter 14

After lunch, they all walked down to the village to see the New Year's market. Niro bundled herself back into her coat and followed Vimal out of the villa and down the corridor to the main exit. The others were milling around by the door. Kerry was talking to Magda.

The young man from yesterday was back at the reception desk. Not wanting to stand with the others, Niro paused to smile at him. Vimal said, 'Hello, Martin.'

The guy evidently knew Vimal. He closed the book he had half-heartedly put down and said, 'Hello. Are you going down to the village?'

'Yes, apparently, there's a New Year's market on?'

'Ah yes. There is a market. It is mostly for Christmas, but this week there are still the food stalls and some things like New Year's Eve hats. It is very good fun.'

'That does sound good,' said Niro.

'Did you take the photographs that you wanted at the hotel?' He inclined his head towards her.

'How did you know about that? It wasn't you here this morning.' She did a quick mental check. The other guy had the same colour hair and eyes, but she was pretty sure it was someone different.

Martin grinned. 'In the morning, it was my brother Tobias. We are a family business. Me and my brother do the front desk. My aunt runs the catering. My girlfriend, Helga helps her sometimes.'

Niro thought of the blonde girl who had been serving them. 'Oh. I know who you mean. She's lovely.'

Martin looked pleased.

Lucien came down the corridor, with Felicia and the others in tow. 'Are we all here? Good, good. Come along then, everyone.' He swept past the rest of the group – Niro had forgotten most of their names. All the men worked in finance, or management of their family companies. The women had all taken one look at her and dismissed her, so she had dismissed them right back. Her priority was Vimal and Kerry. Although, she was starting to worry about Lucien's interest in Vimal. It seemed … out of place.

Niro noticed that Lucien had completely ignored Martin. She and Vimal both said goodbye and followed the rest of the party out.

Outside, the sun was shining, the melting snow making every-thing slightly damp. Niro's hands itched to take a few photos, but she kept her focus on the group. As they walked, she nudged Vimal's arm with her elbow and slipped her hand into his. He looked at her, surprised, then seemed to remember that he was supposed to be pretending he was her boyfriend. His fingers tightened ever so slightly around hers.

'How come you know the guy at the reception desk?' she asked him, by way of making conversation.

'I popped down earlier to get a map from there. So I stopped to say hello.'

Interesting. She liked that he didn't just ignore people who weren't useful to him, like Lucien did. 'Do you always talk to everyone?'

'I try.' He gave her a confused glance. 'I'm not good with social interactions, so I had to learn. Why?'

'No reason. I like that you treat everyone the same. It's refreshing.'

'Refreshing.' He smiled, rather abstractly. 'Kerry liked it too. She said it was endearing.'

'Well then, let's hope she noticed earlier.'

His face brightened. Bless him. Niro gave his hand a squeeze.

They fell into pairs as they walked, with Lucien and Peter at the front, talking loudly about cars. Magda and Kerry appeared to be talking about opera. Felicia, looking stunning in a powder-blue-and-white jacket and matching trousers, was falling behind because she was taking photos of herself posing in front of all manner of things.

'Do you want me to take a photo for you?' Niro asked her.

'Oh yes, please. I've done some lovely selfies but a full-view photo would be great.' She passed over what looked like a very expensive phone. 'I want to get that view in the background,' she said.

Niro took a few photos and passed the phone back. The others had walked a fair way in this time. Vimal was walking slowly, as though trying to keep them in sight without leaving the two women behind.

'We'd better catch up, I suppose,' said Felicia.

Niro grinned and they both jogged down to join Vimal.

'Are all those going to go on Instagram?' Vimal asked, when they reached him.

'Only the best ones,' said Felicia. 'I've only been here two days and I've got some ah-mazing pics. Living the dream, you know.' She threw her arms wide and beamed at them. Niro took a picture.

Felicia's eyes were immediately alert. 'Can I see?'

She showed her the photo as they walked along. She had caught Felicia at a slight angle, not looking directly at the camera, her smile wide and sincere.

'Oh, I like that,' said Felicia. 'Can you send it to me?'

'I'll post it on my Insta and tag you, how about that?' Niro pulled up the app. 'What's your handle?'

'I'll have to follow you.'

They exchanged Instagram details. As soon as Niro shared the photo, Felicia started typing, her thumbs moving rapidly, even though she was still walking. Niro, who had to stop walking to text or talk, was hugely impressed. Within seconds, Felicia had liked and shared.

'Your photos are so beautiful,' Felicia said.

'Thank you.' She decided she liked Felicia.

They were nearing the village now. Niro caught up with Vimal and nudged him to get hold of his hand again.

He leaned towards her and muttered, 'You don't have to keep reminding me to hold your hand, you know.'

'I have to remind you, otherwise you forget,' she replied in an undertone.

'Just because we're going out, we don't have to hold hands all the time.'

She gasped with mock indignation. 'Sometimes, I think you're not very committed to this fake relationship.'

He looked at her for a full second, then laughed. 'Fine. Fine. I'll hold your hand.' He lifted their clasped hands up between them. 'See.'

Niro chuckled. That was better.

'What are you two lovebirds giggling at?' Lucien called from a few feet away.

'Nothing,' Niro said. 'In-joke.' Standing not far from Lucien, Kerry was watching them. Her face was expressionless. Niro noticed that when Vimal turned in her direction, she quickly looked away. She hoped that was a good sign.

*

The smell of waffles preceded their first view of the market. When they turned the corner, they were in a small square lined with little huts, lit with fairy lights. There was still a Christmassy flavour to the decorations. The snow helped too.

'Oh, how lovely!' Niro fiddled with the camera settings and started snapping away. She had only intended to photograph landscapes, but the combination of lights and high spirits was impossible to resist.

'What are you doing?' Felicia was beside her. 'Can you take a photo of me with these adorable hats?'

The 'adorable hats' had panda ears and long scarves attached. Niro obediently photographed her, using Felicia's phone. She watched as Felicia tweaked the pictures to fit her aesthetic before posting them. It was quite impressive how quickly she decided what she wanted.

'How did you decide on the look of your Insta profile?' Niro said.

'Oh, I've been refining it for years,' said Felicia.

'Does it pay off? All the work?' Niro herself hadn't done much with her Instagram. She had started off posting regularly, but nowadays, she rarely left the house to take photos, so there wasn't much that was interesting to post.

Felicia shrugged one shoulder. 'I get the odd offer to promote something and free stuff occasionally. But I'm still working on it. One of these days, I'll get some sort of big sponsorship and I'll be well away.' She flitted across the stall. 'Oh, look at this one. It's so adorable.' This was a hat shaped like a fox, the russet a lovely complement to the hints of strawberry in her hair.

'Do you like that, Filly?' said Lucien. 'It suits you.'

'It does, doesn't it?' Felicia flicked the scarf portion over her shoulder.

'Then you should have it.'

'Oh, darling, thank you.' Felicia threw her arms around Lucien and kissed him.

Niro sidled away to catch up with Vimal, who pointedly grabbed her hand.

127

'You keep disappearing to take photos,' he said. 'Anyone would think you weren't committed to this fake relationship.'

She grinned at him.

They stopped to look at a stall selling pastries.

'Stollen,' said Vimal. 'I love stollen.' He glanced over to where Kerry was looking at some jewellery. 'So does Kerry.'

'It's got marzipan in it, right?' Niro pulled a face.

'Ja,' said the stallholder. She pointed to a tray of adorable pig-shaped sweets. 'Or we have the marzipan pigs. It is a tradition to exchange them at the New Year.'

'Then, I should get some for everyone.' Vimal was already fishing his wallet out of his pocket.

'None for me,' said Niro. She lowered her voice. 'In fact, that's an idea. You can offer them around and I can pretend to be offended that you didn't consider my likes and dislikes before you bought them.'

He frowned. 'And that would show ... what exactly?'

'That we don't know each other very well. Sow the seed of doubt that we're suited.' She shook her head. He was making this such hard work.

He nodded slowly. 'I see. I think.' He took out his wallet, frowning. 'May I buy some?'

'Can I take photos of your stall?' Niro asked. When the stall-holder nodded, she crouched down and took a few photos of the rows of tiny pigs. 'They're cute.'

At the stall next door, Kerry pointed a piece of jewellery out to Magda.

'Yes, that's very quaint, darling. I prefer real stones though.' Magda pushed her hair back to show Kerry her earrings. 'These are diamonds.'

From behind the camera, Niro could see Kerry's face. She looked disappointed as she returned the piece to the stall. Why did she need Magda's approval? She should just buy what she wanted. She took a photo of the jewellery stand, with Kerry and

Magda blurred into the foreground. The lighting was wonderful.

They meandered some more. When they came back into contact with Kerry and others in the group, Vimal pulled out a paper bag. 'Stollen, anyone?' He shared them round. 'It's the marzipan sort.'

'Ugh,' said Niro. 'I can't stand marzipan.'

'Oh, come on,' said Lucien. 'Who dislikes marzipan?'

'Me. I dislike it. Bleurgh.'

'I ... I'm sorry,' said Vimal. 'I didn't know.'

'You could have asked. Well, you enjoy your stollen,' Niro said, with bad grace. 'I am going to go have a look at the ice rink.' She stalked off, leaving Vimal with the others.

She leaned against the barrier, taking photos, until someone came to stand beside her.

'That wasn't very nice of him,' a voice said.

Niro lowered her camera and found Felicia next to her. 'Pardon?'

'Vimal. That wasn't very nice of him to buy something for everyone when you can't have any. Surely, you must have mentioned it to him when you were looking at the food earlier.'

'I don't think I did.' She rapidly ran through how she should respond. Her character should be upset. Or annoyed.

Felicia sniffed. 'And anyway ...' She glanced over her shoulder. 'I think he might be flirting with his ex. Also, not on.'

'Is he?' Niro said, cautiously. 'Flirting with his ex, I mean?'

'Well, not flirting exactly, but looking at her with big puppy-dog eyes.' Felicia shook her head. 'He shouldn't be doing that.' Even Felicia's frown was charming. 'Lucien said yours was an arranged set-up thing. Are you sure that's a good idea?'

Ah. The perfect feed line! 'Actually, we are just getting to know each other better. This holiday – we haven't told our families about it. We thought it would be a good idea to spend some time together to see how we get on. You know, check out how we'd be as a couple.' She gave Felicia a sidelong glance. 'I can see that it was a good idea to do this.'

'Because he's not exactly measuring up well?'

Niro nodded. 'Better to find out now, before we tell our families we agree to get engaged, right?'

Felicia leaned closer. 'So what are you going to do?'

'I'm going to give him another day or two. I'll decide on New Year's Eve.'

'Wow, that's very business-like.' Felicia's expression changed. She now looked impressed.

'We have to be, really,' said Niro. 'It's an arrangement. Not love. Not at first, anyway.'

'I suppose,' Felicia said. 'I hadn't really thought about that before.'

'Mind you,' Niro said, with a sigh. 'It would have been a hell of a lot easier if the villa had single rooms. Or at least one with twin beds.'

'It does. Kerry's in it. I know because she mentioned it. She made a joke about it being a good job she and Simon had split up.' Felicia gave a little giggle. 'Simon would have been furious if he'd turned up. I think Lucien just wanted to mess with him. But he didn't show, so that was a waste.'

Niro said nothing, but filed this piece of information away to think about. Lucien had told Vimal that there were no twin rooms. He had put Vimal, and consequently Niro, in an awkward position just so he could prank his school friend. This was not normal behaviour.

'Hey, Filly, look at this!' Lucien called.

'Don't you hate that he calls you Filly? Like some sort of prize horse?'

Felicia laughed. She waved to Lucien. 'I don't mind. I got called that at boarding school anyway. I'd best go see what he wants.' She patted Niro's arm and tripped off towards Lucien.

Niro shook her head. Posh people. Sometimes she didn't think she'd ever understand them.

130

*

Later on, back in their room, Niro told Vimal about her conversation with Felicia. He sat on his side of the bed, leaning against the headboard, and listened with focus. 'So … Felicia thinks I'm a bad boyfriend.'

'Yes. Which is good, because we want people to think we're not well suited.'

'I guess.' He didn't look very happy about it. She didn't blame him. No one liked to look bad. Besides, Vimal was rubbish at lying.

'This was the plan,' she reminded him gently.

He sighed. 'I know. I know. There must be another way to make us look incompatible. I just hate being the bad guy.'

'You're being the racy, unpredictable guy. And that's—' She was interrupted by her phone ringing. 'Oh, it's Sam. I'd better get it.' She had tried to call Sam earlier to tell her about the change to the plans, but it had gone straight to voicemail.

'Niro! I got your message.' Sam's face appeared on the screen. She seemed to be in her office. 'What's happened? Is now a good time?'

'Yes, it is.' Niro sat back, leaning against the headboard on her side of the bed. Vimal sat on his side and scrolled through his phone.

'What's going on?' Sam asked.

She explained what had happened and outlined the new plan.

'That sounds shaky,' said Sam. 'I mean, the most logical solution would be for you to leave.'

'Yes, but wouldn't that be too obvious?' Vimal said.

Niro instinctively turned her phone, so that he appeared on camera. There was sudden silence from Sam. Niro turned the phone back. 'Well?'

Sam appeared to be craning her neck, trying to see through Niro's phone.

'What's up, Sam?' she said.

131

'Nothing really,' Sam said. 'It just looked like you were sitting on an enormous bed.'

Damn. Sam was going to tease her mercilessly when she got back. Niro glanced across at Vimal, who looked alarmed. 'Oh, yeah.' She rolled her eyes. 'There aren't any twin rooms, just doubles, apparently. So we got this humongous bed.'

'So, you're in a fake relationship and there's ... only one bed?' Sam was making huge eyes at her.

Niro glanced at Vimal's puzzled expression and mouthed *sorry*. If anything, that made him even more confused.

'Are you guys ... *sharing*?' Sam said, a grin starting at the edges of her smile. Yup. There it was. She was never going to hear the end of this.

'It is huge. And there's the pillow wall.'

'Pillow wall?'

'Yes. There's a load of spare pillows, so we made a wall down the middle of the bed. It's completely sane and above board. Can we get back to the main point, please?'

Sam narrowed her eyes at her, then said, 'Fine.'

'So, we thought it was too obvious if I flounce out immediately. So I was thinking we'd make it look like I'm a really bad choice for Vimal.'

'How are you going to do that?'

They looked at each other. 'We need ideas.'

Sam frowned. 'Hmm. Vimal?'

He shifted closer and peered at the screen by Niro's shoulder. 'Yes?'

'What's important to Kerry? Like ... what does she judge people on?'

He looked taken aback. 'I don't ...'

'I mean. What does she care about in a partner?'

'If I knew that, we wouldn't be having this conversation. Clearly, I don't know.'

Niro turned and found his face right next to hers. She quickly

132

shifted back to look at the phone. 'You must have some idea.'

Vimal looked stunned. 'Okay. She likes food. Bit of a foodie. Really likes pretentious stuff.'

'So ... if I taste things and go "not as good a burger"?'

'Yes!' said Sam. 'That's the sort of thing I mean.'

'Okay,' said Vimal. 'High-brow art, obviously. But you're better at that than she is.'

Niro wasn't so sure, but she let him have that one.

'Fashion? She likes to buy clothes ... like with a personal-shopper appointment, every six months.'

Niro snorted. 'Being unfashionable is no effort at all for me.'

'I dunno, mate,' said Sam. 'You've got your own unique style.'

Niro shrugged. 'I like what I like. But it ain't high fashion.'

'Yes,' Vimal said, slowly. 'But you know what you like. I think that's something else that Kerry might envy, just a little bit.'

Interesting. 'Well, I can be a bit more myself. That's easy. What else?'

'How about life ambitions?' Sam asked. 'Like, did you and Kerry plan to have kids? Maybe that's something we can use.'

Vimal opened his mouth, then shut it.

Niro tilted her head. 'Did you *not* want kids?'

'We ... didn't really discuss it.'

'You went out for four years. How can you be together that long and not discuss it?' That seemed unlikely.

He shrugged. 'It just never came up. We were both young and starting new jobs, so it seemed presumptuous. And then, I dunno. It seemed like something to think about at some point in the future ... and we never got around to it.'

'That's ... interesting,' said Sam.

'So, maybe not that then.' Niro still had trouble believing that he'd never thought about it. Perhaps he had, but felt that Kerry would disagree with him, so he'd avoided it. Or maybe he wasn't telling the truth.

Except Vimal was not good at lying. Amazing.

133

'I don't like change,' he said, suddenly. 'Could we make it sound like, if we stay together, you're going to make me move out of London?'

'That's worth a try.'

Soon they had a list of things that Niro could do or be to show Kerry that she was completely unsuited to Vimal. Handily, one of them was being too childish. Niro smiled. She could do childish. The new, updated character was even more fun than before. Besides, feigning attraction to him was becoming a little bit too easy. It would be much simpler this way.

She hung up, put her phone away and rubbed her hands together. 'So basically, I no longer have to be cool and interesting. I just have to be myself and have fun. In fact, if I manage to embarrass myself, then so much the better.'

Vimal knitted his eyebrows together. 'How do you mean, embarrass yourself?'

She shrugged. 'Don't know yet.' Mainly, she intended to treat this as a holiday for herself. She didn't have to worry about making Vimal look good. 'Now, if you'll excuse me. I'm going to go and get changed before dinner.'

'Seriously,' said Vimal. 'Don't embarrass yourself.'

She grinned, grabbed her change of clothes and locked herself in the bathroom.

When she came out, Vimal had already changed into a shirt-and-jumper combo that looked … very good on him. Nope. Nope. Not noticing.

He held something out to her, in a small paper bag. 'I nearly forgot. I got this for you. Sorry, it's a bit squashed from being in my pocket.'

'What is it?' She took it and unfolded the bag.

Vimal bounced off the bed and stood up. 'Apple stollen,' he said. 'There's no marzipan in it. I checked with the lady.' He gave her a smile.

Niro stared at the small square of sugary bread. 'Oh.' The

thought that had gone into his buying this caught her unawares. 'That's so nice.'

'It didn't seem fair that you should miss out while you're helping me. I know you have a sweet tooth,' he said, and smiled at her. 'Shall we go?'

'I … You go ahead,' she said. 'I'll be there in a minute.'

After he'd gone, she stood still, staring at the small piece of stollen. She put her hand against her chest, where her heart had picked up speed. She folded the paper bag back up and put the parcel down on the dressing table. She couldn't be catching feelings for Vimal. That would be stupid. The man was in love with someone else and would never look at her that way.

Looking in the mirror, she told herself off. She had to pull herself together. Otherwise there was going to be nothing but trouble.

*

When she got to the living room, she found the others already there, already drinking. Vimal disappeared to go and fetch wine. Niro hovered, out of place in the polished company. She amused herself by looking out of the window and trying to make out the snow-covered patio outside. A movement beside her made her turn. Kerry had arrived. She seemed surprised to be so close to Niro and looked like she was about to run away.

Niro smiled. 'Hi,' she said. 'We met earlier. I'm Niro.'

'I remember. I'm Kerry.'

'You're Vimal's ex, right?'

Kerry nodded. 'Yes. Yes, I am. I'm sorry. That must make this very awkward for you.'

Niro didn't reply, merely carried on smiling.

'He's a great guy,' Kerry said.

'I'm glad I met you, in fact.' Niro bent her head towards the other woman. 'Would you mind if I ask a personal question?'

135

Kerry blinked. 'Er ... sure.'

'You said he's a great guy. So why did you break up?'

Kerry's face was a mask of surprise.

'I'm sorry,' said Niro. 'I realise that's a weird thing to ask. But Vimal and I ... It's an arranged-match-type thing. We're still trying to work out if we can make it work. So, it makes sense to do a bit of ... what's it called? Due diligence?'

Kerry nodded slowly, a worried crease in her forehead. 'I see ...' She seemed to come to some sort of conclusion and smiled. 'Okay. Like I said, he is a great guy. He's clever and driven and kind.'

'And you split up because ... he was boring?'

The other woman winced. 'He told you about that? I probably shouldn't have said that. I was upset. I didn't mean it like that.'

Niro waited.

'He can be a little set in his ways,' said Kerry. 'When we met, he was full of ambition and drive and was up for trying new things and being fun, but ... we changed. He likes his work.' She rolled her eyes. 'Loves his work. But outside of that, he has his comfort zone and he prefers to stay in it.'

'Whereas you want to get out there and do more fun things?'

'Exactly. But if you were wanting to settle down ... comfort zone is great.' Kerry studied Niro's face. 'Is that what you want? To settle down.'

She felt a flash of discomfort. Did she want to settle down? She hadn't really thought about it. Her parents wanted her to and she'd fought against that on principle. But wait. This wasn't about her. This was about Vimal and Kerry. 'I quite like the freedom of being single, but I guess I'm not completely averse to settling down,' she said. 'So long as it's with the right man.'

Kerry's attention switched to someone behind her. 'Speaking of,' she said. 'Hi, Vimal.'

Niro turned. Vimal was carrying two drinks. His expression was a cross between longing and panic. Poor guy.

'Kerry.' He handed Niro her glass, without even looking at her.

'We were just talking about you,' Kerry said. She was smiling, her expression soft. Clearly, she was still fond of him. She just thought he was too stuck in his ways to be the one for her. They could work with that.

'Oh, really? I hope it was all good things.' He couldn't have been more awkward if he tried. Still, it was good. Kerry would have to be daft not to realise that he still cared about her – far more than he cared about Niro.

'Of course,' said Kerry. She moved the hand holding her drink to gesture towards both him and Niro. 'You guys make a cute couple.'

'Thank you,' Niro said.

Vimal seemed to snap out of a trance. 'Yes,' he said, quickly. 'Thank you. I'm sorry to hear about your guy.'

Kerry made a face. 'Ah. Just one of those things.' She looked at the far end of the room. 'If you'll excuse me, there's someone I need to talk to.'

She hurried away. Vimal came closer to Niro and they watched Kerry weave her way through the people and out of the room.

'What did you learn?' Vimal asked, quietly.

'She's still fond of you. She said you were a great guy. Just a bit stuck in your ways.'

He nodded. 'Boring.'

''Fraid so. I think I've sown the seeds of doubt about us being right for each other. We need to do something about this image of you being stuck in your ways.'

'What's the plan for tonight? Still stick with you being picky with your food?'

Niro shrugged. 'Let's go with that,' she said. 'We'll come up with something better for tomorrow.'

*

If anything, dinner was even more awkward. Now that everyone was there, most of the table was occupied. There were a great many more bottles of wine out and the conversations were louder. Niro was sitting opposite Kerry now. She wasn't sure how that had happened, but it was maximum awkward. Vimal, sitting next to her, was practically hyperventilating with tension.

Everyone was dressed like they were going to a nice restaurant. She was wearing a shift dress with a starburst pattern on it, which she had considered nice but looked drab next to the ultra-smart clothes of the others. Even Felicia, who was in jeans and a relatively plain cashmere jumper, looked more dressed up than Niro was. But then again, Felicia would look good in anything. Magda seemed to be wearing a twinset and actual pearls.

As before, Lucien kept up a steady stream of smooth chatter, which, Niro couldn't help but notice, was aimed at Peter and Magda. Whenever Peter responded, it seemed to spur Lucien on. Weird. Was he worried that they might get bored or something?

The caterers were serving today. A blonde girl slid a plate of something in front of her. Niro looked at the two perfect circles of pinky grey stuff that sat alongside skinny melba toast, cornichons and some sort of relish.

'What is it?' she asked.

'Foie gras, I believe,' said Lucien.

She had a mental image of force-fed geese. It must have shown on her face.

'You don't like foie gras?' Lucien asked, his tone amused.

Kerry was watching her keenly. Niro remembered that Vimal had said Kerry was a foodie. Time to be an unsuitable girlfriend, then.

'I mean, it's just liver, isn't it?' she said to Lucien.

'Oh, hardly! The taste, the texture. You can hardly compare this to a plate of liver.' He smoothed a portion over a piece of melba toast and topped it with relish.

She made a face. 'Still though, I'll pass.'

She nudged Vimal with her foot. Hopefully, he would get the message.

'Try it,' he said, quickly. 'You might like it.'

'No, thanks. It still sounds like liver to me. And they make it by force-feeding geese.'

Vimal looked lost.

'Actually, they're a lot more humane these days.' This was from Kerry. She was saving Vimal from an embarrassing situation. Niro resisted the urge to look at Vimal. Kerry clearly felt kindly towards him. Good. The plan would work. She ignored the stab of disappointment she felt.

Lucien appeared amused. So did Peter. Magda looked too aloof to care. A burst of laughter came from further down the table.

'I'm having vegetarian pâté,' Felicia piped up. 'I sorta agree with you.'

Everyone turned to look at her. She gave them a bright smile. 'I prefer the veggie version to the real thing anyway.' She went back to daintily eating her meal.

Niro pointedly buttered her melba toast and put a dab of chutney on it and ate that.

She couldn't help noticing Lucien's glance at Peter, as though checking for approval. So odd.

There was a brief pause in the conversation as people ate. Lucien broke it by saying, 'So you two lovebirds went to my uncle's hotel to take some photos.' He looked intently at Niro and Vimal and put a peculiar emphasis on 'lovebirds'. 'Did you get everything you needed?'

'Nearly,' said Niro. 'I'd like to go back early one day, to catch the dawn.'

'Niro is a photographer,' Lucien said to Kerry. 'She takes pictures of buildings.' He frowned. 'Is that a hobby, or …?'

This again. Clearly, none of them considered her to be someone who had a real job.

'No. I'm an artist. It's my job.' She might have been creatively blocked for a couple of years, but she wasn't going to let these people take away her artist badge. No way.

'Do you exhibit?' Kerry leaned forward, suddenly keen.

'Only at a few indies off the West End.' She managed to stop herself from adding, *and not for a couple of years.*

'I go to indie galleries often. Would I have seen anything of yours? Where have you been shown?'

She named the galleries, which Kerry didn't seem to recognise.

'She's very good,' Vimal piped up.

Bless him. She gave him a grateful smile, but his attention was on Kerry. 'Reminds me of that guy who took pictures of doorways. Only with whole buildings.' The familiarity with which he said it was not lost on Niro. Nor on Kerry, it seemed. She looked uncomfortable.

'Oh yes.' She thought for a moment and came up with a name.

'I know his work,' Niro said. 'I can see why you felt that. We both work with light and shade a lot. Although, I like a bit of movement when I can get it.'

Kerry's attention focused on her. 'That's so interesting. What do you mean by movement?'

'Something alive or suggestive of a person. Something that you can imagine moving in your mind's eye. One of my best ones was of a skate park. It was early in the morning, so it was empty apart from this one kid who was just about to kick off into a half-pipe. I got a shot of him just as the skateboard was tipping forward. He transformed the photo from something static to something dynamic and full of possibility.'

Kerry's eyes sparkled. 'Fascinating.'

Niro smiled and looked down at her still-full plate. Kerry really did want to be into art. Excellent. It was a lovely little ego boost to have someone interested in what she did. Besides, it should stop Kerry thinking Vimal was boring. Niro reminded herself that this was a good thing. After all, a deal was a deal.

Chapter 15

After dinner, Lucien and Peter suggested that the men all go to the games room, ostensibly to play pool. 'You joining us, Vimal? I'm sure you can show us how it's done.'

Vimal, who hadn't played pool in years, said, 'Ah, no, thank you. I'm not very good.'

'Hah, I bet you're just being modest,' said Lucien. 'You must have angles and patterns all worked out in that boffin head of yours.'

What was that supposed to mean? 'I don't think it works like that.'

'Come on, old chap, don't be a wet blanket. What are you going to do, hang around with the girls?' This was said with a hint of derision.

He really didn't want to play pool. He didn't mind spending time with 'the girls', as Lucien put it. He looked over at Niro, who was still sitting at the table, talking to Felicia. She noticed him.

'We're going to watch *Pride and Prejudice*,' she told him.

Kerry had just walked into the room. 'Which version?'

'Keira Knightley and Matthew Macfadyen, obviously,' Felicia said. 'I found the DVD collection and that's the one they've got.'

'I've not seen that version,' said Kerry.

'I have,' said Niro. 'But I don't think anyone can be a better Darcy than Colin Firth.'

'Sacrilege!' said Felicia.

Lucien turned to Vimal. 'Well, there you go. Come on, Vimal.'

Vimal looked from Lucien to Peter. It was exhausting trying to work out how to behave around them. He had thought that more people arriving would make the Peter and Lucien club seem less exclusive, but it had only made things worse. The rest of the guys all seemed to know both of them through university, or school or various clubs. Vimal felt like a complete outsider. He really did not want to sit in a room with them while they talked at each other. The more he got to know them, the less he liked them. The way they talked about people they knew, but no one else did. The way they seemed to always need to top whatever he was talking about. The constant drinking. The more he thought about it, the more he realised that he didn't want to be friends with Lucien and his crowd at all. It was as though he'd been possessed by some inner demon that told him his worth would increase, in Kerry's eyes at least, if he got in with them. It might, but it wouldn't be worth the terminal boredom. Besides, they would never 'let him in'. At most they would tolerate him. He would have to prove himself over and over. It wasn't worth it. Not even for Kerry.

'Actually,' he said. 'I think I'll watch *Pride and Prejudice.*'

Niro came over and looped her arm through his. 'Excellent,' she said. 'Another one for romcom movie night.' She grinned at the other two men. 'Excuse us.' She steered him away.

Lucien said, 'Whipped' in a none-too-subtle voice and Vimal knew he had made exactly the right decision.

A few minutes later, they were sitting on the white sofas. Three of the other women in the group had joined them. They were sitting squashed together on the sofa, and topping up their glasses.

Felicia found the remote control. 'Let's see,' she said and pointed it at the wall at the far end of the room.

Vimal was impressed at how smoothly the wall slid to the side and the TV screen rose into place with a barely audible click.

'How on earth did you know that was in there?' said Niro.

'I looked around when I was in here by myself.' Felicia opened a cupboard, which contained the DVD player. She was in what passed for casual clothes. Trousers and a fluffy jumper that didn't quite come down to her midriff. She was a beautiful girl, but gosh she looked young. What was Lucien thinking?

His initial thought was that there wasn't much to Felicia apart from her looks and apparently posh upbringing. But he noticed that she was friendly towards Niro in a way the others weren't. Niro seemed to like her, too. He was fast coming to realise that Niro was a much better judge of character than he was.

Kerry came in, carrying a tray with some bowls on it. She handed them out. 'Popcorn,' she explained as she passed one to Vimal.

'Thanks.' He smiled at her and got fleeting eye contact and a tiny smile in return. His heart gave a little skip. She took a seat at the end of one of the other sofas. When she pulled her feet up and tucked them under her, the movement was so familiar that it made his chest ache. He missed so much about her. How was it possible that all those things he'd taken for granted were not gone? Having permission to put his arms around her, to lean against each other on the sofa, to hold her hand. They had to sit on different sofas now, as though they were strangers.

Felicia turned the movie on. Vimal turned his attention to the film and tried to concentrate, which was hard to do when his eyes kept wanting to flit back to Kerry.

He and Kerry had met at a work orientation week. They had been put on a team, to do an exercise which had a large logic problem component. Vimal had tackled the logic side of things and Kerry, who was good at reading a room, got everyone to work together so that the team aced the challenge. That night, in the bar, they had started talking. They were both new and adrift in

London. Both were older than the fresh-faced graduate recruits – only by a couple of years, but it seemed to make a difference. Since they didn't quite fit with the others, they gravitated towards each other. The weekend after that, they'd gone on their first date and gently drifted into a relationship. No fireworks. Perhaps that was what the problem was. It had happened all too smoothly. Maybe he had taken for granted that it was going to be that easy.

The Kerry that he'd started going out with had been different to the woman sitting opposite him now. She had been clever and ambitious, sure, but she'd been softer, both physically and in demeanour. She had always been keen to improve herself; she studied all the time, which suited Vimal perfectly, because he tended to study a lot in the evenings, too. Although, he did it more from curiosity than drive. Kerry's self-improvement had made her fitter, more glossy but, it seemed, less happy. Even now, from the way she was fiddling with her cuffs, he could tell that she was tense.

She turned her head towards him and he quickly looked away.

Niro was sitting cross-legged next to him, her knee was almost touching his thigh, but they weren't actually in contact with each other. Compared to Kerry, she looked more relaxed. How strange that Niro, who did not fit in this glossy, opulent place, could be more relaxed than Kerry, who probably wanted to.

When he looked back, Kerry was watching the film again. She seemed sad. He hated that he was unhappy. He hated that Kerry was unhappy. Most of all he hated that they couldn't cheer each other up anymore.

*

Niro had seen the film before, so she didn't need to concentrate on it, but she forced herself to, because if she turned her head slightly, she would see that Vimal was staring longingly at Kerry. It was fine, really. In fact, it was a good thing. For the plan to work, Kerry needed to realise that he still loved her. Mind you, she'd have to be a complete idiot not to. The way he looked at her made it abundantly clear. But then again, she had dumped him before.

Niro picked at her popcorn. What had he done to deserve being dumped? He said he had no idea, but of course he would say that. All he'd said was that she'd accused him of being boring. Surely, there was more to it than that?

Vimal was, as far as she could tell, methodical and fastidious. He was terse when he was nervous, but when he relaxed he was funny and relatable. And he cared for people. Surely, Kerry knew all that. So why would she call him boring? Did she not know a good thing when she saw it?

And the way he looked at her, with all that longing in his eyes. Niro stifled a sigh. What wouldn't she give to have a guy look at her like that? Even just once.

Niro sneaked a glance at them both. Kerry seemed to be watching the film. Vimal was facing the TV, but his eyes were on Kerry.

She felt a stab of irritation. What a waste. He was such a nice guy. Caring and kind. He must be a great boyfriend. If only … No. She could not go there. She forced herself to focus back on the film.

*

When the film finished, Vimal went into the kitchen, taking the empty popcorn bowls with him. The women were discussing Mr Darcy, which was not a conversation he could usefully contribute to.

In the games room, which was only a short distance away, he could hear the guys talking, their voices and bursts of laughter muffled by the closed door.

The dishwasher was already running, so he left the bowls by the sink. He was getting himself a glass of water when Kerry came in.

'Um. Hi,' she said. 'I was just going to get myself a hot chocolate to take to my room.'

He moved out of the way so that she could reach the cupboard that had a variety of hot chocolate–related paraphernalia. She took out a Velvetiser and set about making herself a drink.

'I … should go to bed.' Oh, that sounded so lame. Now was his chance to talk to her. Why did he just say that? He could have kicked himself.

'Can I ask a question?' she said, looking up suddenly.

The hairs on his arms stood up on end. He froze, mid-step. 'Sure.'

'Have you been running here? I know you normally run every day.' She looked down. 'I was wondering if it was safe to … go for a run. For me, I mean.'

Vimal's mind raced. She ran every day, too. They used to run together. 'It's safe enough, I think.' Niro would kill him if he didn't take this opportunity to spend a bit of time with her. Going for a run would be a perfectly innocent way to talk to her. 'I'm going tomorrow morning at around six,' he said. 'You could come with me, if you want to.'

The silence went on for longer than he liked. Then she said, 'Are you sure you don't mind?'

'Not at all. It's nice to have company.'

'What about your girlfriend?'

For a split second he didn't know what she was talking about. Oh. Niro. Of course. 'Oh, Niro doesn't run. She won't mind at all.'

'That's not—' She frowned and shook her head. 'That's very kind of you, Vimal,' she said. 'I will take you up on the offer, if you don't mind.' She finally looked up to meet his gaze. 'I promise I won't slow you down.'

'I know you won't.' He smiled. She gave him a small smile back and it warmed him to his core.

'Goodnight, Kerry,' he said.

'Goodnight, Vimal. I'll see you tomorrow morning.'

He held it together until he got to his room before punching the air. He got ready for bed feeling the most cheerful he'd felt in a long time. The only slight damper on his mood was that Niro wasn't there, so that he could tell her how cool he'd been.

*

When Niro got back to the room, Vimal was already in his pyjamas, sitting in bed, reading. He was wearing his glasses, which made him look like a hot rumpled professor ... like Indiana Jones. She pushed the thought out of her mind.

He looked up. 'Have you settled your debate with Felicia about Mr Darcy?'

'We have agreed to disagree,' she said. 'I like Felicia, but she has dubious taste in men. She's definitely far too good for Lucien.'

Vimal lowered his book. 'How do you reckon?'

Niro went over to her side of the bed and picked up her pyjamas. 'She's bright and young and quite interesting. Lucien is treating her like she's just a piece of ass. Which, in fairness, is what she's letting him think.'

'Why would she do that? That doesn't sound so bright.'

He genuinely didn't see it, did he? 'Free holiday.'

The expression on his face was priceless. He seemed unable to decide if he was shocked, horrified or determinedly neutral. In the end, confusion won out. 'That seems so wrong. She's using him?'

'He's using her. Or, arguably, they are both consenting adults and they have agreed to use each other.' She pointed to herself and to him. 'We are not in a position to criticise.'

'But why would Lucien do that? He doesn't need to hire a girlfriend.'

'She's very hot,' Niro pointed out. 'I'm sure you've noticed.'

He looked faintly embarrassed. 'She is also quite young. It seems odd.'

147

'I think your Lucien might not be as glamorous and popular as you think he is.' She took her pyjamas and bathrobe into the bathroom. While brushing her teeth, she examined her reflection. She had nice features, but her skin was very dark brown, which she hated. You rarely saw properly dark brown people in film and TV. It was as though the only brown people allowed to play 'beautiful people' on screen were paler ones. Niro took her hair out of the topknot she'd put it into and let it fall to her shoulders. She didn't think she could pass for gorgeous. Kumudhini Aunty was always going on about what a pity it was that she was so dark. *She doesn't have a good job or prospects. She doesn't even have good looks to fall back on. She's so dark. And she's getting fatter. What options does she have, really?* Sometimes, when her defences were down, Niro thought that Aunty wasn't wrong.

She looked around the tastefully appointed bathroom. She might not be a looker, but that was irrelevant here. Right now she was here doing an acting job. Her task was to show Vimal's ex that he was desirable boyfriend material. She had to focus on that. She could not afford to be distracted by how nice he was. Or how he had incredible muscular legs. Or the general hotness. She splashed cold water on her face. No. She must be immune to all of that.

She could do that.

She took off her clothes and rubbed moisturiser on herself. Despite it being colder than in England, it was less damp, so the cold didn't sink into the bones in quite the same way. On the other hand, the dryness was hell on her skin, so her limbs had taken on an ashy sheen. Moisturiser soon restored her to her normal gleaming brown. Her bra had started to rub under her boobs, so she put a thick layer of Sudocrem there. It was a blessing she was single. It would be so awkward to have to hide all this from a boyfriend. She put on her pyjamas, packed everything up in her washbag, firmly tied her bathrobe – which she was using as a dressing gown – and went back into the room.

Vimal put down his book. 'I rebuilt the pillow wall,' he said, gesturing proudly. The cleaners, who had mysteriously turned up at some point, had put everything back in the cupboard. Vimal had restored the wall to its stern glory.

'Thank you.' She slipped the bathrobe off and quickly slid into bed. 'I mean it,' she said. 'I really am grateful to you for taking the wall seriously.'

'It's a serious wall,' he said. 'I wouldn't dream of messing with it.' His eyes caught the light when he smiled.

She returned the smile. How on earth could anyone think this man was boring?! She snuggled down under the covers. 'Good.'

'I'm done reading. Shall I turn the light off?'

She rolled onto her side, so that she was facing away from him. 'Sure.'

The sheer domesticity of their chat wasn't lost on her. She hadn't had this kind of conversation in a long time. It was a little scary how easily they'd slipped into it. This wasn't a real relationship, but sometimes, it felt like they'd been going out for years. Weird.

Vimal turned the light out and the room plunged into darkness. She listened to him settling down.

'By the way,' Vimal said. 'You'll be proud of me.'

Niro frowned. 'Why?'

'I arranged to go for a run with Kerry tomorrow morning. Just the two of us.'

He sounded so pleased with himself, she had to sound happy for him. 'That's great.' It was great. That was the plan. Why did she feel irritated?

After a few seconds, Vimal said, 'I'm not sure what to say to her tomorrow, though.'

Niro rolled onto her back. How on earth did she answer that? 'Just … go with the flow?'

'I'm not very good at that. I always say the wrong thing.'

'You managed to talk to her for four years. What did you do differently?'

'I don't know.' His voice was a whisper, almost a sigh. 'I wish I knew.'

She didn't know what to say, so she said nothing.

'I was going to ask her to marry me, you know,' he said, suddenly. 'When we split up. Like, literally just that day, I was going to ask. But it all went wrong.'

Oh. This was new information. 'Why?' she asked. 'I mean, why did you decide you wanted to get married? Had you discussed it before?'

'I thought … Well, it felt like the right thing to do. We'd been together for nearly four years. It seemed … appropriate.'

'Did she know that you were to propose?'

'I don't know.' Vimal was quiet for a moment. 'I think she might have guessed.'

At that moment, she had a glimpse into what Kerry must have felt. They had both been focused on their careers and suddenly, they weren't so young anymore. Marriage, domesticity, middle age were all things that made your world narrower. Kerry clearly had a different vision for her life. Niro understood what it was like to have your view of yourself shattered. No wonder the poor woman panicked. The question was, a few months later, did Kerry still have her old vision of her life? Or had things changed?

Vimal's side of the bed rustled as he changed position. 'Can I ask you something personal?'

'Okay,' she said, cautiously.

'Do you know if you want to have a family? You and Sam made it sound like everyone worked it out quite young. Have I missed a step?'

Oh, Vimal. 'No … not really. It's just that when a couple has been together for a while, it's usual to think about whether they want to be together for the long haul. Marriage, like you say … and kids.'

'Did you want to have a family with your ex? Before you split up, I mean. When things were fine.'

That stumped her. Had she? 'I think I was still too young. I was only twenty-four. I don't think I was sure he was my one true love, you know. Obviously, at some level I thought he might become the right one ... but ...' She rubbed her eyes and sighed. 'I don't know, Vimal. It's complicated.'

'Sorry. I didn't mean to blunder into hurtful territory.'

'It's fine. Don't worry about it.' Then, because she knew he would worry about it, she added, 'I'm not hurt or upset. And I guess I've just answered your previous question about whether everyone knows what they want. Clearly not.'

There was silence as he mulled it over. Niro sank into her own thoughts. Did she want kids? She didn't have to think very hard to know that at some level she had always assumed she would have them. Younger Niro had taken for granted that a father for those kids was out there and that she would find him when she was ready. What if she didn't? An arranged marriage was a plausible option, really. Attraction wasn't an emotion you could trust. She'd learned that the hard way.

'That's good to know,' Vimal said, quietly. 'Very reassuring.' He sighed. 'It stings when someone you thought loved you says you're boring.'

Niro gave a short laugh. 'Trust me, I know what that feels like,' she said. 'My ex, who was also an art mentor of sorts, by the way, told other people that I was talentless and ordinary.'

'Well, he sounds like an idiot,' said Vimal, sleepily. 'I hope you didn't believe him.'

'He was a tutor on my course, before we started dating ...'

'Regardless,' said Vimal. 'You're one of the most talented people I've met. And practical too. Just look at the way you've taken on my mad idea and turned it into an actual project. As far as I'm concerned, you're making the impossible happen. There is no way in the world anyone could mistake you for ordinary.' He yawned.

151

'If anything, you're a miracle.'

She felt a glow in her chest. No one had ever called her a miracle before. 'Gosh,' she said. 'That's very kind of you to say.'

'I mean every word.' His voice sounded thicker now, as though he was drifting off to sleep. 'You're a good friend, Niro. I'm glad I met you.'

Friend. Yup. That's what she was. A good friend. 'Goodnight, mate,' she said.

On the other side of the pillow wall, Vimal's breathing slowed and settled.

Niro lay there for a long while afterwards, trying not to think about how aware she was of Vimal's presence behind the pillows. Vimal was the polar opposite of Mick. While Mick had love-bombed her about her talent and attractiveness, Vimal didn't do flattery and empty words. So if he said she was miraculous, then he meant it. If he said her photographs were good, it was because he really thought they were. Those things mattered to her. He seemed to understand that the thing she needed the most right now was for someone to believe in her. And he genuinely did.

Vimal sighed in his sleep. Niro turned her head to look in his direction. The vague sense of longing for someone to look at her with love and admiration crystallised into something else. She wanted *Vimal* to look at her that way. The low-level attraction to him that she had been slowly developing suddenly exploded into a fully formed crush. She shook her head in the darkness. That was never going to happen. The man was in love with Kerry. She would be stupid to fall for him. And yet. And yet …

Exasperated with herself, she punched her pillow and rolled over. Then she lay there, listening to Vimal breathing, until she finally fell asleep to dreams of a Mr Darcy made of marzipan.

Chapter 16

The next morning, Vimal got up early and tiptoed around getting ready for his run. Excitement fizzed in his belly. This would be an ideal opportunity to chat to Kerry. He came out of the bathroom to grab his phone.

Niro, who was a mere shape under the covers, stirred. She pushed her hair off her face and said, 'You off running?'

'Yes. With Kerry.'

Niro let go of her hair, so it fell on her face again. She disappeared back under the duvet. 'Good stuff.' Her voice was muffled. 'Have fun.'

'Thanks. Wish me luck.' He grabbed his phone and water bottle and headed out.

Kerry was standing by the front door, stretching. The sight was so familiar to him that it brought the hollow ache back into his chest. He had to be cool, so he merely said, 'Are you ready?'

It wasn't long before they were outside, running side by side at a familiar old pace. For the most part, neither of them spoke. He had waited so long to get a chance to talk to Kerry alone and now he couldn't think of a single thing to say.

They weren't going very fast, partly because they were running on fresh fallen, powdery snow, partly because he wanted to keep the option open for them to talk.

Finally, Kerry said, 'So, how are you these days?'

Oh god, what should he say? 'I'm okay. You?'

'Well, I've been better,' she said. 'I could have done without getting dumped just after Christmas.'

'That sucks.' He slowed and jogged on the spot to check the road. 'Terrible timing too, since you were both meant to come this week.' He was pleased with himself for not mentioning how she had dumped him, not so long ago.

They crossed the road and carried on running. He waited for Kerry to say something more about her recent breakup, but she didn't. Perhaps it was too painful. Besides, he reminded himself, he was her ex. That was bound to make things weird too.

'Niro seems nice,' Kerry said, after a while.

'She is, I guess.' There wasn't a lot else he could say. He didn't want to sound too keen on Niro, because he needed Kerry to see the possibility of their getting back together. But he had to keep up a pretence.

'How are things going? It must be strange for you. She told me the Aunties introduced you.'

He hadn't introduced Kerry to any specific Aunties, but he'd told her about them at some point. 'Yes, we're seeing how we get on before we commit to anything.'

'Wow. That's … serious stuff.' She gave him a sidelong look that he couldn't read. 'I hope it works out for you. I think it might, you know. She seems good for you.'

What? Kerry approved of Niro. Oh, no no no. This was not going according to plan at all. 'What do you mean? She and I have nothing in common, apart from the nosy Aunties.'

'She's the complete opposite of you. She's unstructured and creative. You're all about structure and routine. You're not trying to kill each other, so you must be complementing each other instead.'

'Ah, pop psychology.' They had had this discussion before.

154

Kerry firmly believed in her half-arsed psychoanalyses. Vimal felt a little knowledge was probably more dangerous than none at all.

'Don't knock it. It's not always wrong.'

They stopped talking as they ran up the hill. He chose the route through the hotel garden to the outcrop with the bench, where Niro had stood to take a photo of the valley.

Kerry stared out at the view, breathing hard. 'Wow. This is … amazing.'

'Niro came here to photograph it,' he said. 'I thought it'd be a nice thing to see.'

Another look that he couldn't read. Kerry nodded. 'It is. Thank you for showing me.'

It now occurred to Vimal that maybe he shouldn't have brought Kerry up here. This was a Niro kind of place. She might not like him sharing it with Kerry. No. That was stupid. Niro didn't *own* the view. He could show his ex the view if he wanted to.

Kerry turned. 'Shall we head back?'

Glad to stop thinking about the nagging feeling of guilt, Vimal nodded. 'Yup. Sure.'

They had to be careful running downhill in the snow. They ended up going down the road, where the snow had been cleared. They were nearly at the bottom, when Kerry slipped. She gave a shriek and flailed as she fell backward. She slammed into Vimal and he almost went over too. His knees buckled, but he kept upright. With Kerry in his arms.

Vimal's first thought was that it was a lucky escape. Hitting the ground would have hurt his back. The next thought was that he was holding Kerry. She turned her head and looked up at him. Everything about the moment was so familiar. The movement of her head against his shoulder. The way her ponytail swung down. The colour of her eyes, the weight of her body against his.

Then inexplicably, he thought of Niro and how it felt when she'd fallen and he'd caught her.

Kerry's eyes widened and she tried to get back on her feet.

Vimal stood upright again, pushing Kerry up with him. She dusted herself off and adjusted her jacket, which had slid up.

'You okay?' he asked. He himself was fine, physically at least. Being that close to her had unleashed a mishmash of emotions. The most insistent of which was that he missed her. Closely behind it was that nagging sense of guilt again. He opened his mouth to speak.

'Let's get back.' Kerry started running again. He had no choice but to follow. Now, there was no easy conversation. Kerry's expression was set. He knew that face. She didn't want to talk. She was annoyed. He kept pace with her and kept quiet.

All the things he wanted to say muddled around in his brain. One thing was for sure. He wasn't over her. He had thought he could handle going out for a run with her, but clearly he couldn't. Being with her felt so right. They got on so well together. How on earth had it gone wrong? More to the point, was there a chance that he could fix it?

After the most awkward run ever, they came to a halt outside the entrance to the villa.

Panting from exertion, Kerry stopped for water before she started on her stretches. If he didn't speak to her now, he would lose his chance.

'I miss you.' The words bundled out of him before he could censor them.

Kerry lowered her bottle. 'Pardon?'

'I … I mean, this has been nice. And I miss … I miss having you around. I miss running together and eating dinner together and just—' He looked at her incredulous face and ran out of steam. 'Sorry. Forget I said anything.'

She gave him a serious look. 'Vimal. You're with Niro now.'

He was meant to be, wasn't he?

'I know, but—'

She shook her head. 'This isn't like you,' she said. 'You're a good guy. Why would you string Niro along if you don't actually want to be with her?'

Vimal faltered. He had no good reply to that. This was not going well at all. He suddenly wished he had Niro there to ask for advice.

'Vimal, listen. You and me … It's over, okay,' Kerry said. 'I thought you'd moved on.'

Argh. How could he rescue this? He gestured between them. 'We were together for four years. You might be able to just switch those feelings off and move on, but I can't.' He looked up at the sky. 'I thought I could do the family arrangement thing. I don't meet a lot of people now, apart from work people. And you know what I'm like with new people anyway. I … Niro is nice. I do like her. And, you know, culturally appropriate and all that, but … it's not the same.'

'Of course it isn't. No two relationships are the same. How could they be?' She stood on one leg to stretch the other leg.

'I know. You're right. I'm sorry. Forget I said anything.' He felt like a proper idiot now.

She gave him a small smile. 'It's okay. It's almost a relief to talk about this. It's been a bit awkward, hasn't it?'

He sank into a calf stretch and kept his eyes on his own foot. 'I guess so,' he mumbled. It hadn't just been awkward for him. It had been painful.

Kerry sighed. 'Vimal. I'm sorry, okay. I didn't mean to hurt you …'

He straightened up and looked her in the eye. 'What I don't understand is why. I've gone over everything. All those years and months and there were no indications. If you were unhappy, why didn't you say something?'

'I wasn't unhappy—'

'Then *why*?'

'It's …' She looked around, as though seeking inspiration. 'It's hard to explain. I had an epiphany one day and I couldn't go back. I don't know how else to describe it. I'm sorry.'

That didn't help. 'But what did I do wrong?'

'Nothing. You did nothing wrong. It's me. I changed and we …' She gestured to the two of them. 'We didn't work anymore after that.'

He stared at her. So she just woke up one morning and realised she didn't love him? That made no sense. How could you make any commitment to anyone if people changed their minds overnight?

Kerry shook her head. 'I'm going inside now. I think … tomorrow we'd best not run together.'

That was clear enough. 'Yes. Yes, I'll see you later.'

She went put her hand on the door knob. 'Vimal.' She turned. 'All those things you just said you missed. That's not you missing me. That's you missing companionship.'

'But I miss those things with you. I miss your smile. I think about you all the time.'

Kerry shook her head. 'No. You're used to having those things with me and you don't like change,' she said, firmly. 'You could have all that with Niro. If you give it time.' She pulled the door open and disappeared inside.

Vimal stood there in the deserted drive and felt defeat and humiliation flame through his face. What was wrong with him? He was supposed to be making Kerry jealous, not begging her to take him back. He had ruined everything, hadn't he? Now he had to go and explain all this to Niro. She was going to be bloody furious with him for messing up the plan.

Chapter 17

Niro sat on the bed fully dressed and checked the time again. The trouble with being an hour ahead was that she had to be awake for ages before she could call Sam, even though Sam was one of those insane people who woke up early to get to work 'before the rush hour'. Still too early. Vimal would be back from his run soon, and she would have to go and find somewhere else quiet to talk to her cousin without Vimal overhearing.

Niro put her phone down and looked up at the skylight, where a glow suggested the sun was up. Vimal overhearing hadn't really been a problem before. But it was now, because it was him that she wanted to talk to Sam about. She stood up and slipped the phone into her pocket. She could go and have breakfast. There was no point hanging around here.

Well, there *was* a point if you considered the chance of running into Vimal in Lycra. She smiled. God, she was pathetic. Clearly, she'd been out of the dating game for far too long. Faking a relationship, which involved sharing a luxury room with a guy who was clearly still in love with his ex, was probably not the smartest way to get back into it. She had just been starved of action for too long, that's why she was catching feelings for him. Yeah. That was all.

Breakfast, then. She checked her hair and straightened her outfit. Last night there had been talk of going for a walk or something. She wasn't sure if she could bear that. She picked up her camera and hung it around her neck.

Someone knocked on the door. Her heart gave a little skip. It was bound to be Vimal. 'Come in.'

He used his key to let himself in. She appreciated the level of respect he showed her. Then again, it was as though she were a valued colleague, which was nice in some ways, but depressing as all hell in others.

'How was your run?' She watched him walk across to the cupboard and get his clothes off the shelf. 'How did it go with Kerry?'

He paused, his arms raised to remove a shirt from a hanger. 'Okay. I think,' he said slowly.

She wasn't looking at his bum. She wasn't. Niro deliberately turned away. 'So you talked to her?'

He didn't turn around. 'I did,' he said. 'She … slipped and fell and landed in my arms.'

She could picture it. The romantic moment when Kerry landed in his arms, when their faces were close enough to kiss … The idea tore a strip off her heart. She should be happy for him. That was the plan.

'That's … great,' she said, despite the urge to cry. 'Things are going well, then.'

Vimal went to the bathroom. 'I guess so,' he said. He still hadn't made eye contact.

Niro wondered what had happened. Had they actually kissed? But then he'd tell her, right? Mission accomplished and all that. 'Vimal—'

But he shut the door. The lock clicked into place.

'I'm going to grab some breakfast.' Niro and left the room.

She needed somewhere private to call Sam. When she got to the living room, Felicia and another equally lissom woman were in there doing yoga. No. That would never do. Maybe the games room? She went across and stepped in.

'Oh.'

There was a man sprawled on the sofa, snoring gently. She backed out again quickly and went to the end of the corridor. There was the storage room. No one had reason to go in there. She cautiously opened the door and peered in. After some fumbling, she found the light switch and turned it on. Unlike the luxurious fittings outside, this room was mostly bare concrete, although there was a thin carpet on the floor. The light was just a bulb. This was clearly a more functional room. It was warm though.

She went in and closed the door. The room had several racks, neatly stacked with clear boxes holding spare bedding, cushions, pans and random bits, including ski equipment. In one corner there was something boxed into a cupboard. That must be the water heater. No wonder it was warm in here.

Looking at her phone she noted that there wasn't much mobile reception, but the Wi-Fi signal was strong.

She didn't want anyone to hear her talking and come to investigate, so she moved away from the door, closer to a light well of some sort at the far end.

It wasn't a light well, it was a real window. The pane was set high up in the wall and was mostly white from packed snow, apart from the bottom corner which was ... What was that? She moved closer and looked at the patch of brown. It looked ... furry. Searching around, she found a stepladder and used it to get closer.

It was a creature of some sort, curled up against the glass, asleep. The reflection of the light bulb gleamed off the glass. Hmm. Looking carefully, she found an angle to just about make out the creature's head, tucked away into the curve of its body. A quick google suggested it could be an alpine marmot. Cute.

She took a photo with her phone camera. It wasn't great. Really, she needed to diffuse the light a bit and use a longer exposure, but it would do for now. Besides, there was something else she was meant to be doing.

Dragging a plastic-packed duvet onto the floor, she made herself a seat and called her cousin.

'Niro?' Sam sounded tired.

'Hi, Sam. Do you have a minute?'

'Uh … yeah. Sure. Is everything okay?'

A lump appeared in her throat. Everything was not okay.

'Niro?' Sam's voice was sharper now.

She let out a shaky breath. 'Well. Everything is going according to plan, I think. Vimal went for a run with his ex this morning. It seems to have gone well.'

'But …?'

'I think I've messed up.'

'How? You've taken the photos you want?'

'Yes. I've taken some lovely photos. But … I think I might fancy Vimal. Just a bit.'

There was silence on the other end of the line for a few seconds. Then, 'Oh. Shit. Are you okay?'

'It's stupid, right? We have nothing in common. I wouldn't have gone into this deal if I'd thought that there was any risk that I'd … Ugh. Why do I have to ruin everything?' She should have seen this coming. Everything she touched turned to dust. Everything. 'I thought four days wasn't long enough for me to screw something up, but it looks like I was wrong.'

'Hey. Come on. Talk me through it. When I spoke to you last, you were both properly focused on the project. What changed?'

'I don't know.' She closed her eyes and thought about the apple stollen, the way he seemed to value her *and* her work, the absolute security of knowing that he was looking out for her. 'He's so … kind.'

'Kind?' Sam's voice was full of confusion. 'That's not … what I was expecting to hear.'

'It's hard to explain,' said Niro. 'I think I made the same mistake everyone does. I thought Vimal was intense and a bit boring. You know how it is. Corporate drone, bit of a nerd.'

'He … does come across as that, yes. But quite nice, with it.'

'Oh, Sam, he's not boring at all. He is very intense, because what he cares about, he really cares about. He's a bit weird, to be fair, but that's just part of who he is. He's totally oblivious about some things and then extremely observant about others.'

'You are going to have to slow down. I don't understand.'

Niro opened her eyes, so that she could roll them. 'He has great legs.'

Sam laughed. 'Now *that* I can understand. Go on. Tell me more about the kindness.'

She told her cousin about the things that Vimal did. 'No one's shown me that level of thoughtfulness in years.'

'Hey,' said Sam, who definitely had.

'You know what I mean. He practically forced me to quote twice my normal price for my photos. And it worked. If I tried that without him there, I'd fall flat on my face, but with him, Basty didn't bat an eyelid.'

'Why do you think you'd have fallen flat? He might have said yes. You might just be undercharging,' said Sam.

Too late, Niro remembered that Sam had suggested charging more a few years ago, back when she still believed in her work. 'No. I think there's something about the way he seems so certain that it's worth that. He *is* so certain. He keeps telling me that my photos are good and … he's so sure that I believe him.'

'He's right. I mean, you are really good. You just lost your way a bit after …'

'After Mick dumped on me from a great height.' She rubbed her temple. The beginning of a headache was starting to nag at her. Bloody Mick.

'Yes.' Sam sounded sad. 'You haven't been yourself since then, Niro. I know you've been trying, but honestly, the only time I've seen the real you was when you were preparing to do this "project" as you call it, with Vimal. You were keen and focused and determined. That's the real you.'

'I thought I was getting better,' Niro said. 'I thought ... maybe I was coming out of a bad period in my stars or whatever my horoscope said.' She tipped her head backward and hit it against a shelf. 'Ow.'

'What happened? Are you all right?'

'Yeah. Just bumped my head.' She rubbed it with the palm of her hand. 'But what do I do about Vimal? I can't catch feelings for him. He's not interested. That's the whole reason we're here. He's in love with his ex. He won't be interested in me. And that's as it should be.'

'Wait, wait. Are you saying he won't be interested in you ... just generally? Or in this specific circumstance because he's in love with his ex?'

Niro blinked. What kind of question was that? 'Because he's in love with his ex. Obviously.'

'Okay. Because if he weren't, you'd totally be in with a chance.'

She stopped rubbing her head to throw a hand up in the air. 'How is this helping?'

'Sorry. It's just that you're gorgeous and talented and I don't want you to forget that.'

She doesn't even have good looks to fall back on. 'I love you, Samadhi, but you're still not helping. What do I DO?'

'I don't know. You could say ... you want to come home? That was part of the deal, right? That you could leave any time you wanted.'

'Yes, but that's not fair. He's kept his side of the bargain. I should keep mine. I can't abandon him.'

'Well, you could. He would then need comforting.'

Niro chewed the skin on the edge of her thumb. That was a good point. She could run away and not watch while Vimal and his ex got back together. The thought of them together made her stomach burn. Vimal mustn't know how she felt. He would be kind and thoughtful and let her down gently ... and the humiliation would just kill her. 'I said I would help him show Kerry that he's not so stiff and stuck in his ways. Make him more fun. So … I could do that, right? Make an effort today. And then leave tomorrow night, before the new year sets in.'

'You could.'

'There's bound to be space on the early morning plane. No one wants to fly at silly-o-clock in the morning on New Year's Day.' She nodded. 'Yes. I think that sounds like a plan.'

'Niro …' Sam said, in a hesitant voice.

'What?'

'Nothing. Just … good luck. Luke and I are at home, so we can hang out when you get back. We could have a romcom movie night, if you like.'

'No fake-relationship movies.'

'Nope. Absolutely not. Maybe an enemies-to-lovers.'

Niro smiled, knowing that Sam would now pore over the streaming services to find the right one. 'Thanks, Sam.'

'You look after yourself. Good luck.'

Niro hung up. She felt slightly better now. Not great, but at least she had a plan. It was annoying that her feelings were doing this to her. She couldn't be interested in Vimal. He was completely unavailable. So why did her heart betray her? Hadn't she suffered enough with Mick?

She looked at the time. It had been a while since she'd left their room. It was best to get out there and actually have some breakfast before Vimal wondered where she'd disappeared to. The last thing she needed was him looking at her with those deep, concerned eyes. There were limits to her acting abilities. She got back to her feet, pummelled the duvet back into the right shape and put it back on the shelf. Before she left she went to check on the marmot, asleep, in the shadow she had created for it.

She stood for a few seconds longer, watching the still shape. How nice it must be to sleep through the winter. No running around in the cold, no surviving, just waiting until the spring so that you could go back out into the sunshine.

Wasn't that what she'd been doing for the past two years? Hiding away. Doing the minimum. She thought about the camera that she'd carried around with her every day so far. Before this trip, she hadn't been outside with this camera for months. She had done weddings and engagement parties when she was with Mick. That was good money and she'd enjoyed the social aspects. When the work dried up, she'd blamed it on her lack of talent. But what if it was her unhappiness? Who would recommend a miserable photographer to work at events that were meant to be celebrations? She hadn't been a hermit, but as close as. No wonder Sam kept nagging her to go out.

She made her way back to the door, thinking about how Sam could be a real pain in the arse, but it was only because she cared. Even romcom movie night was part of that. They'd both enjoyed it, so it became a regular thing, but it had all started as Sam trying to get Niro to stop moping and have a little fun. Maybe even restore her faith in love.

Turning the light off on her way out, she whispered, 'G'night' to the marmot before closing the door.

When she reached the kitchen, Felicia was in there gulping down her weird green drink. She looked at Niro and glanced at the corridor behind. She didn't ask Niro out loud why she'd come from that direction, but she may as well have.

'Morning,' Niro said, brightly. She sat down and poured herself a bowl of muesli.

'Good morning. You look like you didn't sleep much.' Felicia leaned on the island, looking like an advert for athletic wear.

'Yeah. I didn't. Too much excitement, I guess.'

'Are you looking forward to the New Year's party tomorrow?'

'I am,' said Niro. 'I haven't gone out for New Year's Eve in a few years. I used to go a lot.' Before Mick. 'So, it'll be nice. How about you?'

'Oh, I love New Year's Eve. There's such a buzz about it,' said

Felicia. 'Normally I got out in London, so it'll be a bit different this year.'

'Good different? Or bad different?'

Felicia gave a graceful shrug and pushed away from where she was leaning. 'Don't know. I guess we'll find out.' She gave Niro a beatific smile. 'I'll see you later.' She waved and walked away, hair swinging in the same rhythm as her hips.

Niro grinned. Felicia knew exactly what she was doing.

She looked at her muesli. She wished *she* did. At least she got to eat her breakfast without Lucien, Peter or Magda there to be condescending at her.

Her peace didn't last too long. Vimal showed up and started making himself toast.

'What's the plan today?' he asked her. 'And do you want more coffee?'

'Tea, please,' she said. 'I don't really know that there is much of a plan today, apart from going down to the village around four for the New Year's Eve parade that happens the night before New Year's Eve, for some reason.'

'Oh yes,' said Vimal. 'Martin told me about that. Apparently, it's a new tradition and no one wanted it to interfere with actual New Year's Eve, so they brought it forward by a day.' He nodded. 'That's very pragmatic.'

Niro smiled. Of course he would think it was pragmatic.

'I think there was a suggestion of going snowshoeing this morning,' said Vimal, busily making mugs of tea.

'Excellent,' she said. 'I won't be going, but you should.' She checked for people and lowered her voice. 'Is Kerry going?'

He nodded, not making eye contact.

'Great. You'll be able to talk to her some more. Work on your rapport-building you did this morning.'

He visibly winced.

'What?' she said.

He shook his head. 'I don't know what to say. This morning,

I'm not sure I didn't just make things even worse. What do I even talk about with the woman who was everything to me, but now acts like we're strangers?'

He brought her tea to her and finally met her gaze. 'What do I do?'

Niro focused on stirring her tea as an excuse to look away. Curse these stupid feelings. Why couldn't she have carried on seeing this as a job?

Vimal pulled out a chair and sank into it. 'Seriously, Niro,' he said, quietly. 'Help me.'

She sighed. 'Could you ... mention some fun stuff you did together?' The words jammed in her throat, but she had to help him. That was the deal. No one had promised it would be easy. 'You were together for a long time. There must be nice things you could bring up. Remind her of why she used to ... love you.'

He nodded, his expression distant. 'I think I see what you mean. Remind her of how we had fun together. We did have fun, early on.'

She nodded into the steam from her tea. 'Yes. Bond over the things that used to make you laugh.'

'Okay,' he said, thoughtfully. 'Okay, I can do that. Maybe I was a bit intense this morning.'

Niro snorted. That figured.

'But you're right. It would be better if I slowed down a bit, tried to be chill ...'

Thankfully, the arrival of one of the other couples saved her from having to hear him talk about how he could charm Kerry. They exchanged polite greetings. Vimal fetched his toast and came to sit by her and they ate their breakfasts side by side.

'Are you guys going on the snowshoe hike this morning?' the woman said.

'I am,' said Vimal.

'I'm not,' said Niro.

'Aw, why not?'

'Not my thing. I might hang around here.' She could walk around to the side of the place and see if she could find her marmot friend. She wouldn't disturb her … or him … Niro frowned. She didn't know how to check the sex of a marmot, and it really didn't matter, did it?

'I want to take a few more photos of the villa.' She didn't want to share the news of the marmot with anyone else. She didn't trust them not to wake it up and some things were best left sleeping.

Chapter 18

The walk in the snow was surprisingly strenuous. Vimal trudged along as part of the group. The snow was deep, but the snowshoes stopped them from sinking in. They were just more difficult to walk in. Snow smothered everything. Even the trees they were walking through had patches of it clinging to the sloping branches. Every so often a clump of it would fall.

He assumed this would be a tranquil walk if he weren't in such a big group. They had started off chatty, but now, all you could hear was people walking and breathing, which was better, but still distracting. He looked over his shoulder and checked on Kerry, who was a few places behind him in the line. She was keeping up okay. He hadn't doubted that she would.

'Nearly there,' said the guide, from the head of the group. 'It will be worth the trip, I promise you.'

A few minutes later, they emerged into the dazzling sunshine. Vimal had to shade his eyes, to let them acclimatise.

'And here, you have one of the best views for miles.' The guide gestured with a flourish.

They were higher up than Vimal had realised. No wonder his lungs were straining. Both above and below them, there was unbroken snow. It was hard to tell how high up they were, because there was so little to give a sense of scale. Niro would have loved this.

Kerry came up and stood next to him, panting. 'Wow.'

'Where's the villa?' Vimal asked the guide.

She looked down at the valley. 'Over there … somewhere. You can just make out the river.'

Vimal squinted in the general direction and wondered if, far away, Niro was looking his way too. He had been so restrained with how much he spoke to Kerry on this walk so far, Niro would have been proud of him.

The river was a mere gleam in the distance. 'Wow,' Kerry said again. She leaned on her ski poles and let her head hang.

'Are you okay?' Vimal asked. 'Do you need some water?'

Kerry swung her head to the side to look at him. 'I'm okay. Just need a moment. To get my breath back.'

'Sorry.'

'No need to apologise,' she said. 'I appreciate you looking out for me.' She didn't look at him when she said it. Of course. She was still feeling awkward about what had happened that morning.

He nodded and moved away, his face aflame. He stuck his poles into the ground and fished out his camera. He took a video of the view. He would never be able to capture it in a photo. When he finished, he put it away and turned to find that Kerry had recovered. She was still leaning on her poles, but she was looking at the view.

He was supposed to engage her in conversation and remind her of the good times they'd had. That's what Niro had said. How on earth was he supposed to do that now?

After a few minutes, they set off to go back. Vimal fell into step beside Kerry. 'Listen. About this morning. I'm sorry. I didn't mean to make things weird.'

Kerry puffed out a breath. 'It's okay. It was bound to be weird anyway, right?'

'I suppose.'

171

'It's a shame your girlfriend couldn't come today.'

'Not really her sort of thing. She's got plans to go and photograph the villa from about a hundred different angles.' Vimal shrugged. 'We don't have much in common.'

Kerry's focus remained in front of her. 'Hmm.'

'Remember the first time we went skiing?' he said. There. That was something from their shared past.

'I do. I was so bad at it.' There was a hint of a smile on Kerry's face.

'So was I, though. Remember that time I fell over getting off the ski lift?'

Now, she was really smiling. 'Oh yes! And you ended up in a heap at the bottom of the off-ramp. I think you might actually have been worse than me.'

'I saved you the embarrassment of being the worst skier there. I'm useful like that.'

Kerry laughed. 'I can't believe you thought you'd learn to ski by reading a book about it.'

'It's always worked for me before.'

'You could at least have tried YouTube,' said Kerry, still laughing. 'But no. A book. Madman.'

He grinned and felt the warmth of a connection restored. This was good. She was laughing, like she used to do. He just had to not ruin it now.

Before he could say anything else, Lucien, who was a few feet away from them, turned. 'What's funny?'

'Nothing special,' said Vimal. 'We were discussing how much better I am at snowshoeing than skiing.'

Lucien's gaze moved from him to Kerry and back again. 'Oh yes? Do you not ski?'

Kerry stopped laughing.

'I try,' said Vimal. 'I'm just very, very bad at it. Kerry's pretty good now, though. She's had more practice than I have.'

As they trekked back, Lucien was walking just ahead of them.

172

'I should have suggested skiing instead,' he said. 'It sounds like it would have been funnier.'

Vimal didn't know what to say to that. Kerry, no longer smiling, said, 'Oh no. I much prefer this. The view back there was spectacular.'

'Wasn't it?'

Kerry walked a little faster, catching up to Lucien. They were, after all, old friends. Vimal reminded himself to remain chilled. They were talking about people and places Vimal didn't recognise, so he tuned out. For most of the walk back, he focused on his feet. The voices and other sounds faded into the background until his world was full of the shuffle-crunch of his own feet. It was oddly calming.

The conversation with Kerry had changed something between them. At the very least, it had undone some of the damage from that morning. That was good. Niro said he had to show Kerry that he had changed. How on earth did he do that? He could do big, out-of-character things, but he'd never be able to sustain that and Kerry would see it for the ruse it was within a week. He needed to do smaller things. Make new habits. But like what?

A voice broke into his thoughts. 'Nearly back,' a man said. 'I can't wait to get these blasted things off my feet and have a drink.'

Vimal looked up. They had reached the edge of the trees. Smoke curled invitingly from the chimney of the cabin that they had started from, which was just visible beyond the brow of a hill.

'Oh. It seemed a shorter distance coming back,' he said.

'I think it was a bit shorter, actually,' said the man. He was one of the guests staying in the villa. 'Going downhill probably helped too.'

Vimal tried to remember his name. Although he'd made an effort to exchange a few words with everyone, he hadn't spoken to this one before. 'Er ... Christopher, right?'

'Yes. Got it in one. You're Vimal?'

They nodded to each other instead of shaking hands.

'So, you know Lucien from Sabatini Putnam Woolf?'

'Yes. You?'

'I sort of know him from rugby … I'm a hedge fund manager. We've done business together a few times.'

Vimal nodded.

'So, what do you do at SPW?'

'I'm a … quantitative analyst. I make algorithms.'

Christopher rattled off a few names. 'Any of them yours?'

'Two, actually,' Vimal said, with a touch of pride. 'I'm impressed you remember that level of detail.'

Christopher grinned. 'Closet nerd,' he said. 'Which two were yours?'

He told him.

Christopher gave a low whistle. 'Hey, Lucien, why didn't you tell me this guy wrote that last algo you sold me?'

A flicker of annoyance passed Lucien's face when he looked over his shoulder. 'Why? Did it perform?'

Christopher laughed. 'Did it perform? I got my biggest bonus ever.' He raised an arm, making the ski poles wave around alarmingly. 'I owe you a drink, my friend,' he said to Vimal.

'You owe me a drink, actually,' said Lucien. 'I persuaded you to use it.'

'But he wrote the bloody thing. Boffin genius.'

Vimal spotted the hint of steel behind Lucien's apparently affable expression. Maybe he felt Vimal was stealing his limelight. 'I guess you owe us both a drink,' he said, quickly. 'After all, I could write the best algorithm in the world, but it wouldn't be useful to anyone if people like Lucien didn't sell them.'

'True, true,' said Christopher, turning his attention back to his walking. 'But Lucien could sell sand to Arrakis,' he added quietly.

Vimal gave him an amused glance, tickled by the *Dune* reference. Christopher winked at him.

Vimal chuckled. 'Quite so.' When he looked back at the group ahead of them, he caught Lucien's scowl before it was replaced by his habitual charm. He made a mental note to talk to Niro about that later. There was something happening that he couldn't understand. Niro was good with people. She would know.

*

The evening was clear and chilly. Niro had managed to avoid the rest of the gang for most of the day and had a wonderful time exploring around the villa. She had even found a path that took her above the villa, so that she could photograph it from that angle. By the time she got back, the party that had been snow-shoeing was back and rested and ready to go out again.

They joined the steady trickle of people, families and groups, heading towards the village. When Niro nudged Vimal's arm and took hold of his hand, he didn't object. Felicia walked with them, telling her about an advertising campaign she wanted to get involved in. Vimal didn't seem to be listening. His attention was focused ahead of them, where Kerry was walking with Magda. Kerry seemed to be hanging on to every word the other woman was saying. That was a strange dynamic. What was going on there?

They neared the village and more people joined. As the sun sank lower, it got colder. Niro had brought her camera with her, but didn't think she'd be taking many photos. Night photography took stillness and patience and she wasn't sure she could be bothered right now. But she'd brought the kit along, just in case.

Was there a moon tonight? She looked up at the darkening sky. Although the sunlight had drained from the valley, it still caught the tops of the mountains, making the snow on the top glow orange.

'Oh wow,' she said. A quick look around and she dragged Vimal off the path onto the driveway of a shop.

'What are you doing?' he said.

'Look up there. I need to photograph that.' She shrugged off her backpack and pulled out the extending tripod. It was small, but she could angle the camera on it.

Vimal cast a last glance towards Kerry's disappearing back and said, 'Can I help?'

She handed him her backpack and gloves. It was difficult to adjust the settings on her camera with gloves on.

Felicia had stopped too and was watching with interest as Niro fiddled with settings.

'What's that for?'

'There's not much light. We can see well enough in twilight, but that's because our eyes adapt. I'm trying to get as much light into the camera as I can, without having too long an exposure. The longer the exposure, the more likely that something will move and the shot will be less clear.'

She bent down to fix the camera to the tripod. She had to tip the camera back so far that she had to go down on one knee in the snow to see through the viewfinder. Her knee was cold. Her hands were freezing. She set the exposure time to a few seconds and pressed the shutter as carefully as she could, so that she didn't shake the camera. She took a few more, at different exposure times, just in case.

'Can't you edit it later? Do you have to get it just right at this point?' Felicia asked. 'There's filters and things.'

'The more I can capture right now, the better. I can fiddle with it later, but it won't be the same as getting it right the first time.' Niro quickly looked through the pictures. 'That's pretty good,' she said. She changed the angle and took one more. 'That'll do.'

She stood up, brushed off her knees and put the camera back around her neck. Vimal held her bag open while she collapsed the tripod and stuffed it back in. Her knees were patches of cold. She shivered.

'Ow. My hands are so cold.' They actually hurt. She stuck her hands under her arms.

'You should put your gloves on,' said Felicia.

'You need to warm them up first and then put gloves on.'

Vimal reached towards her. 'Here.' He clasped her hands in both of his. Niro, too surprised to object, let him, wondering what he was going to do.

He raised them to his face and blew on them. The warmth of his breath hit her fingers and the heat raced all the way up her arm and earthed itself somewhere in her belly. She inhaled sharply. He didn't seem to notice and did it again.

It was warming her fingers up. It was warming other parts of her as well, but he wasn't to know that. He raised his gaze to hers and she saw only concern. He was making sure her hands were warm. That was all. He had no idea what it might look like ... or feel like, to her.

She gave the faintest tug on her hands. He let them go and whispered, 'Sorry.'

'It's fine,' she whispered back. 'They are much warmer now. Thank you.'

He handed back her gloves, which had been in his pocket. She pulled them on, and had to admit it was much warmer doing this his way.

He helped her get her bag back on. She took his arm, which brought more of her in contact with more of him. She tried not to think about how solid his arm felt. Or about how warm he was. She herself was feeling altogether warmer, too. But that was probably because she was so close to him. After all, men were basically radiators with legs, weren't they? That had to be it.

They fell into sync as they resumed their walk into the village. After all, they had to catch up with the others. The whole point of this holiday was for Kerry to see him differently.

*

Vimal craned his neck to catch a glimpse of the parade. They would hear the marching band coming nearer. From where he was, he could just about make out the procession of lights. Niro was standing beside him, clutching a cone-shaped crepe filled with Nutella. She bobbed up and down.

'You'll see them in a minute,' he told her, amused.

'I wish I were taller.' She scowled, but it only lasted a few seconds. She took a bite of her cone and closed her eyes with a rapturous expression on her face. 'This is delicious.'

'Yeah. Not my sort of thing,' he said.

'Oh yeah, I forgot you don't like hazelnut spread. I don't know how you can live without it, honestly.'

He smiled fondly at her. She must have warmed up now. It had worried him when she was shivering. Her hands had been so cold. He knew the reason she took her gloves off all the time was because the fingers in most gloves were too long to cover her short fingers. It seemed like a bad idea. She was an artist. She needed her fingers to be in good working order. There must be a solution. Perhaps there were gloves that had shorter fingers. Or allowed more sensitivity. He would have to look into that.

He scanned the scant crowd for the rest of the group. Lucien and Felicia were a few feet away from the parade route, arms wrapped around each other. Kerry was standing with Magda and Peter. She noticed him looking and gave him a small smile. He returned it and turned around. Kerry seemed to be less tense around him now and he couldn't tell what that meant. He hoped that she was moving past whatever it was that put her off him all that time ago.

'I feel a bit bad standing here wolfing this down without sharing,' Niro said. 'Are you sure you don't want some? This bit here doesn't have any Nutella on it.'

'Surely it's not doing its job, then.'

'It's just sitting there being taunted by its Nutella-bearing colleagues. You'd be doing it a favour by eating it.'

'But it's all one pancake.'

'You have no poetry in your soul.'

He laughed. 'Okay, fine. I'll try a bit of your overly sugary pancake.'

She grinned and tore a piece off with her ungloved fingers. He'd never known anyone so rubbish at using gloves. He had no intention of taking his own gloves off, so he opened his mouth so that she could feed it to him. Her hand touched his face briefly, the contact making his breath catch. He chewed thoughtfully. The pancake was sweet, but not too much because there was no spread on it. But it was still far too sweet for him.

'Oh no,' said Niro. 'I got some Nutella on you.' She gestured to his chin. He wiped it off.

'No. Here. Let me.' She raised her hand to his face and used her thumb to wipe away whatever was on his face. The swiping motion meant that her thumb, very briefly, swept along the underside of his bottom lip and it did funny things to him. Heat flared in his face. If he didn't know better he'd have said the contact was arousing, but this was Niro. She wasn't flirting with him. She was playing a part. She had no feelings for him and he didn't have any towards her.

Niro looked away, as though nothing untoward had happened. *See? Just playing a part.*

'Did Kerry see?' she asked, murmuring out of the corner of her mouth.

He checked. Kerry was watching them, looking thoughtful. 'I think so,' he said.

'Good. The old you would have been far too uptight to eat a crepe with Nutella. Especially as it's not even your crepe.'

'That is true.'

'How did it go with the snowshoeing?' They hadn't had a chance to talk about it yet.

'Not bad, actually,' said Vimal. 'I think I got things back on track.'

Niro didn't reply. She nodded and peered past him, then gave a little jump. 'Oh, look. Here they come.'

The band came round the corner, and behind them was a procession of kids of different ages carrying lanterns decorated with varying degrees of artistry. The crowd clapped in time with the music.

'How lovely,' Niro said. 'They're so adorable.'

Vimal watched, but barely registered anything. He was too busy thinking. In the last half hour or so, wandering around the village, he had barely thought about Kerry. Instead he had been completely immersed in the moment. He glanced over at his ex again. He missed her, but that all-consuming need seemed to have disappeared.

What was it Kerry had said about his missing companionship rather than missing her specifically? Did she have a point? Niro had been with him nearly all day, every day since he'd got here. They shared a room and a bathroom. There was an easy intimacy about being around her. Was that why he was feeling so calm and happy? Niro provided him with companionship, with no romantic demands attached.

He thought guiltily of the frisson he had felt a minute ago. Was he so starved of human connection that he was seeing things in his friendship with Niro that weren't real? Niro was here to help him get back with Kerry and she was very keen on doing that. When this holiday was over, they would go their separate ways and her companionship would disappear as suddenly as it had arrived.

He tried to shake himself and concentrate on the here and now. Kerry was mellowing towards him. She was still fond of him, he was sure of it. New Year's was a special time for them, so if he was to stand a chance of getting back together with her, tomorrow was the day to do it. He needed to stop trying to distract himself and focus on winning Kerry back.

'I love parades,' Niro said.

He looked down at her. Her gaze was fixed on the back of the procession as the lights wound their way to a platform at the far end of the market, near the ice rink. From what Martin had told him, the lanterns were going to go on display and you got to vote for your favourite.

'Have you ever seen a perahera?' she asked him suddenly.

He had, as it happened. As a teenager on holiday in Sri Lanka, his parents had dragged him out in the night to sit upstairs in a café and watch a procession go by. 'It wasn't the big Esala Perahera,' he said. 'But yes. I have.'

He looked around at the people bundled up in the cold and the sedate procession. The perahera had been noisy, with whip crackers and drums that made your chest vibrate. There had been fire eaters and flame jugglers and an elephant covered in lights walking through the haze of smoke and camphor like a vision of calm in a heaving mass of chaos. Even jaded teenage Vimal had been enthralled. 'It was a bit different to this though.'

Niro chuckled. 'Yes. This is a bit colder. And, you know, quieter.'

'Hmm,' said Vimal. 'And not a single elephant.'

'Right? Is it even a parade if there isn't an elephant?'

They both laughed.

'What are you two giggling at?' Lucien's voice cut in. He was walking past, with Felicia hanging off his arm, dragging him towards the stage.

Vimal and Niro exchanged glances. How could they even begin to explain?

'Nothing, really,' said Niro. 'You wouldn't get it.'

A scowl snapped across Lucien's face but was gone so fast, Vimal wouldn't have noticed if he hadn't been looking directly at him at the time. 'Oh, I see – an Asian in-joke.'

It sort of was, but there was something about Lucien's tone that felt odd. Vimal looked at Niro to see how she was responding. She was staring at Lucien, her expression solemn.

'We're going to see the lanterns up-close,' said Felicia. 'Wanna come?'

Vimal looked ahead and saw that Kerry was heading down

too. 'Sure. Niro?'

'Yep. Yep. Just finishing my crepe.' She tagged along, too busy with her food to hold his hand. He wasn't sure why he'd even noticed that.

Chapter 19

They walked back up the hill after voting for their favourite lanterns. Some of the lanterns had been done by kids. Others had clearly had parental help. Vimal was surprised at how much he enjoyed discussing the artistic merits of them with Niro, who was treating it with just the right balance of humour and seriousness. There were things she pointed out in the ones made by kids that he wouldn't have noticed. Attention to detail. Nearly all of the lamps consisted of open wooden frames, decorated with translucent paper, so that the glow from small LED tealights inside shone through. Niro's favourites had been the ones that played with the medium and created effects through light and shadow. Vimal had preferred the ones with the pretty pictures on them.

'I agree with Vimal,' said Felicia. Lucien had got bored and walked ahead to join Peter and one of the other blokes. Because Niro walked slower, Vimal and Felicia were lagging behind too. 'I like the ones with the pictures the best.'

'Fair enough,' said Niro. 'There's no bad reason for liking stuff. If it moves you.'

'I wouldn't say a bunch of lanterns moved me, as such,' said Vimal.

'The kids' faces, though,' said Felicia. 'They were so proud of their work. It was adorable!'

'It really was,' said Niro.

They reached the steep path that led to the entrance. For a few minutes, they walked in silence, their footsteps muffled by the snow. They were halfway up, where the path curved, when Niro said, 'Stop. Stop, stop.'

Vimal turned, alarmed. 'What's wrong?'

'Nothing,' said Niro. 'Just … look.'

The clouds had parted, revealing a waxing moon. The scant moonlight reflected off the snow. Below them, the valley was a glow of lights and above, the mountains rose, etched out in black and silver.

'Just look at it,' said Niro, breathlessly. 'It's so … vast.'

Vimal looked and had a moment of dissonance, where the world was huge and everything was far away. These mountains had been here for millennia and would still be here for millennia to come. They didn't know or care that he was there. He felt, just for a second, insignificant, in the face of nature. It should have been humbling, or frightening. Instead it felt … incredible.

He breathed in. The feeling disappeared and he was back to being regular old Vimal, with regular old feelings and regular old worries. But for that second, he had been … something else. A speck that was part of something huge.

Beside him, Niro exhaled and smiled. Even in the semi-darkness, her smile was enchanting.

'How could you capture that in a photo?' said Felicia, already looking through her phone camera.

Niro turned back towards the path home. 'I don't think you can,' she said to Felicia. 'Sometimes, it's better to just remember how it made you feel.'

Vimal gazed one more time at the valley, which looked like it always looked. Had he just imagined that feeling? Was it even real? He turned and followed the two women up the path. If the feeling was real, was that how Niro saw the world the whole time?

He knew the world was beautiful. He saw it in maths and in patterns. This was the first time he'd seen it in a view. As he trudged up the path, he thought back to Niro's smile. It was the first time he'd seen it in Niro, too.

*

'My hands are a mess.' Niro was sitting at the dressing table, putting moisturiser on. Her skin was dry from the cold and covered in tiny cuts where moisture had frozen in the folds and cracked it. 'I have to stop taking my gloves off to take photos.'

'Why do you?' Vimal was sitting in bed, already in his pyjamas and tucked up. He was reading something on his phone. She hadn't expected him to be paying any attention to her.

'So that I can change settings and press the shutter with the lightest touch.' She put the lid back on the hand cream and leaned forward to check that there was enough moisturiser on her face.

'You can get touchscreen gloves.'

'Not for me, you can't.' She'd had this discussion so many times, with so many people. 'Short, stubby little fingers, remember?' She shook out her hair. 'I tried fingerless gloves, but that was almost worse because I couldn't put proper gloves on over the top.'

She checked her hands again. More hand cream needed. 'Honestly, in the winter, I fantasise about being dipped bodily into a bath of warm moisturiser.' She rubbed in the lotion and turned round.

Vimal looked away quickly. Had he been watching her? That was weird.

She went over to the bed and shrugged off the fleece she was wearing, before getting into bed. It was nice and warm. 'Oooh. Toasty,' she said.

On the other side of the pillow wall, Vimal sniffed. 'I like the smell of that hand cream,' he said. 'My mum uses it. Has done forever.'

Niro reached across and turned off her light. 'Your mum is a wise woman.'

'I suppose.'

She could hear him moving. The pillow wall stopped them from touching, but it did nothing for the sounds. There was so much connection in just being so close. Inhabiting the same room.

'I'm turning in, too.' He switched off his light and the room plunged into darkness.

Niro lay on her back and stared up into the dark. Neither of them was asleep. Something had been nagging at her for a while.

'Why do you want to be friends with Lucien?' she asked.

Vimal moved. 'I … don't especially. I just work with him.'

'But you want him to think well of you, don't you? Why is that?'

Vimal seemed to be thinking about it. 'I guess … he's charismatic and popular. Other people seem to think well of him … I don't know. I'm the wrong person to ask about these things. I don't really understand social capital.'

'He's not a very nice person.' She had noticed the scowl when they'd refused to tell him what they were laughing at. Lucien liked to control a room. He didn't like things happening that weren't centred around him. Then there was the thing about the beds. 'Did you know that there is a room here with twin beds? He gave it to Kerry and her bloke and then forced us to take this room because he thought that would be funny.'

To her surprise, Vimal didn't disagree. 'I didn't know that. That's shitty behaviour.'

She thought back to the comment about the Asian in-joke – couple it with the tone of voice and his general demeanour of hilarity whenever he mentioned their 'arranged match', and well … 'And I'm not sure he's not … a bit racist.'

Vimal was quiet for a very long time. 'Maybe,' he said, quietly.

Interesting. Vimal didn't like Lucien either. She turned her head to face the pillow wall. 'So you're really only here because of Kerry.'

'Yes. Why else would I come?'

'I don't know. To get in with the posh kids? To have a nice holiday?' She was pretty sure Kerry was here for the former reason and Felicia was open about being here for the latter.

'No,' he said, sounding genuinely puzzled. 'I don't want to get in with the posh kids. I would never fit in. If I wanted a nice holiday, I would just go on one, I think.'

'By yourself?'

'I suppose. If I wanted it badly enough.'

She had never been on holiday by herself. The idea felt faintly ludicrous to her. Surely, places were only fun if you have someone to share them with.

'Where would you go?' she asked. She couldn't imagine where someone would go to be alone.

'Paris,' he said, so fast that he obviously didn't need to think about it.

'Paris?' That was ... definitely not what she'd expected.

'Yeah. I'd like to go and spend some time in the museums. There's a lot of interesting science and maths history there. Whenever I went to Paris with Kerry, she made me go to art galleries and cafés and things. Never the really interesting places.'

Oh bless him, sometimes he genuinely had no romance in his soul. She almost felt sorry for Kerry.

'Not that I minded,' he added, suddenly. 'It made Kerry happy. And I like making her happy, so ...'

The chuckle died in Niro's throat. 'I like making Kerry happy' was one thing Vimal was sure about. If that wasn't the most romantic thing she'd ever heard! It was so sweet. No one had cared about Niro enough to sit through things that bored him, just because he knew it made her happy. Kerry was one lucky woman.

If Kerry meant that much to him, he deserved to be with her. She rolled over again, so that her back was to him. Whatever this feeling of interest was, she had to put it out of her mind. Vimal wanted Kerry. She had noticed that Kerry kept looking at Vimal this evening – nothing overt, just quick glances. If Kerry wanted Vimal, too, then this plan of his was completely sensible. She had promised to help him. So she would. Regardless of how she felt about it.

'How about you?' said Vimal. 'Where would you go?'

Niro hunched herself up into a ball. 'I don't know. Everywhere. I haven't narrowed it down much. Goodnight.'

'Oh.' He sounded disappointed. 'Okay. G'night.'

*

It was no use. She wasn't going to get to sleep. As quietly as she could, she unplugged her phone and, using the weak light of the screen to guide her, slipped out of bed. Vimal stirred and she froze. He turned over and went back to sleep.

'Just going to get myself a glass of water,' she whispered, even though he was clearly asleep and wouldn't hear her.

She grabbed her fleece and tiptoed out. The house was warm and still. Even though the main lights were out, the corridor was lit by tiny lights at floor level, which gave off enough of a glow that she could see where she was going. She was suddenly aware that they were sleeping quietly inside a mountain, covered in a blanket of snow. No wonder it felt so snug.

The kitchen was in darkness, so she flicked on the spotlight above the island. Now then, what could she have? Something like Horlicks would be lovely, but there wasn't likely to be anything like that here. So she settled for a hot chocolate. Rather than faff around making the good stuff, she chose to warm up some milk in the microwave and use a sachet of the instant variety instead.

While the microwave was humming, she went to the other side of the island to flip through the *What's On* magazine that had been left there. Voices and laughter drifted down the corridor. She peered down it, a thin rectangle of light came from the door of the games room. There was a clink of glasses. Some people were still up and still drinking. She couldn't help herself; she crept a little closer to listen.

'I thought he'd come by himself.' Lucien's voice. 'But then he produced this girlfriend.'

Niro frowned. Were they talking about Vimal? She tiptoed closer.

'That's just comedy in itself.' That sounded like Magda. Magda? Hadn't she gone to bed earlier? 'Surely, it's a convenience thing,' Magda continued. 'He is obviously still in love with Kerry.'

They were definitely talking about Vimal. She shouldn't eavesdrop, but …

'I'm almost convinced he just talked a friend or a cousin into coming with him,' said Lucien. 'He was so flustered when I asked if he was bringing a partner. And he's clearly not interested in her.'

Peter snorted. 'Who would be? Just look at her. Such a common, dumpy little thing.'

Niro stiffened. Ouch.

'I like how she thinks having a bit of colour in her hair will make up for not having a personality,' said Magda. 'And she has no sense of style.'

'Quite,' said Lucien. 'I honestly didn't expect him to bring anyone. I thought it'd be funny having him here while Kerry was here with Woolberg. But … this is better. Watching him tie himself in knots over Kerry while trying to keep his fat little girlfriend on side is even more entertaining.' He laughed. 'D'you know, he asked for them to have separate beds.'

'So, perhaps your theory about faking the girlfriend is right,' said Magda.

'And the best bit,' said Lucien, amusement still lacing his voice, 'is that they've got to share one massive bed.' In the midst of the ensuing guffaws, he added, 'I imagine he's having to fight her off every night.'

'Unless he doesn't,' said Peter.

Niro went cold. These people were horrible. They were laughing at her. At Vimal, too, but mostly at her.

'I must say, Lucien old chap, you've excelled yourself with the entertainment this year,' said Peter.

Entertainment?

'Yes,' said Lucien, smugly. 'It worked out even better than I thought it could.'

'Going to be hard to top this, eh what?' Peter said. More laughter.

Niro could hardly breathe. Anger, humiliation, horror all churned together. What should she do? Well, she couldn't deal with this by herself. Definitely not right now. She started to step backwards towards the kitchen. The microwave pinged.

Someone said, 'Shh. What was that?'

'Lucien, be a sport and shut the door, will you, old chap?'

She dived back into the kitchen and crouched behind the island. If discovered, she could claim she'd dropped something.

A few seconds passed. The door was pushed shut. She cautiously rose. She didn't want the hot chocolate anymore. She felt sick. How dare they? How horrible.

She made her way back to their room and let herself back in.

Vimal was still asleep. Using her phone screen to guide her again, she made her way back to her side of the bed and lay down.

Common, dumpy little thing.

She thinks having a bit of colour in her hair will make up for not having a personality.

That was the story of her life. Mick was right. There was nothing special about her. She curled up into a ball. What was she doing here? She wasn't this good an actress. Pretending to fancy Vimal was easy, because she genuinely liked him. Either way, it wasn't much of an acting job.

She was probably kidding herself about the acting too. Mick had called her talentless and delusional. After months of coaxing by Sam and making ends meet by selling her digital creative skills, she had finally got to a place where she didn't believe him … but what if he had been right? Lucien, Peter and Magda clearly thought so. Was she so easy to see through?

She sat up and hugged her knees. Tears slid down her face. She rubbed at them with her sleeve. She had to cry quietly so that she didn't wake Vimal up. He seemed to think she was worth something. It would never do to let him see how useless she really was.

In the darkness, every single harsh thing anyone had said to her rose up in her memory. She bowed her head to her knees. A sob rose and, before she could stifle it, escaped. In the quiet room it sounded very loud.

Niro would have held her breath, but the tears wouldn't let her. Now that the gates had been unleashed they came afresh. Another big gulping sob bubbled up.

'Niro? What's going on?'

Oh great. Now Vimal was up. The last thing she and her misery needed was a witness.

'Niro?' He clicked on the bedside lamp. 'What's wrong?'

'Doesn't matter. Go back to sleep,' she said, into the space between the top of her knees and her chest. She rubbed her face with her sleeve. On the other side of the bed, Vimal got up.

A second later, his arm appeared over the pillow barrier, holding a box of tissues. 'Here.'

She raised her head far enough to see and took a couple of tissues. She tried to say 'thanks' but only managed a muffled 'mfph'.

For a few minutes, he said nothing while she cried. When she finally got the tears under control, she said, 'Sorry.'

He made a soft click with his tongue. 'No need.'

It was the sort of thing her parents would have said when they meant *oh, darling, it's okay* and the familiarity of it made her feel better. She gulped a shaky breath. 'You should go back to sleep. I'm okay.' She looked over and saw that he was sitting up on his side of the bed, eyebrows drawn up with worry.

'You're clearly not okay,' he said, quietly. 'Do you … want to tell me what's wrong? You don't have to, if it's too personal.'

She lowered her head once more. Should she tell him? What if he took their side? He knew them better than he knew her. Could she deal with the humiliation? She reminded herself that she was only here because he needed her to do something special. Other than that, she was nothing to him. She shook her head.

'It's nothing.'

He sniffed. 'Clearly, not nothing. You're crying.'

She thought of what she could say. 'I was thinking about … something someone said. They called me common and dumpy and … that I must think having colour in my hair was a substitute for having a personality and … I thought of it just now and it hit me rather hard. It's stupid, I know.'

He was horrified. 'That's a terrible thing to say! Who said that?'

'Why? Are you going to beat them up for me?'

He looked a little sheepish. 'Well, no. But I could tut at them. Mercilessly.'

That made her smile a little bit. 'That'll work. What if it was the Aunties?'

'Was it? I'm not sure I'm brave enough to tut at them.'

She nodded. 'Brave enough or stupid enough.'

He nodded. His mouth was smiling, but his eyes were watching her carefully. Niro wiped away her tears. Now that she had cried herself out, she felt weary and oddly, calmer. 'Besides, it's true. I *am* common and dumpy.'

Vimal drew a breath to speak.

Niro went on, 'And please don't patronise me by saying I'm not fat. I know I am. Okay, I'm not terribly unhealthy, but I am overweight. Always have been. Lying about it doesn't help.'

Vimal pulled the bedclothes up on his side. 'I wasn't going to say that.'

She crossed her arms and raised her eyebrows. Of course he was going to say that. It would be interesting to see how he got out of this one.

Vimal looked down at his hands. 'It's like … mountains,' he said.

Okay. She had not seen that one coming. 'Mountains?'

'Yeah. The ones here, they're sharp and pointy and covered in snow. Then there are ones in Wales and on the way to Scotland that are gentle and rolling and soft. There are mountains in Sri Lanka which are dark, wild, green. They're all very different from each other, but they're all beautiful.'

It was such a ridiculous analogy that her sadness gave way to amusement. 'So, which kind of mountain am I, then?'

'A soft …' He cleared his throat. 'A soft one. Gentle.'

'You know it would have been quicker to say "beauty is in the eye of the beholder".'

He made a very Sri Lankan hand gesture. 'Yeah, but such a cliché, no?' The melodic cadence of his speech was pure Sri Lankan.

This made her smile properly. 'Thank you.'

'You're welcome.'

'Listen, I'm sorry I lost it before. It's not that big a deal, really. It took me years to accept it, but this is me. There isn't a thin person trying to get out. I'm okay, most of the time, but sometimes, if I'm already vulnerable, a single comment can undo all that work.' She wiped another tear away. 'Their opinion shouldn't matter to me much. On a different day it wouldn't. It … it just reminded me a bit of Mick and the stuff he said.'

Hardness returned to his expression. 'Your ex? He made fun of how you look?'

You think you're quirky and cool. You're not. You're just a talentless hack. Wearing weird things doesn't make you cool. They just make you look like the fat girl who's trying too hard. He had been angry that she was leaving. He should have been contrite, not angry. Why was she only just realising this now? He had never loved her. Nothing he'd said about her work, positive or negative, meant anything.

'And other things,' she said. 'And ... Aunty's ... comment really hit a sore spot.'

'He sounds like a real dick.'

'Yeah. I think he liked me well enough, but he thought I should be grateful, that he fancied me, that he rated my art ... and when I took it as my due, he didn't like it.' Sam had made this observation at the time. When she thought about it now, Niro felt she had a point, but it had been hard to remember that when the pain of Mick's comments were raw.

For the longest moment, Vimal didn't say anything, just looked at her with weight in his gaze. Finally, he said, 'If you want me to, I could breach the sanctity of the pillow wall and give you a hug.'

She should say no. It wasn't really appropriate and it was a dangerous indulgence on her part. She looked up to say no, but somehow, 'yes please' came out.

He moved closer, solemnly lifting the pillow at the top and propping it up so that he could lean against it, and put his arm around her. She leaned into him, her cheek resting on his shoulder. The top of her head was tucked into the side of his neck. He gave her a gentle squeeze and rubbed her shoulder. He was warm and solid and smelled faintly of toothpaste and soap. She closed her eyes. It had been such a long time since she'd been this close to a man. It was a shame this wasn't for real.

'Don't let them get to you,' he said. 'You're an amazing photographer, you're clever and friendly and funny and a genuinely good friend.'

He meant well. It would have been a comforting speech if she didn't inconveniently have feelings for him. She wasn't that clever. If she had, she would have remembered that this was all pretend and all she could ever be to him was a friend. So, she said, 'Thanks' and reluctantly moved away.

Vimal moved back to his side of the bed and carefully restored the pillow back to its place on the wall. 'There,' he said.

It was only after she had snuggled back down and Vimal had

turned the light off that she remembered the rest of what she'd overheard. She should tell him about that. After all, it was about him. She rolled over. He seemed to have fallen asleep again, the lucky git. Oh well, she'd find a time to tell him tomorrow.

Chapter 20

Niro overslept, so she missed her chance to catch dawn coming over the valley. She was annoyed with herself, but honestly, she felt better for having had the extra sleep.

She checked on her marmot friend when she went to call Sam. Afterwards, she bundled herself up in her outdoor clothes and went to see if she could find him (or her) from the outside. She and Vimal had a plan for today, one that involved him spontaneously building a snowman with her. Luckily, Kerry was staying in that morning. Most people were having a quiet day, resting up before the party in the evening, so it would be relatively easy to make sure Kerry witnessed it. Lucien was staying in too, keeping an eye on the party preparations.

Niro found the snowbank under which the marmot was sleeping. It looked just like any other stretch of snow, apart from a steep bit of rock next to it. When she tried to get closer, her leg sank into the snow up to her knee. For a second she panicked. Was there some sort of deep well here? She didn't want to die, just a few feet away from the lovely warm house! Flailing, she fell backwards onto the snow. Thankfully, her bum didn't sink any lower. She had obviously stepped into a hole. Carefully extracting her leg, she scooted backwards and stood up.

She turned and looked outwards. From where she was, she could see along the valley. The little window in the storeroom wouldn't be much of a light well, but, if you stood in there at sunrise, you would get to see the light spilling into the valley. It was a sweet little hidden treasure in a house that was built to be a hidden treasure itself.

She really should have made herself get up and go photograph the valley at sunrise. She wasn't going to be able to do it now. It wasn't as if she was going to be around to capture it tomorrow morning.

Her mood dipped and sadness settled on her like an extra layer. Tonight, she would leave. Vimal would get the girl he wanted. She would just have to get over him, quietly, back at home.

Niro brushed off the snow that was clinging to her legs and bum from falling over. It would be fine. Her feelings for Vimal were probably an overreaction to proximity. She hadn't been anywhere near a guy in two years and being this close to him was bound to mess with her mind. She would go home, watch some romcoms with Sam and Luke, eat her own weight in chocolate and then feel better. Easy as.

She walked back round the side of the house. The curving walls of the courtyard were topped with mesh fencing that acted as a net to hold back the snow. The perfect snow had been marred by her tracks. She retraced her steps back until she came to the shallow steps that led up to the small gate at the front of the courtyard. Felicia was standing a few steps down from the gate with a selfie stick, taking a photo of herself with the house behind her.

Niro waved to her.

Felicia lowered the camera and beamed. 'Hello there. Where've you been?'

'I've just been taking a few photos of the house from the side. You can barely see it. It's impressively hidden.' She climbed the next few steps and stopped next to Felicia.

'It must have snowed in the night. It all looks so perfect.'

'Would you like me to take some photos for you?' Niro asked.

'Yes, please.'

They spent a few minutes taking pictures of Felicia looking beautiful in front of the house. As she handed the phone back, Niro looked up. There were people on the viewing platform above the house. One of them waved to her. That must be Vimal.

She looked at the snow. There was plenty of it. Her original plan had been to just start building the snowman herself, but if she got Felicia involved it would look a lot more natural.

'Seems a shame to disrupt this snow,' said Niro. 'But it would be so much fun to build a snowman.' She pointed to a spot outside the courtyard where the ground was less steep. 'Just there.'

Felicia looked at it with her head cocked to the side. 'I haven't built a snowman in ages. We used to do it all the time when we went up to my grandparents' place in Scotland.' She turned, eyes shining. 'Shall we?'

'What? Build a snowman?' Niro looked at the snow all around them. 'Sure. Why not? I'm not sure I'll be very good at it, though.' It took a while to build a snowman, if she remembered rightly. Plenty of time for Vimal to join them.

'Doesn't matter. It's the building it that counts.' Felicia stepped off the path and waded through the snow to the place Niro had pointed out and started to push together a pile of snow.

Niro zipped her camera inside her jacket and joined her.

They worked together for a few minutes without talking. Felicia broke the silence with, 'So, how are things going with you and Vimal?'

Niro frowned. 'What do you mean?'

'Well, it must be weird with his ex turning up.'

'I … yes. I guess it is a bit.' What was the best way to play this? She was going to disappear by the end of the night. Was it best to sow doubts about their relationship now? 'But Kerry seems nice.'

'Oh, she is,' said Felicia. 'Is Vimal finding it weird, do you think?'

'I'm sure he is,' said Niro, carefully. 'They were together for a long time.'

'Right?' Felicia smacked another handful of snow against the side of the growing snowman. 'How do you feel about that?'

'They split up ages ago—'

Felicia laughed. 'Oh, come on. I know you guys aren't really together.'

What? How? Was it obvious? Then she remembered Lucien and his friends laughing at her. Had Felicia been there? 'What gave you that idea?'

Felicia stood back up with her hands on her hips. 'I'm very observant,' she said. 'First, you have to keep reminding him to hold your hand. When you sit next to each other, you're careful not to touch each other. But most of all … he keeps looking at Kerry and you know that. Yet, you seem okay with it.'

Except she wasn't okay with it, was she? It was eating away at her. Niro looked away and didn't reply.

'Oh, no,' said Felicia. 'You're not okay with it? Oh, that's sad.' She put a hand on Niro's arm. 'I'm so sorry. I thought this was some sort of fake relationship to help Vimal save face or something, which … you know, who am I to judge? But if you really care and he doesn't … Oh, Niro.'

She stared at the earnest sympathy in Felicia's expression. 'It's not like that,' she said flatly. Hopefully, that would be it.

'Which part? About the relationship being fake? Or about the way you feel?'

'What makes you think—'

'I much prefer Chamonix.' Magda's voice drifted over the wall, clear and close.

Niro shot Felicia a look and spotted the expression of distaste before it was replaced by a sunny smile. They turned their attention back to the snowman, which looked quite rubbish, frankly.

'I don't really ski.' This was Kerry. 'But I do like the idea of it.'

'You must try it. There's nothing quite like the feeling of speed and control. It's like flying.' This was one of the other women.

'I will definitely try it,' Kerry said.

Felicia rolled her eyes and Niro giggled. 'I don't think we're going to get this snowman to be any rounder,' she said, loudly.

'No,' said Felicia. 'We should do the head. Unless you want to go for a three-ball snowman with a chest.'

'I'm getting cold, to be honest,' said Niro. She was.

'Okay then. Two-ball snowman it is.' Felicia started to roll a ball of snow. As she passed Niro, she whispered, 'We'll talk about this later, okay?'

Niro nodded but she wasn't sure she wanted to talk about it. She focused on her task, her mind whirring. Was there even any point to her staying, even until the evening, if everyone was just humouring her and Vimal? Or worse, laughing at them? Vimal would hate that.

As far as she could tell, the best thing she could do was to leave as soon as she could. She pushed more snow into the ball. Where the hell was Vimal?

*

Vimal stood on the viewing platform. He and a few others had come up with Peter and Lucien, who were currently talking to the catering staff about the set-up for a party up here.

The view from here was spectacular. He must tell Niro. From this vantage point, the village looked like a postcard, all snowy slopes and wooden gables. According to Lucien there would be fireworks from the town square at midnight. From this height they would be able to see them clearly.

Below them, he could just about make out a sliver of courtyard and the slope beyond. Two figures were busy piling up snow. It took a few minutes for him to recognise Niro and Felicia. From this distance, the difference between their shapes was harder to spot. Niro must have roped Felicia into helping her with the snowman. This was his cue to go down and join them. He looked behind him to see if Kerry was around. She had been there a few minutes ago. Where was she?

'What on earth are those two doing?' said Peter, coming up next to him. He frowned and squinted down.

'Building a snowman.' Vimal smiled. How long had it been since he'd built a snowman? Too long, probably. When everyone was wandering around trying to enjoy the snow in the most sophisticated ways possible, trust Niro to pick the most fun instead.

He was about to set off to join her, when Lucien inserted himself smoothly between Vimal and Peter.

'What's going on down there?'

'Felicia and Niro are building a snowman, apparently,' Peter said, with a hint of haughty laughter in his voice.

Vimal didn't like the patronising tone. The more time he spent with these people, the less he liked them. Why *did* Kerry want to get to know them?

Lucien looked up at the view of the mountains and took a deep breath. 'Switzerland always makes me think of chocolate,' he said.

Vimal frowned. That was a weird change of topic.

'There's a lot to think about with chocolate. Texture for one. Thickness for another.'

Since Lucien was talking to him, Vimal couldn't leave. He nodded. He didn't really have much to say about chocolate. It was chocolate. He wasn't super keen on it. He could tell bad chocolate from mediocre, but he wasn't sure he could tell the difference between mediocre and spectacular.

'Do you, for example, prefer regular KitKat or *chunky* KitKat?'

'I don't think there's—'

'On the one hand, with the regular one, it's delicate and there's only a thin coating of chocolate, but you get four fingers. But the chunky one is … well covered. And it's much more solid and …' He made weird squeezing motion with his hands. 'Muscular.'

Vimal was completely lost now. He tried to apply logic. 'I imagine there's the same amount of chocolate in both. But there's more surface area in four fingers than in a chunky bar ...'

A look passed between Lucien and Peter. He couldn't see Lucien's expression, but he could see Peter's smirk. Behind Peter one of the other guys ducked his head and hid a grin. There was a joke he was missing. He looked to where Peter's gaze was aimed. The two women were standing side by side. Felicia slim and pretty in her sky blue and Niro far chunkier in her red-and-purple coat.

The fury that blazed up from his chest surprised him. He gripped the railings in front of him until the urge to punch Lucien's smug face subsided. It only took a few seconds to get a lid on it. 'I see you're not talking about chocolate at all,' he said, tightly. 'I don't like body-shaming people.'

'Obviously not,' said Lucien. 'You don't discriminate because of size and nor should you.'

'And I don't appreciate you trying to get me to say things I don't mean.'

'Calm down, old man. We're not insulting your fat girlfriend.'

'I think you are. And I like my girlfriend, thank you, and at least she likes me. It's not like I bribed a poor undergrad to come with me.'

Lucien looked startled and Peter guffawed. Vimal stamped off to the door that led back to the house. In the stairwell, he breathed out slowly and let his feelings simmer down. As he clattered back down the steps, he wished he was good at pithy put-downs. It would have been so nice to slap Lucien back with a better placed insult. But he hadn't been prepared and he'd blurted out the obvious instead. By the time he got to the bottom of the stairwell, it had occurred to him that Lucien was still his host and it would have been quite rude. That wasn't really the done thing.

He pulled on some shoe covers to walk through the house. When he went back outside again, into the courtyard, he spotted Kerry and Magda. Ah, perfect.

'I'm going to help the ladies build a snowman,' he said to her. 'Want to come?'

He saw the surprise and the temptation in her expression, but she cast a swift glance towards Magda, whose grimace was clear, and said, 'No. Not for me.'

The anger still burning in his veins gave him a moment of sudden clarity. Kerry was trying so hard to be someone she was not to fit into another person's vision of what was best. She wanted him to do the same. And here he was pandering to it.

He would never be what Kerry wanted. Even if he managed to persuade her that he was, he would know inside that he wasn't and the effort of keeping up the façade would destroy him. He was bad at telling lies. He could only imagine how much worse it would be to live his life as one.

Vimal marched on, towards the gate. If Kerry wanted to give up on doing something she knew she'd like to stay in Magda's good books, then more fool her. Niro didn't expect him to be anything more than himself. When it came to her, she could be his friend even if he did whatever he wanted. And right now, what he wanted was to go out in the snow and have fun.

He opened the gate and stepped out. 'Hello, ladies. May I join y—'

A snowball hit him in the face before he could finish his sentence. Brushing snow out of his eyes, he saw Niro laughing. Right. That was how it was, was it?

He scooped up a handful of snow and hurled it back. He missed her. Suddenly, they were throwing snowballs at each other in earnest. Felicia seemed to be on Niro's side. Glancing back at the house, Vimal realised that Kerry had moved into the middle of the courtyard and was watching. There was a strange expression on her face. Envy. She was wishing she could come and have fun too. Another snowball hit the side of his face. He turned to see Niro punch the air. He aimed his next one at her.

Vimal was no match for the two women; they had a ready-gathered supply of snow and there were two of them. Within minutes, he had forgotten all about the people watching him and was fighting to keep upright from the barrage. Eventually, he slipped and fell over and that was the end.

He crossed his arms above his head and said, 'I give up! You win!'

'I hate to say this,' said Felicia. 'But you suck at throwing snowballs.'

He peered through the gap between his forearms. 'I don't get to do it often.'

'In fairness, there were two of us against him.' Niro came up and stood next to him. She leaned down. 'It's okay. We've stopped now.'

He uncurled himself and sat up. 'Well, that's put me in my place.' He brushed some of the snow off his chest. Niro offered him a hand. He took it and tried to get up, but ended up pulling her down instead. She landed facedown next to him. Vimal flopped back onto the snow, laughing.

She pushed herself onto her knees. 'You git.' She picked up a handful of snow, with the clear intention of throwing it at him. He caught her wrist, so that she missed and the snow went in his hair instead. Still holding her arm, he made eye contact and felt a thrill of connection; a tingle ran right through him and made his breath catch. Her beautiful eyes, creased at the edges with amusement, widened. She stopped laughing, but the smile remained on her lips. Vimal's world narrowed. Suddenly, there was only Niro and him and snow and laughter ... and the world felt uncomplicated.

'Oh, you guys are so cute together,' Felicia said.

They both turned, just as she took a photo of them. He let go of Niro's hand and they got up, no longer laughing. The sudden intimacy seemed awkward now. The other sensations that had somehow been chased away a minute ago, rushed back in. He was cold. He dusted snow off himself again and shook it out of his hair.

Beside him, Niro did the same. She didn't look at him.

He heard male laughter. Lucien and Peter had come down to join them. Their laughter had an entirely different quality to it.

'I see you got a pasting from the girls,' Lucien said, the sneer just below the surface.

'There were two of them,' Vimal protested. He wasn't sure why he was protesting. He didn't mind. Not at all. He had forgotten how much fun it was to lose yourself in something silly like that.

'And Felicia is a pro,' Niro said, from next to him. She pulled off her gloves. 'My fingers are freezing. I'm going to go and warm up.' She stamped off into the house. Vimal finished brushing snow off himself and went back into the courtyard. He noticed that Kerry was watching him, her expression thoughtful. It should have made him happy, but right now he was too distracted to care.

Inside, he knelt to remove his boots. Something had changed with Niro and he didn't know what to make of it. He was used to her being his friend, but this newfound awareness of her as more than a friend was unsettling ... and exciting. He needed time to think about what it meant, what she meant and how he was going to deal with his feelings.

Removing his boots, he placed them next to Niro's ones. He was pretty sure she didn't feel anything more than friendship towards him. From the moment she agreed to this deal with him, she had been diligently helping him; in fact, she was the driving force that made any of it work. She reminded him to hold her hand, pushed him to talk to Kerry, engineered scenarios to make Kerry see him in a different light. She was helping him. It would be stupid of him to read more into that.

He reached the bedroom room and hesitated before he knocked. Niro had promised to help him get Kerry back and she was the sort of person who kept her word. A deal was a deal, she'd said. So that was all there was to it. He couldn't afford to lose focus at this point.

He knocked. When there was no response, he said, loudly, 'I'm coming in now' and went in.

*

Niro leaned against the door in the bathroom and fought the urge to cry. She had let her guard down. The snowball fight had thrown her right back to a more carefree time and she'd forgotten to be careful. In those few seconds, lying in the snow next to Vimal, breathless with laughter, she'd let him see how she felt and he had been surprised. Shocked, even.

She groaned and rubbed her face with her hands. Ouch, they were cold. She opened the hot tap and put her hands underneath it. The warmth turned her fingers red. As she dried her hands, she reflected that her face wasn't cold. It was burning.

She heard the door to the main room open and Vimal call, 'I'm coming in now!'

She shouted back, 'Okay' and leaned against the sink. What did she do now? She couldn't hide in the toilet. Pulling herself together and talking to him was her only option.

Patting her face dry of all the melted snow, she gave herself a stern glare in the mirror. She'd made a deal. If Kerry's thoughtful expression a few minutes ago was anything to go by, Vimal now stood a very good chance of winning her back. So, Niro had essentially fulfilled her side of the bargain. It was time for her to leave.

Steeling herself, she opened the bathroom door and went into the room. Vimal was sitting on his side of the bed, with his hands tucked under his armpits to warm up. He didn't quite look her in the eye. Oh dear. Niro's face felt hot all over again. Okay. She had to deal with this now before she made things worse.

Before he could say anything, Niro said, 'I think I should leave this evening.'

He blinked. 'You … you do?'

She nodded. 'I think my work here is done. You need me out

of here before the New Year's party gets going, so that you can talk to Kerry. You don't want her rebounding by pulling some random.'

He drew a breath as though to speak and then closed his mouth again, looking confused. Bless him, the thought that his beloved Kerry might choose solace in the arms of a stranger hadn't even occurred to him.

'There's a plane in the small hours tomorrow. I've checked online and I can use my open ticket to book in,' she said, quickly. 'We can arrange to have a big argument.'

Vimal sighed. He finally looked at her. 'What would we argue about?' His voice sounded weary. Resigned.

'I don't know … maybe I realised that you weren't genuinely into this arranged-match thing and got annoyed at you wasting my time.' A brainwave. 'Even better, we could pretend we'd already had the argument. That way, we don't have to do the shouting bit. Just be off with each other.'

'That would be better,' Vimal said. 'Less … drama.'

'Then if someone asks, you can say we decided it wasn't working out. We've been telling people we're using this holiday as a sort of trial run to see if we're compatible, right? So our deciding we're not, because you're clearly in love with your ex, would track.'

Vimal sighed. 'What if …'

She crossed her arms and waited for him to finish the sentence.

He didn't. Instead, he shook his head and said, 'You're good at reading people. Do you think Kerry is likely to change her mind about me?'

Ouch. Still, at least that told her that her intuition had been right all along. The man was in love with Kerry. It wasn't like he'd ever pretended not to be. She looked at him. He had tucked his hands under his thighs and was frowning at a spot on the floor. Poor, awkward Vimal. He didn't know how to read a room, so he erred on the side of kindness. How could you not love a man like that? But he trusted her opinion. So he deserved an honest answer.

She thought about all the interactions she'd seen with Kerry. 'In all honesty, I'm not sure. She's clearly fond of you. But you don't go out with someone for four years and leave without some feelings of fondness. Also, I suspect the thing that made her dump you in the first place was more about her needing to spread her wings and explore, rather than anything you'd done. She's done that now. Dated a few guys that she thought were glamorous and none of that lasted. Plus, she's seen a new, more adventurous side to you. So … I think you're in with a chance.'

He was still looking at the floor, thinking. Had he given up hope? She should go over to him and pat him on the shoulder reassuringly. Or say something motivating, but she couldn't bring herself to go near him. He wasn't for her. After this evening, she wouldn't even see him again. Her throat felt swollen and tight.

'You can never guess for sure how someone else feels,' she said, firmly. 'The only way to find out is to tell her how you feel and ask.'

He looked like he was about to say something. She wasn't sure she could bear to be there any longer.

'I'm going to go get a hot drink,' she said, and left the room before she gave in to the urge to blurt out her feelings.

Chapter 21

Vimal pulled off his T-shirt and glared at the shirts laid out on the bed. He was having his first ever fashion crisis. They had to dress smartly for the New Year's party. Niro had taken the bathroom, leaving him with the room to get changed in. He was trying to decide what to wear under his shirt.

The main event was outside, on the viewing platform, where they'd been setting up tables and heaters earlier. It would probably be cold. He picked up a thermal T-shirt. But part of the event was also inside, in the living room. Which would be warm. He didn't want to overheat. He clicked his tongue, put the thermal top back and picked up the short-sleeved T-shirt. The material felt thin in his hands. He would freeze outside. He put that back and put his hands on his hips. Seriously. How was this decision so difficult? He couldn't think straight. Everything was going wrong. The whole point of this week was for him to get Kerry back. Somehow, he'd managed to lose sight of that and develop feelings for another woman who wasn't interested in him either. On the plus side, Niro at least liked him as a person and didn't think he was boring. On the minus side, she was his friend and definitely not interested in him romantically, given how invested she was in helping him with Kerry.

He shook his head. All this wasn't helping him choose what to wear and he was getting cold standing there without a shirt on. The bathroom door unlocked. He grabbed the short-sleeved T-shirt. Behind him Niro gave a small squeak.

He turned to see her back away, a hand over her eyes. 'Sorry.'

Quickly, he pulled the T-shirt on. 'It's okay. You can come in now.'

'I'm sorry. I didn't think ...' She stepped back into the room, her hand still over her eyes.

'I'm decent now,' he said, amused. He took his shirt off the hanger and pulled it on.

Niro lowered her hand. She was wearing a black swing dress with a low-cut square neck. It drew attention to her magnificent cleavage and he had to concentrate on buttoning his cuffs so that he wasn't staring at it. 'You look nice,' he said. 'That dress really suits you.'

'Thanks. It's the wonder of shapewear.' She walked briskly across to the dressing table and sat in front of it.

Vimal finished getting dressed in silence. Every so often, he would look at Niro's rigid back and catch her eye in the mirror. She always looked away. Tonight, her hair was down, sitting in glossy waves on her shoulders. He wondered what it would be like to run it through his fingers.

He lifted his chin and did up his tie. 'I'm a bit worried about getting cold, when I go out onto the balcony,' he said. 'Aren't you?'

'I will be, in this dress,' she said. 'Which is why I have a shawl to take with me.'

'That's a good idea. We men don't get much choice in accessories.'

'Yes, but you have warmer clothes.' She put down her mascara and reached for her make-up bag again. 'A few years ago, I bought a men's jumper by mistake and it was so warm! And it had lovely big pockets. Now I always wear men's jumpers at home.'

He thought of her penchant for huge jumpers. He could see that.

'It's not like anyone's going to see me to judge,' she carried on, her voice carrying an undercurrent of defiance.

'I hadn't realised there was such a difference.' He sat down on the bed, looking away from her.

'Could you do me a favour?'

He turned. She was holding up a necklace. 'Could you put this on for me?'

'Oh. Of course.' He went over to her. It was going to be hard not to stare at her being this close. *Get it together, man. It's just putting on a necklace.* He used to do that for Kerry all the time.

Sitting on her stool, Niro lifted up her hair and moved it, releasing the scent of her perfume. It filled his nostrils and set his heart racing. He took the necklace and reached around her to put it on her. For this, he had to lean very close. From his distance, it would be easy to dip his head and kiss her. Focus. He had to focus.

A tendril of hair that had escaped when she gathered up her hair lay against her collarbone. He moved it out of the way, careful not to touch her. On her smooth, dark skin, goose bumps appeared where his fingertips had skimmed past. What if he ran his fingers over them? Would they disappear under the warmth of his hand? What if he leaned down just a fraction and pressed a kiss onto her shoulder? Or to the delicate place at the side of her neck where he would feel her pulse?

Breathing suddenly required extra concentration. He brought his arms around her, to raise the necklace into place. He wanted to touch her so badly. So badly. He looked up at the mirror. She was staring at his reflection, her eyes wide, lips slightly parted. For a second they held each other's gaze in the mirror, before she looked away, a frown creasing her forehead. With huge effort, Vimal managed to pull his concentration back to the task and fastened the necklace. His fingers grazed her neck and he heard her breath catch. He moved back quickly. What was wrong with him? Bad enough he'd been thinking about kissing her all afternoon, he didn't have to do inappropriate touching as well. She clearly didn't welcome it. He stood up straight, pushed his hands in his pockets and cleared his throat.

'You look great.'

It was a beat before Niro answered. 'You said. Thank you.' She cleared up her make-up things, her motions quick and precise.

He pulled out his phone and replied to a few more new-year messages. Niro stood and picked up a shawl that was lying on the bed. 'Shall we go?'

'Sure. Yes. Let's.'

She walked briskly past him. 'So, the plan for tonight is that we pretend we've fallen out. You get close to Kerry sometime before midnight. I'll leave the party around eleven thirty. So you can manoeuvre yourself into a place where she has to kiss you at midnight.'

That was the plan. He had known that for days, so why did each word feel like it was slamming into him?

'Yes,' he said. He didn't want that to be the plan anymore. 'Niro—'

She gave him a hard stare, her mouth set into a firm line. 'What?'

What could he say? She had promised him only that she would play a part. And she was clearly going to do that beautifully. He couldn't suddenly put her on the spot with his confused feelings for her. 'Are you sure this will work?'

'No, but it's the best plan we have,' she said.

'What if—'

She rolled her eyes. 'Come on. Be more positive than that. After she saw you eat a chocolate crepe and spontaneously join a snowball fight, she's bound to know you've changed. Have more faith in yourself.' She opened the door. 'Okay?'

A slight shift in the way she held herself and she was the old Niro again, back in character. Vimal followed her out, feeling several kinds of awful.

Chapter 22

Niro strode down the corridor, all too aware of Vimal's presence beside her. This was it. The last night. She just had to get through this and then he would be with Kerry and she wouldn't see him again. Well, she might, but not for a while. He should be pretty easy to avoid anyway. She sneaked a glance at him. The man could really rock a suit. A brief memory of him in just his trousers flashed through her mind. He wasn't bulky, but he was toned. Just the way she liked.

Not helping. Not helping. She had to stop thinking about that. She definitely had to stop thinking about his proximity when he'd put her necklace on her. It had taken everything in her power to not lean against him, or to turn her face to his and kiss him. It had been the most excruciating and most thrilling torture.

Suddenly, he caught her hand. She looked at him, startled. He gave her a small smile. Oh yes. The pretence. They were still doing that. This was their last night together. Halfway through this evening, she had to leave. She couldn't hold his hand. She just couldn't.

Niro stopped walking. 'Vimal,' she said, in an undertone. 'Maybe we shouldn't hold hands? If we've had an argument …'

'Oh. Right. Yes.' He dropped her hand like it had burned him.

It was a little insulting. He was clearly very nervous in anticipation of talking to Kerry. 'It'll be okay,' she said quietly. 'If it doesn't work out, at least you've tried everything and we'll go out for a drink and talk about it next year.'

He nodded, but he didn't look any happier. A giggle came from the living room. Someone was clearly amused by something.

Vimal let out a long breath and pulled himself upright. 'Okay. Let's go.'

Niro took a deep breath too. She joined him and they arrived at the living room door together, not holding hands.

Lucien gave a small whoop. 'Mistletoe!!' He pointed above their heads.

Niro looked up. Sure enough, there was a small bunch of mistletoe pinned to the doorframe.

'You have to kiss,' said Felicia, grinning delightedly.

'It's tradition,' said Lucien.

Niro looked at Vimal and saw the absolute horror on his face. He didn't want to kiss her. Of course he didn't. He looked at her with wide eyes. Right.

She fixed Lucien with her most withering glare. 'What are you? Twelve?'

Lucien spread his hands wide. 'Oh, come on. It's—'

Niro rolled her eyes and marched off towards the canapés. She didn't have time for Lucien's bloody mind games today. She stared, unseeing, at the stuff laid out in front of her and picked up something at random. It looked like a cheesy pastry. It was probably delicious, but she wasn't hungry. She picked up a plate and put the pastry on it. At least now she had something to hold.

A heightened sense of awareness told her that Vimal was approaching her.

He handed her a glass of white wine.

'Thanks.' She took it in her plate-free hand.

His eyebrow rose a fraction. She knew he was checking that she was all right. She tried to smile, but her mouth wouldn't cooperate, so she gave her head a little wobble that most South Asians would understand to mean 'okay'. Vimal gave the tiniest of nods.

A low whistle from Lucien made them both turn around. Kerry had arrived. She was wearing an emerald-green playsuit, which set off her dark hair and looked amazing. Niro suddenly felt fat and ungainly in a way that she hadn't done for ages. She glanced at Vimal; he was watching Kerry with a faintly worried air about him. She couldn't be here to watch this. Quite apart from it ruining the plan, seeing him being in love with Kerry just hurt too much.

'I say, Niro,' said Lucien. 'Would you mind taking a photo of all of us, before the rest of the people arrive?'

'You can't ask her to do that,' Vimal said. 'She's a professional. She charges for that sort of thing.'

'He's right, Lucien,' said Felicia. 'You can't expect Niro to do pro work for free.'

Niro wasn't sure what to say. On the one hand, they made an excellent point. On the other, it was a bit rude to refuse to take a photo.

Lucien threw up his hands. 'Well, fine, I'll pay her if she wants paying. But only if it's a bloody brilliant photograph.' His tone implied that it couldn't possibly be.

Cheeky bugger. 'Tell you what.' Niro put down her plate and glass. 'Let me get my good camera and tripod and I'll take a few photos. If you like one, you can buy it off me.'

'Can't argue with that, old chap,' said Peter.

Lucien waved a hand at her, as though to say 'go ahead'.

Niro fetched the camera and tripod and arranged people so that they were sitting or standing in a group. For a few shots, she set a timer, so that she could be in them too.

'For this last one,' she said. 'When I say "now" I want everyone except Lucien to get up slowly and walk away. Lucien, I want you to sit very still and look directly into the camera.'

'Whatever for?' said Magda.

How to explain it? 'I'm … trying to capture the sense of Lucien being the centre of activity. If he stays still, he will be in focus. Everyone else, won't be.'

Magda sniffed. 'I'm going to get myself a drink.' She left the room.

'Well, *I* think it sounds fun,' said Felicia.

When everyone remaining was seated in the right place, Niro did a few last-minute checks to make sure Lucien was clearly visible in the middle. 'Okay, now three, two, one … now!'

The resulting photo was exactly what she'd been hoping for. Lucien, in the middle of the picture, remained crystal clear, while everyone else was in motion around him, splashing outwards as they moved away. It made him the centre of attention. Almost as though to confirm it, Lucien's resting face had a hint of a smirk, giving him an air of smugness.

The minute she showed it to him, she knew he loved it.

'How much?' he said.

Across the room, Vimal raised his eyebrows. She named a price three times what she'd usually charge.

'Done. Send it to the office and I'll pick it up from there.'

'I'll keep the original, though,' she said. 'I might want to use it in an exhibition. Is that okay with you?'

'Sure. Whatever. So long as I get something to hang on my wall. Now, I need more wine.'

When Lucien had gone, Vimal came over and said, 'Well done.' She knew he was talking about having the courage to charge more, rather than the photo itself. That was all due to him. If he hadn't piped up, she would probably have taken the photo for free. She certainly wouldn't have charged that much for it. 'Thank you,' she said. She meant it. Vimal had been very good for her.

She showed him the photo. His eyebrows rose. 'That's impressive. You've somehow captured something that's very Lucien.'

'Let me see,' said Felicia, nudging Vimal, so that he ended up pressed into Niro. She looked up at him, disturbed by how close he was and her own urge to get closer. Vimal took a step back, making space for Felicia.

'You're right,' said Felicia. 'It has captured the essence of Lucien. Wow. That's really good.'

'Essence of Lucien,' said the man himself. 'I should bottle that.'

'There is such a thing as being too entrepreneurial,' said Peter.

'Have you got a photo that captures the essence of me?' said Felicia.

'I took one,' said Niro. 'It's the one I took of you when we walked into town the first time.'

'Oh yes, I like that one.' Felicia nudged her gently. 'You're good. How about Vimal? Do you have a photo of him?'

Niro gave her a sharp glance. She hadn't forgotten her conversation with Felicia earlier. Apparently, neither had Felicia. She glanced back at Vimal, who shrugged.

'As it happens, I quite like this one.' She scrolled back to the photo she'd taken on the first day. He was laughing, in the cold. There was something about the moment, his shoulders descending, his head rising, that spoke to the way Vimal held himself in the world. Not quite comfortable, but not really bothered.

'Oh, Vimal, look.' Felicia turned and dragged him back next to Niro. Vimal looked so uncomfortable, that Niro felt she had to rescue him. He just wanted to get close to Kerry and Felicia was trying to push him towards Niro. The poor guy was probably very confused by all this. She wasn't overly impressed either. She didn't need reminding that her time with him was over.

'I think I'll take the camera back to the room.' She turned the screen off, gave Felicia an apologetic smile and hurried away.

As she went back, she noticed that in the kitchen, the caterers were busy putting things on trays. Helga was one of them. Niro smiled at her and got a quick smile in return. She watched the methodical way they worked. It suddenly occurred to her that she could record this. Until now, she'd only taken photos of the main party and how they interacted with the setting. But if she intended to record this 'break' with any kind of accuracy, she should record some behind-the-scenes stuff.

She carefully positioned herself far enough from the caterers to not be in the way. 'Can I take some photos of you working?'

Helga said, 'Yes, of course.'

She could hide away in here, taking photos and avoiding having to spend time out in the living room with everyone else. Thank god for the camera. It gave a good excuse to be anywhere and gave her something to do when she didn't want to make eye contact. She was happily snapping away, when Vimal came to find her.

She crouched down to get a better angle on the food. 'Have you spoken to Kerry yet?'

'Not yet,' Vimal said. 'Listen, Niro. I—'

Thankfully, Felicia came in at just the right moment. Niro turned to her and said, 'Hi' with slightly more enthusiasm than strictly necessary. Vimal scowled briefly before his normal polite expression returned.

'What are you two doing hiding in here? Come and join the party.' Felicia made ushering motions with her hands.

'Who are all the extra people?' Niro murmured to Felicia as she was being hustled out.

'Some of them are guests from Basty's hotel. Some of them are … oh, I dunno. Randoms that Lucien knows, who flew over just for the party. Who cares?' She thrust a glass of champagne into Niro's hand. 'It's a party. Have fun!'

Fun was the last thing Niro felt like having right now, but she had to try. Kerry, standing by the big glass window, drew the eye immediately. The artist in her got the better of her and she took a photo. Wait, was Kerry wearing Magda's earrings? She almost turned to Vimal to whisper something about it to him, but realised just in time that she was meant to look like she'd fallen out with him. So she caught Felicia's arm and asked her instead.

'I think so.' Felicia raised her glass in front of her face to hide her smirk. 'They suit her much better than Magda, right?' She took a sip and smiled at Lucien, who was talking to someone on the other side of the room.

'I … She does look incredible.'

'She does,' said Felicia. 'And you're not the only one to notice. Excuse me a minute. I must go and remind Lucien that I'm the one he's brought as a guest.' She grinned and sashayed across the room, the sequined hem of her very short dress flicking from side to side as she walked.

Niro took a sip of her drink. She could only dream about that level of self-confidence. Felicia reached Lucien, flicked her hair and put a hand on his shoulder, a move that got his attention. Niro raised her camera and took a photo. Felicia looked beautiful and young. Lucien was clearly staring down her cleavage like a perv. Niro took another picture of Felicia waving at her. When she was done, Vimal had turned to talk to someone. Everyone she knew was distracted, so she took the opportunity to leave the room.

The balcony upstairs had been transformed. Half the area was under a white canopy. There was a small booth to house the DJ and temporary heaters and lights had been put up to make the space an oasis of warmth and colour, set against the dazzling white of the snow around it. She didn't want to think about how much energy it would be wasting. The people who had designed Villa Cachée had gone to great lengths to minimise the environmental impact of it, and here was Lucien burning up energy just to add to the area's sound and light pollution. She shook her head.

It was quiet up here. She found a corner and fiddled with her camera to get a decent exposure time. If she was lucky, she could capture the light and still have a hint of the dark mountains behind. It would require some messing around with the image later.

It occurred to her that this would be ideal fodder for a show titled, *The Son of His Lordship Has a Party*. She could showcase the waste and the disregard for the local landscape. Hmm. That wasn't a bad idea. She had permission to take photos. Dammit, though. She'd have to be nice to Lucien to get him to sign the release waiver ...

She lowered her camera and looked back out at the village below. Why not? She disliked Lucien intensely, but she did sort of owe this holiday to him. Being 'nice' wasn't such a hardship, was it? She would be leaving in a few hours, anyway, so it wasn't for very long.

She scrolled through the images on the camera and pulled up the photo she'd taken earlier – the one Lucien had loved. She could use that as the main image. It conveyed so much of his attitude. Swapping over to her phone, she quickly drafted up an email, attached her usual waiver and hit send. He probably wouldn't check his email until the next day.

It was chilly out here. Niro moved closer to the heater and watched. A few people drifted up the stairs. Most of them stood at the edges of the balcony, enjoying the view of the village that was a pool of light in the darkness. It felt late. She yawned and checked her phone. Not even ten. If she left now, she would have time to kill before her 2am flight. It was so cheap because no one wanted to fly out at that time. She took one last look at the party and crept back downstairs.

It was noisier and busier than before. When she peered into the living room, she spotted Vimal, with his back to her, talking to some random person. If he was going to talk to Kerry, he really should get on with it. Still, it wasn't something she could help with. She had done what she'd promised to do. The rest was up to him. Kerry, standing at the other side of the room, spotted her and gave her a quizzical look. She quickly smiled, waved with her fingers and fled to her room.

Once back, she found the number for the reception desk and called Martin.

'Ah, hello. Yes, we can ask your taxi to come early. They will be about twenty minutes.'

'Thanks, Martin, you're a star.'

Packing didn't take long. She crammed everything into the case and zipped it shut. Pulling it to the floor, she was faced with the sight of the enormous bed, with the pillow wall still in place. Her heart gave a painful squeeze. She sank down onto the stool by the dressing table. For a minute, she allowed herself to indulge in the memory of Vimal solemnly talking about mountains and beauty. He was so intense. Tears made the pillow wall distort in front of her. So intense. So kind. He reminded her of all the things she'd forgotten that she was. When she was with him, she felt … alive and powerful. It was like he was the polar opposite of Mick. Where Mick had taken away her confidence, Vimal had given it back.

A tear spilled over. She quickly dabbed at it before remembering that her make-up didn't matter anymore. No one would care at the airport. She cleared her throat and stood up. This had been an adventure and it had done her some good, she knew. When the pain subsided, she would appreciate it. There was no point sitting here. Felicia might decide to come looking for her. Or worse, Vimal might, and she just couldn't give him a pep talk about approaching Kerry. Not again. Not now.

She felt bad about not saying goodbye, but she couldn't face him. So a note was the best she could manage. She had told him that she was leaving on the early morning plane, so he wouldn't be surprised if she was gone. After all, she was only going a little bit earlier than planned. Should she tell him how she was feeling? Perhaps she should. Before she could change her mind, she added, *I simply can't pretend any more* in between the last line and her signature.

After gathering her things, she poked her head out the door. There was no one there. The sound of music and laughter came from the main part of the house and followed her all the way until, safely booted and zipped into her coat, she stepped into the corridor.

The wheels of her suitcase sounded deafening as she walked down to the exit. Helga was sitting on the desk, talking to Martin. Although, judging by the state of her hair, they had been doing something else before they heard her rolling her suitcase down the corridor. They both smiled at her.

'You are leaving?' said Helga. 'Before even the fireworks?'

Niro wanted to speak, but there was a lump in her throat, so she nodded instead and swallowed.

'She has a plane to catch,' Martin explained.

'I do.' Niro nodded again.

'But your boyfriend is not going?' Helga peered behind her, as though expecting Vimal to appear.

'No. He's not. And he's not my boyfriend ... anymore.'

Both their faces were portraits of horror. Helga recovered first. 'I am sorry to hear that.'

Niro shrugged. Tears were threatening again and she couldn't cry here. That would be too pathetic, even for a drama queen like her.

The crunch of tyres over gravel alerted her to the car arriving. 'It's here,' she said. 'I ... Thank you very much for all your help.' She gave Helga a quick smile. 'I have some lovely pictures of you. Just DM me on Instagram and I'll send them to you.'

'I will do that.' Helga hopped off the desk and suddenly, Niro was enveloped in a hug. 'I am sorry you are leaving this place with sad memories.' Helga squeezed her. 'The taxi is driven by my cousin. I will tell him to take good care of you.'

Moved by the unexpected hug, Niro felt her eyes fill with tears. She brushed them away. 'Thank you. I'll be okay.'

It was much colder outside than she'd thought. Those heaters on the balcony must have been quite effective. She looked up. From here, she could see one side of the balcony, especially as it was lit up in contrast to the dark mountain behind it. Music drifted down. There was warmth and light and beauty up there and she didn't belong. Vimal didn't really belong there either, but he fitted in far better than she could. Besides, with Kerry at his side, he would be fine.

Chapter 23

Her phone rang. It was Sam. Thank god. She had left three messages already. Being alone with her thoughts in the back of a taxi to the airport was not fun. She needed to talk to someone.

'Sorry I didn't get your call,' Sam said, instead of saying hello. 'I was talking to Gihan. You know, seeing as it's New Year's Eve. What's going on? It's the big plan tonight, right?'

'Yeah.' Her voice wobbled, even in that one word.

'Oh, Niro. What's happened?'

When she gave her a rundown of the evening, Sam said, 'So … you've left him with Kerry and you're running away?'

'That was the deal. I was going to leave a bit later than this, at about half eleven, but apart from that, this is exactly what the deal was.' She wiped away tears.

'Did you talk to him at all? How did he seem?'

Niro closed her eyes. 'I dunno. He was a bit wired, but that's understandable. Probably nervous. He … Oh god, Sam. Lucien had put up this mistletoe and when we walked in he said we have to kiss and you should have seen Vimal's face. I've never seen anyone look so horrified. If the thought of a peck on the lips under mistletoe is so awful to him, imagine how embarrassing it would have been if I'd told him how I felt.'

Outside the countryside slid quietly by. The roads were eerily quiet. Everyone must be inside, celebrating. Sam was quiet for so long that Niro thought they'd been cut off. 'Sam? Are you still there?'

'Yes. I am. I don't know, Niro …'

'He and Kerry … I can see how it went wrong, but they are so well suited. They're both work-focused and successful. She'd be a much better person for him than I ever would.'

'Wait, no! You can't say that.'

'Why not? It's true. I … I don't have a real job. I haven't sold any art in a long time. Hell, I haven't even taken any decent pictures in ages. The only way I can even afford to go on holiday is to pimp myself out to be a fake girlfriend.'

'Niro!' Sam's voice was shocked. 'That is categorically not true. Didn't you sell a bunch of photos this week? To that guy who owns the hotel?'

'Yeah, that was Vimal.'

'What? He took the photos, did he?'

Niro shook her head. She could almost picture Sam's expression. 'You *know* what I mean.'

'You took the photos that the man liked. Not only that, he liked them enough to pay the higher price. It seems to me like he knows good photography when he sees it. So does Vimal, by the sound of it. The only one who doesn't is you.'

Niro drew a breath to respond, but Sam wasn't finished.

'You know, if I ever see Mick again, I'm going to throttle him for what he did to you. I don't just mean the cheating on you. I mean destroying your confidence. He did a proper number on you, that bastard.'

Niro sighed. 'Anyway. I'll be home at some godawful hour in the morning.'

'Do you need Luke to come and meet you at the airport and see you home?'

'Nah. It's New Year's Eve. There'll be lots of people everywhere.'

'Still though. Tell me when you land and we'll come meet you off the shuttle bus from the airport.'

'Thanks, Sam. You're a good mate.'

'I feel bad,' said Sam. 'I encouraged you to go on this mad trip. I thought you might enjoy playing a role and getting out a bit. You hardly ever leave the flat these days and I was worried ... I'm sorry.'

Now Niro felt bad for unloading on her cousin. Sam might have odd ideas sometimes, but she had always been in Niro's corner. Especially after Mick left. She remembered all too well the hundreds of cups of tea, the favourite meals pushed into her hands even when she had no appetite, the hours and hours of romcoms. Sam had always looked out for her. 'It's not your fault. It wasn't a bad idea. I got to take some nice photos.'

'Did you get anything you could enter into the competition?'

Niro thought back to the photos she'd taken. 'Yes, actually. I have a few contenders. It's an impressive building, the way it's almost invisible until you look at it from certain angles.' She nodded to herself. 'Yeah. I took some really nice photos. You know, I even did a few walks and just took photos of interesting things. I haven't done that in ... a very ... long time.' Not since Mick. She frowned. She hadn't done that since Mick left. It had been the thing that kickstarted her creativity. The thing she loved. Seeing the extraordinary in the mundane. She touched the bag containing her camera, which was never far from her. She had found her eye again.

'Niro? Niro? Did we get cut off.'

'No. No. I'm here. I just thought of something.'

There was a pause before Sam said, 'What?'

'I took a lot of photographs, Sam. I felt a real buzz doing that. I had forgotten what it was like to take a really nice photo and just love it.'

'That's good. You got your mojo back. That makes the trip worthwhile, even if everything else went a bit wrong.'

It felt like something had creaked open and let in a chink of light. 'You're right. I know you're right.' Niro sniffed and dried the last of her tears. 'At least I got my photography back. That's something.' She sat up a little straighter. She could hear Luke ask something in the background and Sam, muffled, as though she'd put her hand over the phone, reply. It was New Year's Eve. They must have had plans.

'Listen, Sam,' she said, when her cousin came back. 'You get on with your evening. I'll text you when I get on the plane.'

'Call me when you get back to Blighty,' said Sam. 'I mean it. We'll come and meet you.'

'Sure. I will. I promise. You go have a good time.'

'If you're sure you'll—'

'Go already. I'll be fine.'

Once she'd hung up, she stared out of the window, where the view was mostly darkness. Sam was right. She had recovered her art and she *had* sold her photographs to someone who clearly thought they were worth the price. Had her work always been worth that price? Was she underselling herself like Vimal said she was?

She patted the camera bag again. If she had underestimated her skill, what else had she underestimated?

For a moment, when Vimal had been putting her necklace on her, she thought there had been something. When his eyes met hers in the mirror, she could have sworn there was a flash of hunger. It had only been brief before he had looked away, but she had felt it to her core. But then he'd rushed off, leaving her to second-guess the evidence in front of her own eyes.

She rubbed a hand over her eyes. He had been trying to talk to her and she hadn't been ready to listen. Come to think of it, she might even have talked over him a bit because she wanted to get her own part over and done with. What if he was trying to tell her that he'd changed his mind about Kerry? Or that he wasn't so sure that Kerry was the only one for him? She hadn't dared to listen.

He didn't see her the way Mick saw her. Mick had always made her feel like she was a work in progress. Like she could be improved until she was worthy. Vimal treated her like she was already worthy of his respect. Even when she didn't believe she was.

Maybe Mick's way of seeing things was nothing to do with her. It was all to do with Mick and his baggage. The more she thought about it, the more she saw that he'd undermined her with his actions. It was all about making him look good; even helping her and praising her when she was a student had been about making himself out to be a great mentor. She had mistaken it for genuine interest in her and her work. She'd felt buzzed by being with him, but never ... valued.

Vimal, with all his awkwardness, made her feel safe and valued. He had called her beautiful, in his own weird way. So why was she so sure that she'd imagined the want in his eyes? Why was she listening to the Mick voice in her head, when she could be listening to the Vimal one instead?

Her phone buzzed. Idly, she opened her messages and found that Felicia had sent her photos of them when they fell over in the snow. There was one where both she and Vimal were looking at the camera, Vimal's eyes were wide as though he was surprised by the camera pointed at him. She scrolled past. There was another photo, taken a second or two before. Niro had her face turned away. Laughter still lingered at the corners of Vimal's mouth, but his expression was a mixture of surprise and ... something that looked like tenderness. Just a few days ago, she had wished someone would look at her like that. And here was evidence that someone had. She shook her head and turned the screen off. How was that even possible?

After a few seconds, she turned the screen back on again and studied the photo again. Yes. Tenderness and maybe a bit of surprise. The fact that it was her he was gazing at with that expression on his face ...

She had accepted his look of horror under the mistletoe

instantly, but wasn't this expression just as valid? Again, she thought of the hunger in his eyes when he'd glanced at her in the mirror.

It had taken her a few days to realise how she felt about him. Why wouldn't it be the same for him?

'Excuse me.' She leaned forward and patted the seat in front. 'Excuse me. We have to go back.'

*

Vimal stood to one side in the living room and tried to work out what to do. There were more people here now, people he didn't know, and he hated that. Even the music, which would have been fine under normal circumstances, felt overwhelming.

At first, he'd assumed that Lucien's party would be intimate, including only the small group who had been there for a few days. But seeing the preparations had made him realise it was bigger than that. For some reason he'd thought he would cope. He might have, if Niro or Kerry were there to quell the anxiety, but they weren't and he was feeling trapped.

He hadn't seen Niro in ages. He wondered where she could be. Upstairs, maybe, trying to find the perfect shot to capture the atmosphere for the party. He wished she were holding his hand. There was something very grounding about Niro. She didn't mind that he was uncomfortable with social situations. She just let her own personality bubble up around them, insulating him. He gave an abstract smile to someone who nodded to him. Thankfully, they didn't stop to talk to him. His brain was reeling too much for him to come off as anything but weird.

Out of the corner of his eye, he saw Kerry move across the room. She looked amazing tonight. Everything about her was so familiar. How many times had he watched her cross a room and noticed the way her hips moved when she walked in high heels? Except, all those other times, he had been her boyfriend.

He had marvelled that she had chosen him, out of all the people in the room, to be with. That wasn't true anymore. Looking at her now, he felt … nothing. No sense of longing. Nothing more than the echo of their shared past. Kerry was wonderful and they had once had something amazing, but she didn't want him now. Not unless he changed who he was. She had told him that over and over and he just hadn't understood … until that afternoon. The strange thing was that he *had* changed who he was, but he'd done it because of Niro.

He knew he'd been less tense since he met Niro. He'd become the sort of guy who joined a snowball fight knowing he had no hope of winning. He made jokes – okay, they were lame ones – but Niro got them. He loved making her laugh. He had come on this holiday wanting to get Kerry back, but now all he could think about was Niro. Somewhere along the way, something had switched and he couldn't imagine how he'd ever managed to be ambivalent towards her. What was wrong with him?

He was convinced that Niro didn't want him, though. Her reaction to the mistletoe had proved that.

But he was bad at reading people. He knew that. So what if he'd got it wrong? What if Niro's reaction was just part of her acting? Only minutes before, they had agreed to pretend to have had an argument. His heartbeat picked up. He looked around the room, hope dawning. No Niro. If he had read the situation wrongly, then … there was a chance that Niro saw him as more than a friend. Hadn't she told him not to guess how people felt? He would have to find her and ask her. At the very least, he had to call off the plan so that they had one more night to sort things out.

He put his glass down and eased his way out of the living room. It was slightly quieter in the kitchen, but Niro wasn't there. Okay, upstairs. Now that he'd decided, it was vitally important that he saw her. She wasn't due to leave for the airport until later. So she would be around here somewhere, taking photos. He took the stairs at a run.

On the balcony, people were milling around. A few people were dancing. He scanned the place. He couldn't see Niro anywhere. He did a quick walk around, just in case.

'Vimal.' It was Felicia. 'Hey! How are you enjoying the party?' She sounded drunk.

'Have you seen Niro?' he asked. 'I have to talk to her.'

Felicia's eyes narrowed, suddenly sharper. 'Is something wrong?'

'I don't know. I need to talk to her urgently.'

'Um. The last time I saw her, she was heading back to your room. That was a while ago now. What's wrong? Did you guys have a fight?'

Of course, they were meant to have argued. That was part of the cover story. He didn't have time to explain. 'Something like that,' he said. 'I have to find her.'

'You guys are so cute together,' she said.

Vimal nodded, distractedly. 'I can't stop right now, I'll chat to you later, okay?'

She shouted, 'Good luck' and he raised a hand to acknowledge it and plunged down the steps. A quick sweep of the games room, the kitchen and the living room failed to produce Niro. He even checked outside on the patio, which was full of people bundled up against the cold, standing around the fire. Not there either.

She couldn't have left already. It wasn't eleven thirty yet. She would have messaged him to say goodbye at the very least. He checked his phone as he went back to their room. Nothing. She had to be in the room. That was the only place left.

He knew the moment he entered the room that she was gone. The clutter of her various bottles and tubs had disappeared from the dressing table. The phone charger was no longer plugged into the socket by the bed. He knew without looking that her coat wasn't hanging up in the closet behind the door. He walked further into the room, reaching for his phone.

There was a note on his bedside shelf. Putting his phone back into his pocket, he unfolded the note.

231

Dear Vimal. I've decided to go to the airport a bit early. I've done what I promised to do. You don't need me for the next part. Good luck.

I simply can't pretend any more.

Niro.

He sat down on the bed. Well, that was clear enough. He'd been wrong. She definitely was only holding up her side of the bargain. And now she was gone.

He read the short note again. *I simply can't pretend any more.* Was it so hard pretending to be his girlfriend? She had seemed so relaxed and comfortable the whole time. But then again, she saw it as an acting role; she had been very clear about that. Seeming relaxed was part of the job. He had thought that he could tell when she was in character and when she was being herself, but that was him deluding himself. Who was he kidding? He wasn't good at reading people. He never had been.

He got up and walked over to her side of the bed. The pillow wall was still in place, just as he'd built it. The cleaners had stopped dismantling it now.

Thank goodness for the pillow wall. It had been a stern reminder that what they had was a deal. Not a relationship. Or even, it seemed, a friendship. He stared at the space Niro usually occupied; mostly, in the mornings, all he saw was the top of her head poking out from under the duvet.

He sat down. The last time he'd encroached onto her side of the bed, she had been in tears. That couldn't have been an act. Perhaps that moment of vulnerability was the only time he'd seen the real Niro. He put a fist against his stomach, which burned. All happiness drained out of him. How could he be so stupid?

She was out there, alone. He couldn't let that happen. Even if she didn't want him, she was his friend. As a friend, he should check that she was okay. Yes. That's what he'd say. He'd got her note and he was just checking in. He could casually ask her if pretending to be his girlfriend really was so hard that she could no longer bear it.

He rang her number, but the line was busy. 'Leave your message after the tone.' What should he say? Panicked, he hung up.

Chapter 24

When Niro arrived back at the entrance to Villa Cachée it was nearly midnight. The driver followed her into the foyer and spoke rapid German to Martin. There was probably some explaining to do. Yes, she knew she was asking a lot of him, making him drive to and fro. She'd got that from the various hand gestures and bits of English. She had to tried to explain, but her German was worse than his English, so she had no idea if she'd succeeded.

Helga was still there. Niro thrust the suitcase towards her. 'Please can you look after this for ten minutes?' When the girl nodded, Niro set off at a run up the sloping corridor to the main house. She still had her camera and handbag, which she had to clutch to herself so that they didn't bang against her as she ran. This was another reason not to take up running, frankly. Where did you put your stuff?

At the door, she paused to catch her breath before she punched in the entry code. She had no idea what she was going to say to Vimal. She just had to get there before he kissed Kerry. Reminding herself that she was at least as good for him as Kerry, she let herself into the house. Rather than go through the hassle of taking off her boots, she pulled some shoe covers on from the much depleted basket and set off towards the living room at a determined pace.

As she rounded the corner, she saw the door to their bedroom. Kerry was standing outside, hand raised to knock. Niro quickly ducked back round the corner. Heart pounding, she peered round to see Kerry knock.

A heartbeat and Vimal opened the door, his expression eager. Niro pulled back and flattened herself against the wall. Bile rose in her throat. She was too late. It wasn't even midnight. He must have told her early. She edged round cautiously, in time to see the door close. No. She rested her head against the wall. *No, no, no.*

This was not how it was supposed to end. The mad dash at the end was meant to be enough to prevent disaster. Clearly not. This was not a movie and her feelings didn't trump everything. Vimal was still in love with Kerry. He had never told her otherwise. She was stupid to think that he might have changed his mind. Stupid. Stupid. Stupid.

She had to get out of there.

Within a minute, she was walking down the corridor to the exit again. The taxi driver was still there, talking to Martin and Helga. At the sight of her dragging her feet down the corridor, Helga turned to Martin and whispered something.

Helga walked up to meet her. 'Are you okay?'

Niro shook her head. Tears threatened. She blinked them back. 'I am ready to go to the airport now.'

The driver rolled his eyes and said something in German to Martin.

'I'm sure this time,' Niro said. You didn't need to speak the language to understand what he'd said.

The driver looked at his watch and said something else.

'He says your plane will go soon. There might not be enough time to get there ...' Martin looked worried.

'Please.'

Helga snapped out some rapid-fire comments. Niro didn't understand it, but she heard the tone of voice and saw the hand gestures. It was loosely, *Look at the poor girl and stop being an a-hole*. She remembered that the man was Helga's cousin. Perhaps cousins were the same the world over.

The driver looked abashed and mumbled something.

'The roads will be quiet, but you must hurry.' Helga pushed her case towards her.

'Thank you so much.' Niro grabbed her case and ran out to the taxi.

When she finally got into the taxi, her limbs felt like lead. She had made the dramatic dash to declare her love and failed. As she was driven away for the second time, the sky exploded in colourful sparks. Her phone buzzed. Somehow it seemed like the whole world was trying to rub it in. With a sigh, she turned her phone off.

*

Someone was knocking on Vimal's door. Irrationally, hope rose. Maybe Niro had changed her mind? Maybe pretending wasn't so bad after all? He practically ran to the door and threw it open, stepping out to meet her as he did so.

It wasn't Niro. It was Kerry, who smiled at him and said, 'Er ... hello.'

Momentum had taken him too close to her. He stepped back. 'Kerry.'

'I think we need to talk,' she said. When she moved forward, he automatically stepped back, which meant he couldn't stop her when she walked in.

Vimal's heart rate accelerated. No. No. This would never do. A few days ago, Kerry coming to his room would have been a dream come true, but now, it was the last thing he needed. He wanted to be alone to think about what he was going to say to Niro to get her to come back, or at least get her to meet him in London later to see if he could talk to her under different circumstances. He couldn't do that with Kerry here. He had to explain – but after the way he'd been for the last few days, mooning over her, unsubtly, he realised now ... how could he tell her?

Kerry opened her mouth to speak.

He interrupted her. 'Kerry, listen. I'm really sorry if I gave you the wrong idea.' Honesty compelled him to add, 'I admit that when we started this holiday, I did want us to get back together.' Now that he'd started talking, his mouth seemed to be on autopilot. 'I was a bit mad with it, to be honest. I sort of arranged for Niro to come with me and pretend to be my girlfriend to make you jealous.' He looked up at her. Why was he confessing this? And *why* was she smiling at him like that? 'What?'

'I know,' she said.

'How—'

'I've been watching you guys together. You were so ... odd together to start with.'

How were they odd together? What had given them away? If Kerry had worked it out, who else had guessed? So many questions! Vimal shook his head. He had to focus. The priority here was getting rid of Kerry so that he could call Niro and explain how he felt. He didn't like decisions, but on this, he was clear.

'That's not the point. The point is that things have changed,' he said, firmly. 'I'm not in love with you, Kerry. I thought I was, but no. I'm in love with Niro. I'm really sorry.' Why was she *still* smiling?

'I know. That's why I'm here. I came to tell you that you need to get past whatever it is you're still holding for me. You so clearly belong with Niro and I thought you didn't realise. But it seems you do. So I think you should stop wasting your time and go and find her and tell her how you feel.'

'I can't. She's gone.'

The smile disappeared from Kerry's face. 'Gone? What do you mean, gone?'

He held out the note to her. She took it and read it. 'No. No. That can't be right.' She looked up. 'Have you called her?'

'I was going to, but someone barged into my room to tell me things I already knew.' It came out sharper than he'd intended.

'I'm sorry. I'm just—'

Kerry moved past him to the door. 'You're right, though. I'll leave you in peace. You call her. I've seen the way you look at her. Don't let her get away.' She opened the door. 'Good luck. If Felicia or I can help in any way, let us know.' She left, shutting the door behind her.

Vimal stared at the closed door in confusion. What had just happened? What did Felicia have to do with anything?

It didn't matter. He needed to call Niro and tell her ... what? That he liked her. That he'd been longing to kiss her since ... He wasn't sure since when. It had sort of snuck up on him. It had started with a feeling of being comfortable around her, being part of a team and somehow, at some point, he'd started noticing the way her eyes seemed to contain several shades of brown when the light caught them, the plumpness of her bottom lip, the way she had curves everywhere. Somehow, over the course of a day or so, she'd gone from someone whom he merely liked and respected to someone he adored.

He sat on the bed and took out his phone. When Lucien had demanded they kiss under the mistletoe, his first reaction was fear, because there was no way he would be able to conceal his feelings from her then. How on earth did you fake a nonchalant kiss when you just wanted to kiss the hell out of that person? Thankfully, she'd been playing the part of the post-argument woman and had flounced off.

Wait. Had she done that because she was playing the part? Or because she didn't want to kiss him? Vimal groaned and lay back. What if she only saw him as a friend? She had thrown herself into the role so well and she had been so helpful in trying to get him together with Kerry. What on earth made him think she would be interested in him? He was the loser who was pining so badly for his ex that he'd asked someone to be a fake girlfriend. Who did that, frankly?

He stared at the ceiling for a minute.

You can never guess for sure how someone else feels, Niro had said. *The only way to find out is to tell her how you feel and ask.*

His phone buzzed. 'Niro.' He sat up and looked at the display. It was not Niro. It was a 'Happy New Year' message from his parents. Another text appeared. And another. In the distance, he could hear muffled pops and bangs. It must be midnight.

He impatiently swiped away the notifications and dialled Niro's number. His pulse thundered in his ears. The phone went straight to answerphone. Again. He hung up. Again.

Why wasn't she answering her phone?

Okay. He needed a new plan. He would have to go after her. He pulled out his suitcase and started to throw things into it. He put his phone on speaker and called Martin at the security desk.

'Hi, Martin. I need a taxi to go to the airport.'

'That will not be possible,' said Martin. 'I'm sorry. There is only one taxi working today and he has just gone with your ... um. Your friend. To the airport.'

Vimal stopped in the middle of rolling up his running kit. 'But there must be someone. I'll pay them whatever they ask.'

'No. I am very sorry. There will not be anyone who is safe to drive such a distance tonight.'

Of course. It was New Year's Eve. Everyone would have been out partying.

'I would offer to take you myself,' said Martin. 'But I have to stay here. I am on duty until the morning.'

'No. No. That's okay,' Vimal said. It was kind of Martin to offer. 'Happy New Year to you and Helga.'

'Thank you. I hope ... I hope you mend your relationship in the new year.'

'I hope so too.'

He hung up and looked down at the suitcase. Now what? He tried Niro again.

'Niro, it's Vimal. I need to talk to you. Call me back.'

Then, because he was getting desperate, he called Sam.

'Hi, Sam, it's Vimal.'

'Yes?' Sam sounded cold and distant.

He faltered. 'I ... I'm trying to get hold of Niro.'

'Have you tried her phone?'

'She's not answering.'

'Perhaps she's busy.'

'Is she okay? I just wanted to check that she was safe.'

'She's fine. I've spoken to her. You need not worry.' Sam sounded cautious, almost wary.

'She's on her way home ...'

'I know,' said Sam.

Vimal gave up. Clearly Niro had been in touch with her cousin and told her the plan. Even more clearly, Sam wasn't going to tell him anything. 'I ... Tell her I'm worried about her. Okay?'

There was a crackling sound, like Sam had sighed. 'I will. Don't worry, Vimal. We'll look after her.'

'Can you tell her that I need to talk to her?'

'Yes. I'll tell her,' said Sam. 'Thanks for checking on her, Vimal. Goodnight.'

He hung up and lay back on the bed. In his hand, his phone buzzed with New Year's messages. He turned it to silent and lifted his head to look across at the empty side of the bed. How had he managed to spend so many days with Niro and fail to realise that he was slowly falling for her? Everyone else had noticed, it seemed. Kerry knew.

If he'd realised a day earlier, he could have done something about it ...

Except, he'd known this evening and he'd done nothing to stop her from leaving. He thumped a fist against his forehead. What an idiot.

*

By the time Niro was on the shuttle bus home, she was exhausted. Everything seemed pointless. The worst part was that she only

240

had herself to blame. Vimal had been completely honest about wanting to get Kerry back. He had been courteous and respectful of her the whole time, despite the crushing awkwardness of their situation. They had even joked about it. It had been monumentally stupid of her to let herself catch feelings for him. So stupid.

No doubt, she would hear from him in the next few days, thanking her for helping him get back together with Kerry. She had no idea how she was going to bear that. Right now, all she wanted to do was to curl up and crumble into dust.

It was very early morning when she stumbled off the shuttle bus. Sam rushed forward and enveloped her in a hug. Niro held on to her cousin and buried her face in her shoulder.

'Oh, Niro,' Sam said. 'It'll be okay.'

The pressure behind her eyes was almost painful. She blinked it back. 'Are you sure? I didn't think I could feel worse than when Mick left, but … I do.'

Luke came up, carrying her bag. He too put an arm around her. 'Let's get you home.'

No one said anything for the short drive home. Outside the car window, people staggered home after a night of fun. Somewhere in a valley in Switzerland, Vimal would be falling asleep in Kerry's arms. The pillow wall would have been thrown to the floor. The thought made her feel sick.

The tears that she'd been holding back finally came. She wiped her cheeks with her palm. Sam turned around to look at her from the front seat.

'I'm okay,' Niro lied.

Sam wanted to talk to her when they got home, but Niro begged tiredness. Tears were still leaking out of her eyes at odd intervals and she knew there were more to come. When she finally crawled into her own familiar bed, she gave herself up to the tears. This wasn't pretty, dainty crying. This was proper ugly crying. Eventually, exhausted, she fell asleep.

Chapter 25

Vimal rolled over and came up against the pillow wall. For one second, it seemed like everything was normal. It was still dark and he had no idea if he was remembering a nightmare or real life. Awake now, he reached across the pillow wall to touch what was on the other side. Niro's side of the bed was smooth and empty. Disappointment fizzled through him. He flopped backwards and felt on the bedside shelf for his phone. It wasn't there. He was still in his suit from the night before. He had fallen asleep while wallowing in self-pity. After a few minutes of scrabbling around, he found his phone in the bed. It was early morning.

Niro would be home by now. He folded his arm, so that the phone nestled on his chest. Was she even thinking of him? Was she sitting with Sam and Gihan telling them how hard it was to pretend to like him?

Surely, they had been friends, at the very least? He thought of all those moments of conspiratorial friendship, the laughter. That *had* to have been real. He lifted his phone up again and found her number. Should he call her? Would she even answer?

Of course not! They were an hour ahead here. She would be asleep. Waking her up wasn't going to make her think any better of him.

Vimal sighed and sat up. He wouldn't be able to go to sleep now anyway. He glanced at the light well – darkness. The sun wouldn't be up for another forty minutes. Dawn made him think of Niro. He had told her he'd take her to the hotel at dawn so that she could photograph the sun coming up over the valley. He groaned. He had forgotten about that. No wonder she found it hard to be with him, if he forgot basic promises like that.

He plugged his phone in to charge and spent a few more minutes trying to get to sleep. It was no use. There was no point wasting time lying here. He may as well burn off some of this nervous energy and go have a run.

Partway through getting changed, he had a brainwave. He could take some photos of the sunrise for Niro. They wouldn't be as good as hers, but if he took a lot, she might be able to salvage something. Besides, it would be a good excuse to meet up with her again.

*

Vimal had just finished getting dressed and was packing his suitcase when someone knocked on his door. He opened it to find Felicia standing outside.

'Um … hello. Happy New Year,' he said.

Felicia frowned impatiently. 'Have you heard from Niro since last night?'

He blinked, surprised. 'No. But I spoke to her cousin last night and she was on her way home.'

'I can't get through to her. Haven't been able to get to her last night or this morning.'

Now Vimal was worried too. He fetched his phone and tried Niro. It went to answerphone. He hung up and tried Sam instead.

'Hello?' Sam sounded tired.

'Hi, Sam, it's Vimal. I'm sorry if I woke you. I'm just calling to check that Niro's okay. I haven't been able to get in touch with her.'

'Yes, she's fine. She didn't get home until early this morning. She's probably asleep.'

'But she's at home? Safe?' He needed to know.

'Yes.'

'Is she ... okay?'

'I have to go,' Sam said. A click and she was gone.

Vimal lowered the phone. 'She's home. She must have turned her phone off.'

Felicia, who hadn't come into the room itself, slumped against the door frame. 'That's good. I was so worried.' She tipped her head to one side. 'What happened with you two?'

What should he say? He couldn't admit that they hadn't really been a couple. 'We ... decided it isn't working,' he began.

'But why?' Felicia wailed. 'You guys were clearly meant to be together! Did you see the photos I sent you?'

Photos? He turned to his phone again. Felicia had sent him a photo last night. He had thought there was only one: a picture of him in the snow, laughing, his hand around Niro's wrist. But there was another, taken a few seconds later, where the laughter was fading from his face as he realised what Niro meant to him. Somehow, Felicia had captured the exact moment that he'd realised that he was falling in love.

He looked up to see Felicia glaring at him, her arms crossed, as though she blamed him for everything.

'But she left,' he said. 'She said it was too difficult.'

'What did you *do*? She liked you. I know she did.'

No, she didn't. She was good at acting a part. Felicia must have believed it totally. He shook his head. 'I didn't do anything. It just didn't work out.'

Felicia shook her head. 'You can't give up!'

Vimal sighed and stepped out of the room, closing the door behind him. 'Can we take this conversation to the kitchen? I need coffee.' He set off. He could feel the disapproval radiating off Felicia. Why was she blaming him? He hadn't done anything.

Niro was the one who had left. She was the one who'd found it too difficult to pretend to care about him.

I simply can't pretend any more.

Was it so hard to feign interest in him? He'd thought they had got on well. They *had* got on well. They were friends. He thought of the familiarity that they'd fallen into, each fitting around the other's peculiarities, the in-jokes, the conversations in the dark; he missed her so much it burned.

'What are you going to say to her, when you get back to London?' Felicia was not giving up on this.

When he hesitated, she said, 'You can't just leave things like this. You like her. She likes you. It's silly that she's left.'

He shook his head. 'She doesn't like me. Only as a friend. She told me that herself.'

Felicia looked taken aback. 'Really? Because that wasn't what it looked like to me.'

He thought again of her angry reaction to the mistletoe. It had looked like that to him. 'She left a note.'

Felicia's phone rang. She made an exasperated noise. 'I have to take this. Don't go away. I'm not done.' She walked away towards the games room answering the phone with, 'Hello, Mummy'.

Vimal got himself a mug. Lucien came in, looking very well groomed, and not at all like a man who had been up partying half the night.

Vimal nodded to him. 'Morning.'

'You're in a good mood for someone whose girlfriend walked out on you,' Lucien said.

Vimal picked an espresso pod. 'Well, that—'

'Mind you,' Lucien continued. 'It wasn't like you were really going out with her anyway.'

Vimal froze. How did *Lucien* know? Kerry had known too. Were they that unconvincing? He set the mug into the machine, inserted the pod and turned.

Lucien laughed. 'Oh come on,' he said. 'Did you think I didn't realise? It was obvious when you said you were bringing someone but you hadn't a clue who.' He smirked. 'To be completely honest, I'm impressed that you found someone at short notice. Who is she? A cousin or something?'

'What? No!' He was appalled. 'Why would you think that she's my cousin?'

'Well, you guys have big families. And you clearly know each other very well.'

His mind reeled. Lucien thought he'd brought his cousin along? And he'd made sure they had to sleep in the same bed? That was ... not nice.

'I know it was short notice and you were trying to save face, but really. I'd have thought that you could find someone better than your fat cousin.'

'We're not cousins,' Vimal said, flatly.

Lucien wasn't listening. 'Someone should tell her that having colour in her hair doesn't make her look like she's got a personality. It just makes her look like she's trying too hard to make up for something.' He shook his head. 'You really could have done better. There are people you can hire, you know. Attractive people.'

A movement in the corridor behind Lucien distracted Vimal. This prompted Lucien to look over his shoulder, too. Felicia stood there, her hand to her mouth, looking horrified.

Vimal glanced back at Lucien, who looked annoyed. Not embarrassed or remorseful. Annoyed.

What Lucien had said about Niro's hair reminded him of something. He had heard that phrasing before. Those were the same words Niro had used, that night when she was upset. She'd implied it was an Aunty who said them, but it clearly wasn't. It made more sense now that she'd heard those words from Lucien. Vimal felt heat burning in his stomach and rising.

He wasn't a naturally confrontational person, but the idea of someone being cruel to Niro made him want to hit something. Or someone. In the back of his mind, a voice reminded him that he had to work with Lucien. Weirdly, that voice sounded like Niro's.

He focused on extracting his coffee from the machine. A quick glance showed him that Felicia had unfrozen and was looking worried.

'What's interesting to me,' he said, keeping his voice calm, 'is that you assumed that I had brought along a cousin.'

'You people have huge families.'

Good god. 'First of all "we people" also have friends and lovers and casual acquaintances, just like all people,' he said. 'Second of all, you thought we might be close relatives and you thought it would be funny to force us to share a bed. That was a weirdly perverted move.'

Lucien scoffed. 'There are no rooms with separate beds—'

'But there is.' Felicia stepped into the room. 'There's a twin room. You forced that onto Kerry. Because you thought it would be funny for her and your old school chum – who *were* together – to not be able to share a bed.'

Lucien looked even more annoyed. He didn't reply, merely shrugged and took his phone out. He had been found out and it seemed he didn't care.

Vimal wanted to throw something at him. He took a deep breath. Remaining calm when provoked was one of the few social skills he excelled at. Just as well, really.

'Lucien, why would you do that?' Felicia came in and stood between them.

'Filly, come on, it's just a joke ...' Lucien said.

'But it's not funny.' Felicia's voice was climbing higher.

There was something in Felicia's voice that wasn't right. Vimal couldn't tell what was wrong, but something was. If only Niro were here, she'd know how to deal with all this. Niro had been fond of Felicia and protective of her. He looked at Lucien's girlfriend and was struck anew at how young she looked. Especially right now. Oh. Perhaps that's what Niro was worried about. If they riled Lucien too much, he might take it out on Felicia. He wouldn't have thought Lucien was that kind of guy, but now, he really didn't know.

Vimal cleared his throat. 'I have to go and pack now,' he said. 'I've got a taxi to the airport coming soon.' He turned to Lucien with a forced smile. 'Thank you for the invitation to visit, Lucien. The villa is amazing, and tell Basty I will definitely be leaving a good review on TripAdvisor.' He smiled at the younger girl, who was looking at him with a frown on her perfect forehead. 'It was nice to meet you, Felicia.'

Felicia came round the kitchen island and kissed him on the cheek. 'It was nice to meet you too.'

'Well, thanks for coming,' said Lucien, his voice unusually toneless.

'If you need a ride to the airport, there's room in the taxi,' Vimal said to Felicia.

'Oh, Felicia's staying a few extra days with me,' said Lucien. He reached across and picked a pastry out of the stack.

Vimal glanced at Felicia, who was chewing her lip.

There was the sound of hurrying footsteps and Kerry ran in. 'Oh good,' she said to Vimal. 'I was hoping to catch you. Did you find her?'

Vimal shook his head.

'Oh no. That's not good.'

'She's okay though,' said Felicia. 'Vimal checked in with her cousin.'

'See what I mean about cousins,' Lucien said.

Everyone ignored him.

'Are you going to go and find her when you're back in London?' said Kerry.

'Kerry …'

'Oh, come on, Vimal. You can't let her get away.'

'Hah!' said Lucien. 'Looks like Kerry bought your fake girlfriend act completely. I have news for you, Kerry, they were faking it.'

Kerry glared at him.

Vimal ignored him and said to Kerry, 'I'm going home today. I was just saying goodbye to Lucien and Felicia.'

'Oh, yes. What time are you taking the taxi to the airport? Can I come with you?' said Kerry.

'Sure.' Vimal looked at Felicia. 'There's plenty of room, if you want a ride to the airport too,' he said again.

Lucien frowned. 'You're leaving today?' he asked Kerry.

'Yes. Something's come up and I have to be back at work tomorrow. I managed to get an earlier flight.' She didn't bother looking at him. 'So, what time, Vimal?'

'Forty minutes.'

'Excellent. I'll finish packing and come join you. Thanks.'

Lucien seemed annoyed at being ignored. 'It's a shame everyone's leaving,' he said. 'I did invite you for the whole seven days.'

'I don't have enough leave,' Vimal lied.

'It's been lovely. Beautiful area,' said Kerry. 'And such a special house. Thank you so much for inviting me.'

'Technically, I invited Woolly,' said Lucien, with bad grace.

They all knew that wasn't true. There was an awkward silence.

Vimal took a quick glance at Lucien's face. His legendary charm seemed to have deserted him. That scowl made him look like a spoiled brat.

In that second Vimal felt the world shift, just a fraction, and he realised that what he'd taken for charm had merely been confidence. Lucien was so sure that he was right and everyone would agree with him, that somehow they believed it too. He liked being in the centre of attention. He needed to look good, even if it meant putting other people down to achieve it. Right now, with everyone treating him like an optional extra, he was looking like a petulant child.

Felicia eyed her phone. 'I suppose I should go and phone my mother back,' she said. 'Cheer up, Lucien darling. Your friends have to go home sometime.' She gave him a kiss on the cheek and walked off.

Lucien watched her leave and muttered something under his breath.

'I'll be off now,' Vimal said. 'There are a few last-minute things to sort out. Thanks again for the invitation. It's been a very interesting time.'

Lucien didn't reply.

It was probably better that way.

He turned to go.

'Won't it be awkward sharing a taxi with your ex?' Lucien said, his voice teasing, but unfriendly.

'I don't think so,' Vimal said. 'Just because we used to go out, doesn't mean we can't be friends.' As he hurried back to his room, he reflected that just a few days ago, the idea of being on a long taxi ride with Kerry would have caused him all kinds of anguish. It was likely he would have blurted out something inappropriate at some point on the journey. But now, almost overnight, his feelings towards her had softened. He was still fond of Kerry. That was only natural. But he didn't want her anymore. He sighed and rubbed his chest. *Oh Niro.*

Not long afterwards, Vimal was helping Kerry load her suitcase into the taxi. Neither Lucien nor the others had come to say goodbye. Kerry got in. Vimal was standing outside trying to decide whether he should sit in the back with Kerry or in front with the driver, when there was the sound of footsteps and Felicia appeared, dragging a bright-pink suitcase.

'Oh thank god, you're still here,' she said. 'Can I still come to the airport with you?'

'I thought you were supposed to be staying for a few more days,' Kerry said, poking her head out of the car.

'I was, but I think I might go see a friend in Zurich instead. Or something.' She cast a quick glance back at the house. 'Lucien is being a real misery guts and ... after what I heard this morning, I don't think I want to spend more time with him.'

He saw the look of resignation in her eyes and remembered Niro telling him how she was dependent on Lucien for this whole holiday. 'If you want to go home, I can lend you the money for a ticket.'

She brightened up. 'Would you? That would be brilliant. I'll pay you back. I promise.'

'Sure.'

The driver was making impatient noises, so Vimal got in the front, leaving Felicia to sit in the back with Kerry.

Once they set off, Kerry asked Felicia, 'What happened this morning that made you dislike Lucien so much?'

Felicia outlined the gist of the conversation in the kitchen. 'I thought he was really rude and maybe a bit racist to you, Vimal.'

'I agree,' said Vimal. He knew he wasn't the greatest at picking up cues, but that conversation had been obviously offensive. And, if his suspicions about Lucien being the one who had insulted Niro were correct, unforgivable.

'How could you stand it?' Felicia asked.

He twisted around in his seat. 'I will see him at work next week. There are a hundred different ways he could screw me over. I have to stand it.'

'But that's bullying! Surely, there must be something your company can do!'

Vimal and Kerry exchanged a glance. 'Workplaces aren't always as nice and supportive as they like to think they are,' Vimal said, carefully. 'They are often set up to protect the people that senior management like. And senior management like people who are very much like them.'

'There are always much higher barriers to being believed if you're a person of colour, for example,' said Kerry.

Vimal would never have said that out loud. Certainly not to someone he didn't trust intimately. He had once tried to tell a teacher at school about racist bullying and the teacher had warned him against 'playing the race card'. He had been wary ever since.

Felicia was staring at him, aghast. 'I thought that didn't happen anymore.'

He made a noncommittal noise in his throat.

Kerry gave him a thoughtful look. 'Is that why you hate socialising with work people so much? Because you have to put up with people like that?'

'I'm not good at reading people. It's easier to assume they mean no harm. But Niro *is* good at reading people and she didn't like Lucien from the start.'

'She's very astute, isn't she?' Kerry said. 'Amazing that of all the people your family could set you up with, they found her. The perfect match.'

His mood plummeted even further. 'She didn't think so,' he said, and turned back to face the front.

'Oh, but you're going to persuade her, right?' said Felicia. 'You have to!'

I simply can't pretend any more.

'I don't know how. She doesn't think we're right for each other. Then there's not a lot I can do, is there?'

'Vimal,' said Kerry, 'she made you happy. I haven't seen you loosen up like that for years. You can't let her go without a fight. Sometimes, things are worth fighting for.'

He twisted around in his seat to look at her. Her expression was earnest.

'I've known you for a long time, Vimal,' she said, quietly. 'I want you to be happy.'

'Are you?' he said. 'Happy, I mean?'

'Not yet,' said Kerry. 'But I will be. I just need to work out what I want.'

'Aw.' Felicia reached over and patted Kerry's hand. 'You will,' she said. 'I think you're pretty awesome, you know. You don't need the approval of people like Lucien and Magda. They're just rich, entitled people. That doesn't mean they're better people. Trust me. I should know. I'm one of them.'

Kerry stared at the younger girl. It had been years since Vimal had seen Kerry speechless.

'Oh, come on,' said Felicia. 'You think we didn't notice how you hung on Magda's every word? Magda's a snob and not a very nice person. She doesn't say much, but when she does it's usually to put someone down. You can do better than being friends with her.'

'Oh.' Kerry seemed to still be struggling to process this. 'I … er … Thanks. I think.'

Vimal turned to look ahead again. Niro had been right when she said Lucien was punching above his weight with Felicia. He pulled his phone out of his coat pocket and tried calling Niro again. Still nothing. He was sure everything was okay, but he couldn't help worrying. Even if she didn't want to see him again, he had to go and check that she was all right. She couldn't possibly object to that.

Chapter 26

When Niro woke up, it was nearly midday. Her phone was dead, so she plugged it in to charge. Once she'd showered and dressed in her usual comfy outfit of joggers and chunky jumper, she felt better. Sam was already out, so she was not coming back that evening. Niro pottered around the flat for a while, making herself toast. She thought about the plentiful breakfasts in the villa. All those pastries. She should have eaten more of them while she had the chance. Would Felicia be doing her yoga this morning? Or sleeping off a hangover? She didn't want to think about what Vimal might be doing … with Kerry.

But now that she'd thought of it, she couldn't shake the memory of him opening the door, his expression keen. Excited. What a fool she'd been to think he would feel anything for her. He obviously had eyes for only Kerry. He thought of Niro as a friend. She had mistaken his fondness as something more.

She opened her computer to check her emails but couldn't focus. In the end, she gave up and decided to go outside. There was about an hour or two of sunlight left. She may as well make use of it.

It was one of those sharp winter afternoons, where the light fell at an oblique angle and picked everything out in light and shade. It was cold enough for the pavements to be icy. Being this late in the day, every single puddle had been stamped on so that the ice shattered. She paused to take a photo of one.

Even though it was warmer here than in Switzerland, the damp made it feel a lot colder. Niro shuddered and carried on walking. Past familiar pubs and storefronts. Everything was the same, but felt different. It was as though she'd removed a filter. A dog, tied to a sign outside a shop, whined at her. She took a photo of him looking forlornly up at her.

Going for a walk had been a good idea. Bringing her camera had been an even better one. Her camera felt like a part of her again. Which was how it should be. Surely, it didn't matter if Vimal didn't want her. She'd got something incredibly valuable out of her trip. She took a photo of an abandoned crisp packet being blown along by the biting wind. Thinking about Vimal hurt right now, but it would stop after a while. Wouldn't it?

There was nothing waiting for her at home. She would be alone for the evening, because she'd persuaded Sam to go to Luke's. So she took a detour to go to the small park that was two blocks away.

It was one of those tiny urban parks that provided a green space in the middle of the concrete. It had been renovated in the last couple of years. She hadn't seen it since then.

A winding path ran in between bushes, shrubs and waist-high planters. Every so often, a bench was set into a recess. Even though it was still light, the streetlamps were on. Lights had been strung through the foliage, giving the place a magical feel. Niro wished she'd brought her tripod with her. She could get it and come back tomorrow.

Looking up, she could see the pink in the sky as the sun dropped lower. She felt the quickening in her pulse that came with inspiration. It was comforting.

Perspective was everything. What did this particular path look like from a higher angle?

She looked around. No one was watching, so she brushed the

light dusting of snow off the bench and carefully got up on it, mindful of how she'd slipped the last time she'd stood on a bench. How had she landed in Vimal's arms and not been moved by the experience? If she was being honest with herself, she had … a bit. But at that time she hadn't even considered him as relationship material. He had been a nice guy, quite attractive, but entirely unavailable. The whole point of her being there was for him to save face in front of his ex. That hadn't changed.

She adjusted the settings on the camera to take account of the low light and took a photo. Hmmm. Not quite right. She changed them again. Experimenting. That was what it was all about.

She would just have to put her feelings for Vimal down as a failed experiment and get out there again. In fact, she should apply the same logic to the whole trip. Sure, she was 'common and dumpy', but so what? Just because people like Lucien were horrible about her weight, or Kumudhini Aunty was horrible about how dark and plain she was, it didn't mean that she was worthless. She was talented and generous and even pretty in her own way. She knew this. She had known this for years. Mick had somehow made her forget it. It had taken Vimal with his nagging about valuing her art and his weird metaphors about mountains to remind her again.

'Screw that guy,' she muttered and immediately wondered which one of them she was talking about. Screw Mick, definitely. He could go die in a ditch for all she cared. But Vimal, not so much. He was still a nice guy. A great guy, in fact. It was just a shame that he was in love with Kerry.

She shivered. Now that the daylight was draining away, it was getting much colder. She would have to go home soon and warm up. It was too dark for good photos, but she could do some trial ones, to give her ideas for tomorrow.

From her elevated position, she saw a man approach the park. He was staring at his phone and didn't look threatening. A couple came in behind him, so she decided she didn't need to worry about him.

She turned in the other direction, placing her feet carefully. Oh, now she could see the curve of the path better. The buildings behind the trees were more obvious, too. This could make an interesting juxtaposition.

She was still taking photos when someone said, 'Niro?'

She looked up and saw Vimal, dressed in a long overcoat and a woolly hat, with his hands on his hips. Her throat went dry.

'Vimal.' Very carefully, she got off the bench. She had hoped to come up with a plan before she saw him next. She needed more time to shore up the collapsing walls around her heart. He was going to thank her for helping him get Kerry back. She had to pretend to be happy. Dammit. This was going to be hard to do with zero preparation time.

'You left,' he said. He sounded angry, but there was something in his voice, a tremor that ran underneath the anger. 'Without even saying goodbye!'

Well duh. What did he have to be angry about? She'd fulfilled her part of the deal. 'I left you a note.'

'You're not answering your phone. I was worried about you.'

Her phone was still in silent mode. When she had turned it back on to send her parents a new-year message, there had been a hundred other notifications of missed calls. She had turned the phone off without looking at any of them. 'Why?'

'Why was I worried? Bloody hell, Niro. You just disappeared on me, with no explanation. No goodbye. Of course I was worried.'

She pulled her shoulders back and lifted her chin. 'We had reached the end of the deal. You knew I was going home. Why on earth—'

'I expected you'd at least say goodbye!' His voice was sharp and very unlike his usual calm.

She had. 'I left you a bloody note!' She was shouting now.

'Oh yes. The note. Really. Was it so much of a pain pretending to be my girlfriend that you had to run away as soon as you felt you could?'

257

She couldn't look at him anymore. She stared at the yellow-lit path, not seeing any of it. He thought she'd left because pretending to be his girlfriend was too much hassle. Now that he said it, she could see how her note was ambiguous. Should she mention what she really meant? He was with Kerry now. How would that help?

'Well,' he said, 'I'm sorry it was so hard for you to pretend to love me.' There was a catch in his voice. Bitterness, almost.

'That wasn't it,' she said. What was she doing? Now that she'd started, she had to carry on. 'I wasn't tired of pretending I was in love with you. I was tired of pretending I wasn't.' She looked at her feet. She might as well tell him everything now. It was embarrassing, but it was better than him thinking he was a difficult person to love. 'It's not you. It's me. I somehow caught feelings for real. And I'm sorry about that. I know that wasn't supposed to happen.'

She finally looked up at him. He was staring at her, mouth slightly open, as though he couldn't believe what he was hearing.

'I'm sorry,' she said again. 'I shouldn't have mentioned it. It's not your problem. You're with Kerry now and I have no place—'

'I'm not with Kerry.' he shook his head vigorously.

'But the plan worked. No need to lie.' Why was he even bothering to hide it? 'I saw her go into our ... I mean, *your* room last night.'

He took a step towards her and shook his head. 'She came to our room and I told her to go away. I told her I wasn't interested in her because I'd accidentally fallen in love with you.' He had the strangest expression on his face. Half worried, half hopeful.

For a second her thoughts skidded in all directions. What? That made no sense. 'But you didn't want to kiss me under the mistletoe.'

'You didn't seem too keen either,' he retorted.

'I didn't think I could fake it being fake.'

His mouth made an oh. 'Well, I ... I thought you didn't want to because you specified no kissing in—'

'The deal,' she said at the same time he did.

They stared at each other. Niro's pulse grew louder and faster. Her breathing made puffs of fog in front of her face. All she could think about was how she could have kissed him and that she'd missed the opportunity. How she could perhaps kiss him now.

Vimal took a few steps until he was standing right in front of her. 'Niro.' There was no anger in his voice now. 'Forget the deal. Can I kiss you now, just ... because I want you?'

Her gaze locked to his and she saw the burning in his eyes. She was definitely not imagining it this time. She wanted to say something clever and witty, but all she managed was, 'Uh-huh'.

He leaned down and she closed her eyes. His mouth met hers, warm and moist after the freezing air. The camera dug into her, she moved it to the side. He grabbed her waist and pulled her closer, making her breath hitch. She ran her camera-free hand up his chest and cradled his neck. It was a long, delicious kiss.

When they finally came apart, he rested his forehead against hers and said, 'I've been wanting to do that for ages.'

'Ages?' She smiled. 'We've only known each other for a few weeks.'

'For a couple of days, then.'

'Why didn't you?'

'As we've established, we had a deal,' he said. 'And you said no kissing.'

'Oh, so it's my fault now?'

'Well, you could have said the deal was off.' He kissed her nose. 'Can we discuss this somewhere warmer? Like in your house?'

That sounded like a very good idea. 'Sure. Of course. Let's.'

They set off. She understood his confusion. After all, she'd been confused too and she was much better at dealing with confusion than he was. 'Vimal,' she said. 'Just to clarify. This ...' She gestured to the two of them. 'This is real. I like you. I want to go out with you for real.'

His smile was a thing of beauty. She wished she had enough

light to capture it. But no photo could do it justice.

'I really like you, Niro. I mean, really, really like you. And I want to go out with you for real too.'

She grinned at him. 'Well, that's okay then.'

He took her hand. 'Bloody hell, woman. You're not wearing gloves. Again.'

'I was taking photos until a minute or so before you arrived.' She pulled her gloves out of her pocket.

'Actually, I got you something.' He took a small paper parcel out of his pockets. 'Here.'

Puzzled, she opened it. It was a pair of gloves – fingerless, but with a hood that flipped over to cover the fingers, turning them into mittens. The gloves were black and grey, but the hood part had a penguin face printed on it.

'They're for kids,' he said, apologetically. 'But they're very stretchy. I thought they might get around your problem of needing the control of fingertips. And I thought you'd like the penguins.'

She put them on. They were snug, but comfortable to wear. She flipped the tops over and found two adorable penguins looking at her from her hands. 'They're brilliant,' she said.

'Oh good.' He looked relieved. 'I wasn't sure if it was okay. I know it's not the most romantic gift. I went out to Basty's hotel this morning to take some photos of the sunrise for you, but then I realised that I'd missed the point completely and they wouldn't be any use to you unless you took them yourself.'

'You went up to the hotel … to photograph the dawn?' It was the sweetest, most thoughtful thing. Misguided, yes, but so sweet.

He nodded. 'I didn't think it through properly until I got there. Then I didn't have a present for you. I probably should have got you flowers, but I saw those gloves and—'

'Vimal. Stop stressing. They are perfect.' She kissed his cheek. 'I love them.'

'Good. I'm … glad.' He reached down and took her hand in his big warm one. 'Shall we?'

She looked down at their joined hands. '*Now* he remembers,' she said.

'I'd like you to know,' he said, solemnly, 'that I'm fully committed to this real relationship.'

Niro squeezed his hand and grinned. As they walked back to the house, she couldn't stop smiling. This was ridiculous. She was a fully grown woman. She shouldn't be walking around dizzy like a teenager. Except she was. She glanced sideways at Vimal and felt warmth swirling in her chest. This delightful weirdo liked her and wanted to be with her.

When they got into the house, it took a few minutes for Niro to peel off the layers of warm clothing.

'I take it Sam's still at work?' Vimal put his shoes neatly together next to Sam's slippers.

Niro's slippers were left at the bottom of the stairs from when she'd kicked them off to put shoes on. She stepped into them. 'Yes. She's going to Luke's this evening, so we have the place to ourselves.'

He gave her a wicked smile. 'So, what could we do? In this place. All by ourselves.'

Niro felt a little flutter in her belly. 'I can't think. Any ideas?'

He stepped closer. 'A few.' He cupped her cheek with one hand and kissed her. With his other arm, he tugged her closer. She put her arms round his neck. As the kiss deepened, she stroked the side of his face, stubble rasped under her fingers. He moved, kissing her jaw and then, softly, her neck. Sensation ran down her spine and pooled in her belly.

'Vimal.' She reached round to his hand that was on her back, pressing her to him, and moved it, tangling her fingers through his. He looked at her, his pupils huge, making his eyes dark and fathomless. She led him up the stairs.

'I should warn you,' she said, as she went into her room. 'I only have a single bed.'

He pulled an expression of mock confusion. 'But … but how

261

will we fit in the pillow wall?'

She turned to look at him. 'I don't think we can,' she said, laughter lacing her words. 'I think we're going to have to make do without one.'

Vimal grinned. 'Ah well.' He slipped his arms around her. 'I guess we'll just have to cope.'

*

Later that evening, Vimal was on the sofa, eating cheese on toast because that was what Niro had made him. She sat cross-legged next to him with her own plate in her lap. The flat was still decorated with fairy lights and Christmas decorations and smelled of toast and grilled cheese. Nothing seemed to match anything else, but he vastly preferred it to the luxury of the villa.

He finished off his dinner and stretched out, resting his plate on his stomach. 'I know we've had some fancy meals over the past week, but that was the best thing ever.'

Niro dipped the edge of her toast in the puddle of chilli sauce she had on the side of her plate. 'I should have discreetly taken a bottle of chilli sauce. It would have livened things up considerably.'

Vimal grinned. 'Imagine Magda's face if you'd just pulled out a bottle and covered everything in sauce.'

He expected Niro to laugh. Instead the expression became serious. Very serious.

Alarmed, he sat up straight and put his plate on the floor. 'What's the matter?'

Niro looked down at her plate. 'About Magda ... and Peter and Lucien. There's something I have to tell you.'

'Was it them? The ones who said nasty things about you? It was, wasn't it?'

She gave a small nod.

'Why didn't you tell me? Why did you pretend it was an Aunty?'

Niro sighed. 'For one, the Kumudhini Aunty has said similar

things to me in the past. So did Mick. For another ... I don't know. You have to work with Lucien. I wasn't sure how to handle it. So I sort of tried to ignore it.'

He knew that feeling. That's what he did too. Insulting him, he could look past, but being mean to Niro ... that was so wrong. 'I guessed it was him,' he said. His feeling of wellbeing had evaporated. 'I tried to call him out on it. I'm not sure he noticed.'

Niro nodded. 'There's something else ...' She shifted position. 'It's a bit worse than that.'

Worse? What could be worse? 'He didn't try anything? He didn't hurt you.' Now he was alarmed.

'No. Nothing like that.' She told him what she had overheard.

'Entertainment?' He followed the thread to its logical conclusion. 'They invited me simply so that they could laugh at me? At us?' His mind recoiled at the thought of such callousness. Surely, real people didn't do that sort of thing. Then he thought of all the glances between Lucien and Peter. The smirks. Of course they did that sort of thing. 'Those complete bastards.'

Suddenly other things fell into place. 'I thought it was weird that he invited random people from work to his parties ... He was just providing people to laugh at.'

'Isn't that ... workplace bullying?'

'Technically, it's not at the workplace. Besides, no one has complained about it.'

'I wonder why not.' Niro was sitting bolt upright now, fully engaged.

Vimal frowned and thought about it. Why had he been reluctant to call out Lucien's behaviour, even when it had become obvious just before he left the villa? 'Partly, we have to work with him and he's charismatic and quick ... and popular. The senior management like him and if it ever came down to believing one of us over Lucien ...' There was no contest. The senior management were mostly public-school types as well. 'There's always a group of people around him and you don't want the whole lot

263

of them to turn against you.' He thought of Richard in his office who had been invited to one party and lived in hope of being invited to another. 'I think some people might not even realise they're being made fun of ... and the others ...' He wouldn't have said anything at work. It made him look stupid and wouldn't do anyone any good. 'The others think it's just them. They don't know that he does this as a regular thing.'

A sudden thought struck him. 'The New Year's thing was small, sometimes he has much bigger events. I wonder how many of the other guys are in on it.'

'That's a terrible workplace culture.'

It hadn't seemed like it before, but he was rapidly seeing that it was. 'What can we do about it?'

'You could start by warning off the other people he invites.'

He nodded. 'I could. It would be nice if I could somehow confront him with his own crap though. In front of his cronies.' An idea began to form. 'When you do your print that he's buying from you, could you bring it to the office?'

Niro gave him a puzzled frown. 'Sure. Why?'

'I think I have an idea.'

Chapter 27

Three weeks later

Vimal waited until he heard the door open in the meeting room and the sound of laughter trickled out. Good. The team meeting was over and Lucien would now be holding court with his lackeys. He had been waiting for this time. It had been the devil's own job to concentrate on anything all morning.

He intended to confront Lucien. Not in an antagonistic way, he wasn't built for that sort of thing, but he had to do something. Lucien couldn't treat people like that and be allowed to get away with it. He stood up and picked up the carefully wrapped parcel that Niro had delivered to him. It was a large picture frame and quite heavy. His heart pounded and his chest felt tight. Perhaps he wasn't built for mild confrontation either.

'What's that?' Richard asked, as Vimal made for the door of the office.

'It's a photo that Lucien bought off my girlfriend.' He was doing this, in part, for Niro. The idea of Lucien and his cronies laughing at her put steel in his spine.

'Can I see?' said Richard, always Lucien's biggest fan. If only he knew.

'I'm sure he'll show it to everyone later,' Vimal said and rushed out. He didn't particularly want Richard there when he spoke to Lucien. He still wasn't sure whether Richard was better off not knowing what Lucien was really like.

He knocked on the meeting room door, which was ajar, and pushed it open.

'Hi. Lucien. Have you got a minute?'

Lucien's gaze took in him and then the parcel. 'Vimal.' He gave a condescending smile. 'Have you taken up lugging furniture around now? Are they not paying you guys enough here?'

There was a smattering of laughter.

'This is that photo you ordered from Niro.' Vimal held the parcel out to him.

'I didn't realise you were still in touch with her. I thought she dumped you.' Lucien took the parcel. 'Or sort of did, since you weren't really going out in the first place.'

There were a few smirks around the table. Lucien must have told his minions a version of the story.

'No, no,' said Vimal, mildly. 'We're still together.' He nodded towards the picture. 'I saw it last night, before she wrapped it. It looks good.'

As he'd predicted, someone in the group called out, 'Let's see it, then.'

Lucien shrugged and tore into the paper wrapping. Vimal noticed that he turned the photo so that he would see it first.

He knew the photo had come out really well. Lucien was the centre of the image, surrounded by blurry people. Niro had fiddled with the saturation levels at the edges so that Lucien looked even brighter than everything else. It was exactly the sort of photo that would appeal to the man's ego.

Lucien grinned. 'Oh. You're right. That is good. Your little cousin is talented.'

'We're not related,' said Vimal. 'No need to be a dick.'

'Steady on,' said one of the guys.

Vimal didn't bother looking at the guy. He wasn't enjoying this, but he had to do this. 'I thought it captured Lucien well. The centre of attention at a party where he'd invited a few people specifically so that he could laugh at them. Isn't that right, Lucien?'

'You're making a fool of yourself here, Vimal,' said Lucien, in the loudest of whispers.

Someone sniggered.

'Maybe,' said Vimal. 'But I'd like you to stop using people in my team to be the butt of your jokes. It's not big. It's bullying. That's no way to treat your work colleagues.'

Someone else scoffed. 'Hardly. Now, come, man. He invited you to a party, out of the goodness of his heart. Just because you didn't have a good time … that's hardly bullying, is it?'

'You're right. It isn't. But spreading rumours that I'm in some sort of weird incestuous relationship with a cousin is,' said Vimal. He drew a deep breath and made eye contact with the guy who had just spoken. 'It's interesting that you knew exactly what I'm talking about. You think it couldn't happen to you. But can you be sure?'

'I think you should leave now, Vimal. Before I report you for slander.' There was no warmth in Lucien's voice.

'It's not slander if it's true. There are enough of us in this building that could say it was. I'll see you later.' Vimal walked out. He went back to the office, picked up his coat, not responding to Richard's query about what Lucien thought of the photo. If he stopped now, the adrenaline comedown would reduce him to a wreck. He signed out, walked from the office and down the road. He didn't stop until he'd reached the pub where he was meeting Niro for lunch. She was already there, sitting at a table, looking at the menu.

When he arrived, she stood up and, without a word, hugged him. Vimal wrapped his arms around her and held on tight. He felt the tension leave him and his hands start to tremble.

'Did it go okay?' Niro said, her voice muffled.

He released his hold on her. 'Yes. I said what I wanted to say. Hopefully, I've seeded doubt in the minds of his gang.'

Niro reached up and kissed him firmly. 'Well done. That was so brave.'

'He's still going on about you being my cousin.'

Niro snorted. 'Idiot.' She untangled herself from him and sat back down. 'I hope there won't be any repercussions for you.'

'There might be,' said Vimal. 'I guess we'll deal with that when we get to it.' He shrugged off his coat and slid into the seat next to her. 'I've dusted off my CV anyway, just in case.'

Niro squeezed his knee. 'It sucks that you have to do that, just because you want some dickhead to stop making snide, racist comments about you.'

He put his hand over hers. 'Maybe it's time to move to something less pressured anyway. The money's good here, but the hours are ridiculous. It would be nice to have time for things besides work.'

Niro laughed. 'You would be so miserable if you had to do other things besides work. You love your work.'

He rolled his eyes. She had a point. 'Okay, then, maybe it would be nice to have a job where I didn't have as much office politics and other shenanigans to worry about.'

'That I can agree with.' She kissed his cheek. 'Now then. Shall we order lunch?'

He looked fondly at her as she went back to poring over the menu. She was so completely herself, it was hard to imagine her ever suffering a lack of confidence, even though he knew that she sometimes did. If she could be brave and get back out there, so could he. She hadn't tried to change him. She just made him want to be a better version of himself.

Vimal leaned in to kiss her and she fidgeted and pushed him away. 'Gerroff. I'm trying to focus on food.'

He laughed. At that moment, he couldn't have loved her more.

Epilogue

One year later

The art gallery was busy, not heaving, but busy enough for the opening night to be a success. Niro wore a 1950s swing dress with boots and the world's tightest shapewear. Between that, a few glasses of champagne and the incredible make-up job that Felicia had done on her, she felt amazing.

'There's so much press here.' Sam was standing beside her, eyeing the crowd. She handed Niro a glass of juice. 'Here. You've been walking and talking for two hours straight, take a break.'

'Thanks.' Niro took the glass and looked around for somewhere to hide. She made a mental note to ask for more seating the next time she had an exhibition. Hah. The next time. That was ambitious. But then again, this exhibition had been ambitious.

When her photo for the architecture and landscape competition didn't get placed, she had felt crushed. But from the ashes of that disappointment had risen this idea. She looked up at the huge display that said 'Influencer', made up of her photos mocked up into Instagram-post styles. Felicia and her network had provided her with ample opportunities to photograph influencers behind the scenes. The resulting photos showed these young people, who appeared super confident and glamorous on social media, worrying about their bodies, planning their themes, setting up their shoots. One of Niro's favourite shots was of Felicia and her friend Ronee peering at a spreadsheet while drinking their green smoothies. It captured the serious professionalism that went on behind the apparently effortless glamour.

As an exhibition, the idea was brilliant. The influencers brought in a younger crowd than would normally come to a photography exhibition and the art crowd got to see into a world they didn't normally bother with.

'Hey.' Vimal appeared. He had been working late at his new job and was still in his suit, his jaw shaded with stubble. He kissed her cheek and stood beside her. 'Wow. This is looking good. Congratulations.'

Felicia bounded up to them. She was in a tiny dress and the most amazing boots. 'Vimal! You made it.'

She grabbed her phone. 'Oh my god, you two look adorable. Say cheese!'

Niro leaned her head on Vimal's shoulder and beamed.

'Aww,' Felicia said. 'That's such a cute photo. I love it.'

'I think Vimal needs a drink,' said Niro, firmly. 'Let me get you one.' She left him chatting and went across the room to get two drinks. On the way past, she checked which prints had discreet dots on them indicating that they'd been sold. Ooh. Quite a few. She counted them under her breath.

Getting across the room and back took a while, because people kept stopping her to talk to her and ask questions about the exhibition. Everyone was being so nice, she felt light-headed with it all.

Her parents had gone home already, which was a shame because they would have liked to have seen Vimal. They had been wild with joy when she had told them about him and their two families were happily back in touch. Amma had had a bit too much champagne and Gihan had taken them home.

When Niro got back to him, Vimal was talking to Sam and

Luke. She handed Vimal his drink and beamed at him before she turned to look at the room again.

'About half of them have sold,' she whispered to him.

He put down his drink and slipped his arms around her from behind. 'I am so proud of you.' He rested his cheek against her hair.

Niro sighed and leaned against him. He tightened his arms around her into a hug. 'Are you happy, Nirosha?' he said, fondly.

Her parents were no longer disappointed in her. She was selling her art. She had a partner who was supportive and believed in her, possibly even more than she believed in herself. Finally, she was winning.

'I am happy,' she said. 'Thank you.' She stood there, cocooned in his hug, and felt a moment of complete tranquillity. This was where she was meant to be. Right here. In this place. With this man.

There was only one thing that would make it more perfect. She leaned sideways and turned to look at him. 'Marry me?'

'What? Right now?' Vimal tilted his head. He studied her face for a second. 'Don't you think that's taking spontaneity a bit far?'

'Why not?' she said. 'I love you. I want to spend the rest of my life with you and have a family with you. May as well make a start.'

He looked her up and down in a way that made her flush. 'I think I'd like that,' he said. 'I can't propose to you right now, though.'

'Why not?' A giggle was rising in her chest. She couldn't stop smiling.

He laughed and hugged her closer. 'A few reasons. I haven't bought a ring, for a start.'

'Wait, wait,' said Sam, who had been listening to the whole conversation. 'Don't move.' She ran off and returned with Ronee, who was wearing all manner of jewellery. Ronee pressed two rings into Niro's hand, grinning.

'Rings,' said Niro. 'Perfect.' She smoothed down her skirt and knelt down on one knee. A murmur went round the room and

271

the hum of conversation died down as everyone stopped to watch.

'What are you doing? That's my job,' Vimal whispered, but he was smiling.

'It's my exhibition,' she whispered back. She cleared her throat. 'Vimal,' she said. 'You make me so happy. Please will you marry me?'

'I told you,' he said, beaming, 'I am fully committed to this relationship.'

She rolled her eyes. 'Is that a yes, you exasperating man?'

'Of course it's a yes.' He took her hands and helped her stand. 'Yes, yes. I will marry you. I can't think of anything that would make me happier.'

They exchanged rings and hugged. There was applause and flashes went off as photos were taken. Niro didn't pay attention to any of it. She buried her face in Vimal's shoulder and held on to him. She had to savour every last second of this night because right now, in this moment, everything was just perfect.

A Letter from Jeevani Charika

Thank you so much for choosing to read *Picture Perfect*. I hope you enjoyed it! If you did and would like to be the first to know about my new releases and see behind the scenes of my works in progress (or even be around to help me out when I get stuck for a name for a bank!), sign up to my newsletter. You will also get a free short story about a woman who wears Doc Martens boots under her saree. The link is at the end of this letter.

If you just want to know when I have special offers on, follow me on Bookbub. If you fancy a chat, catch me on Twitter, Facebook or my website.

Picture Perfect arose organically from Niro's character. This is by far my favourite way to start thinking about a book. I always feel like the characters in my book are a real community of people and I'm slowly getting to know them all. Plus, I get to go and check on the ones from earlier books along the way. Bonus!

I knew that Niro was chubby and dark-skinned. I wanted to write about colourism and the way that lighter brown skin is considered preferable to dark brown skin. It seems like a ridiculous distinction, but it's common in Asian cultures (and in Black cultures from what I've heard). The causes of it are mostly colonial, but, given that people who worked in the sun were darker than those who were wealthy enough not to, it probably taps into something that was already there. For girls with dark skin, it's an extra layer of pain that they really don't need. Niro has come to terms with both her shape and her colouring, but words still have the power to get under the defences.

If you want to find out more about the inspiration behind *Picture Perfect*, I kept notes as I went. I've put all of those and an alternative ending that appeared in draft one and had to be changed into a document that you can get by signing up to my newsletter.

I hope you enjoyed *Picture Perfect* and if you did (or even if you didn't!), I would be so grateful if you would leave a review. I always love to hear what readers thought, and it helps new readers work out whether my books are for them or not.

If you have a friend who would like this sort of book, please tell them! Nothing beats personal recommendations to get the right books into the hands of readers who'd love them.

Thanks,

Jeev

Link tree: https://linktr.ee/JeevaniC
Twitter: https://twitter.com/RhodaBaxter
Newsletter sign up: https://jeevanicharika.com/pp
Bookbub: https://www.bookbub.com/authors/jeevani-charika
Website: www.jeevanicharika.com

Playing for Love

When Sam's not working on her fledgling business,
she spends her time secretly video-gaming. Her crush is
famous gamer Blaze, and she's thrilled when she's teamed up
with him in a virtual tournament.

But what Sam doesn't know is that Blaze is the alter ego of
Luke, her shy colleague – and he has a secret crush too.

Luke has a crush on Sam.

Sam has a crush on Blaze.

How will this game of love play out?

**A fun, feel-good romance for fans of *You've Got Mail*, Helen
Hoang, Jasmine Guillory and Lindsey Kelk!**

Acknowledgements

They say writing is a solitary activity. It is, but researching isn't. So thank you to art fundraising genius Katie Norman for checking the information related to artists – and patiently explaining to me how artists link up with galleries. I hope I've got it right. If not, the fault will be entirely mine. Norman Crighton for explaining to me how quantitative analysts fit into the banking eco system. Thank you to Alexander Last and his colleagues for putting up with my endless random questions about all things Swiss.

The book contained a few banks and I needed inspiration for names for them. So I turned to my newsletter subscribers for help. The suggestions they sent in were brilliant. Very special thanks to Lisa Sabatini, Linda Brown and Cath Allwood whose suggestions ended up as Sabatini Putnam Woolf (the bank Vimal and Lucien work for). Additional thanks to Kay Hensley whose suggestion (Miller Brown) was used as the name of a rival bank and Sherry Brown who suggested Yelvington, which was the perfect fit for a character. So, there's a Lord Yelvington in the book now.

Every author needs a support group – thank you to the ladies of the Naughty Kitchen for the virtual support. Thanks to Jane Lovering and Jenni Fletcher for real-life tea and cake support. Thank you to my agent, Jo, and to Dushi and Abi at HQ for helping me write something about colourism – something I never thought I'd get the chance to sneak into a romcom.

Thank you so much to my family for being so supportive of this writing thing. You're the best.

Last of all, thank you for reading.

Dear Reader,

We hope you enjoyed reading this book. If you did, we'd be so appreciative if you left a review. It really helps us and the author to bring more books like this to you.

Here at HQ Digital we are dedicated to publishing fiction that will keep you turning the pages into the early hours. Don't want to miss a thing? To find out more about our books, promotions, discover exclusive content and enter competitions you can keep in touch in the following ways:

JOIN OUR COMMUNITY:

Sign up to our new email newsletter:
http://smarturl.it/SignUpHQ

Read our new blog www.hqstories.co.uk

🐦 https://twitter.com/HQStories

📘 www.facebook.com/HQStories

BUDDING WRITER?

We're also looking for authors to join the HQ Digital family!
Find out more here:

https://www.hqstories.co.uk/want-to-write-for-us/

Thanks for reading, from the HQ Digital team